NEMESIS

AND
THE

Swan

NEMESIS

AND THE

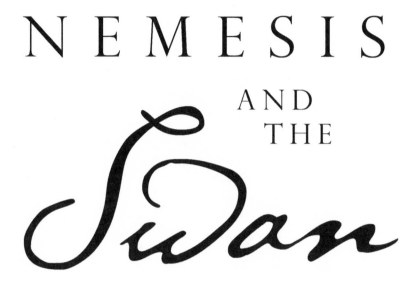
Swan

LINDSAY K. BANDY

BLACK STONE
PUBLISHING

Copyright © 2020 by Lindsay K. Bandy
Published in 2020 by Blackstone Publishing
Cover design by Zena Kanes
Interior design by Amy Craig

Printed in the United States of America

First edition: 2020
ISBN 978-1-09-405947-1
Young Adult Fiction / Historical / General

1 3 5 7 9 10 8 6 4 2

CIP data for this book is available
from the Library of Congress

Blackstone Publishing
31 Mistletoe Rd.
Ashland, OR 97520

www.BlackstonePublishing.com

For Clay.
Je t'aime pour toujours.

PREFACE

Nemesis and the Swan is a work of fiction. All of the main characters are creations of my imagination, but their circumstances are based entirely on true events.

Several minor characters who appear in this story were real-life figures of the Revolution. First, there is singer, orator, and female militia organizer Théroigne de Méricourt. I have also made reference to playwright, feminist author, and abolition activist Olympe de Gouges, who wrote the Déclaration des droits de la femme et de la citoyenne (Declaration of the Rights of Woman and of the Female Citizen) and was sent to the guillotine. She is followed by, among others, the Princess de Lamballe, a close friend of Marie Antoinette, whose body was dismembered and paraded through the streets of Paris, and the Marquis de Lafayette, who fought alongside the colonists in the American Revolution and returned to France to lead the National Guard. No story of the French Revolution would be complete without mention of Maximilien Robespierre, radical leader of the Jacobin Club and principle leader during the Reign of Terror; George Jacques Danton, president of the Committee of Public Safety, who did nothing to prevent the September Massacres of 1792; or Jean-Paul Marat, the physician, politician, and radical journalist who was often forced to hide in the sewers of Paris.

It was Jean-Paul Marat who first pulled me into Hélène's world. In a college art history textbook, I came across a painting of a man stabbed to death while writing radical words in his bathtub. *The Death of Marat* by Jacques-Louis David (1793) portrayed him as an angelic martyr of the Revolution, but by the time of his assassination by twenty-five-year-old Charlotte Corday, his newspaper, *L'Ami du peuple* (*The Friend of the People*), had incited mass murders so brutal that the gutters of Paris ran red with blood. I also found myself drawn to the stories of young women like Charlotte Corday, Pauline Léon (a radical organizer and feminist), and Marie Antoinette, who found themselves desperately trying to walk an ever-shifting line to survive. Their lives and deaths spoke to me of the importance of continually examining the way we draw lines between right and left, good and bad, us and them.

The Fall of the Bastille and the subsequent flight of the aristocracy, the Fête de la Fédération, the Champ-de-Mars Massacre, the Insurrection of 10 August 1792, and the massacres de Septembre, or journées de Septembre, have been recreated from Hélène's point of view with the help of the following sources: *The Days of the French Revolution* by Christopher Hibbert; *Citizens* by Simon Schama; *The French Revolution: Liberté, Egalité, Fraternité; A New Republic Is Born in Blood* produced by the History Channel in 2005; *City of Darkness, City of Light* by Marge Piercy; and *19th-Century Art* (second edition) by Robert Rosenblum and H. W. Janson.

PART I

We have dreamed a lovely dream—that is all!

—Marie Antoinette

I

THE ABBAYE PRISON, PARIS

AUGUST 12, 1792

Just this morning, my basket held three perfect apples and some dry, hard cheese. Like everyone else, I had kept my eyes on the street, watching my feet take one step at a time, watching shopkeepers dump buckets of water over the cobbles to rinse away the blood clotting in the cracks. Blood was smeared in strange places—the trunk of a tree, the side of a horse, on the dress of a child's lost doll.

There is always this eerie quiet after a night of bloodshed. The uncertainty. Who is in charge now? The lowered eyes searching. Who is still breathing?

Just this morning, I had been looking for Jacques. I owed him an answer. He had promised me more than I deserved. Only last night, as the tocsin rang its cold, metallic call to arms, I kissed him. I told him to be careful.

Where is he now?

This morning, his apartment was stiflingly hot, reeking of old dishes, buzzing with flies. I needed to find him, to answer him before I changed my mind. I needed someone to tell me I had made the right decision, even though a priest would call it the wrong one. But my choice was made. I had promises to keep.

The streets were heating up, thickening with armed guards. It was so quiet. I did not look at faces, only shoes. I would recognize his black boots, speckled with drips of cobalt-blue paint.

I kept walking and walking until my feet found home, reasoning that Jacques would find me there more easily than wandering on the street. I went inside, took the apples and cheese upstairs and sat at the kitchen table to wait. I practiced what I would say, whispering it to myself until my throat was sticky and dry and my lips were cracked. When the fist pounded the door, I was ready.

But it was not Jacques.

It was two National Guardsmen, their night uniforms tarnished with blood.

"Hélène d'Aubign?"

I nodded dumbly as their rust-colored hands grabbed me by the arm.

"You're under arrest."

The sun was in my eyes. Everything was happening too fast. "What are you talking about?" I cried. "Why? What—"

But they were shoving me toward a caged wagon. A prison on wheels. Limbs dangled through the slats. Moaning and wailing hung in the air of the otherwise quiet street like tendrils of fog. A man with torn clothes and no shoes put a key in the lock, and the door swung open.

For me.

"What are my charges? You can't—"

The butt of a rifle hit me hard between the shoulder blades, and I stumbled toward the wagon. Who had taken power in the night? Who had accused me, and of what?

I blinked and was inside the wagon, crushed between bodies trying desperately to escape. They pushed me against the closing door, and pain shot through my nose. But I could *see*. I could see the street, the people turning away and pretending not to know me. I could see myself becoming dangerous.

"Help me!" I cried, but no one turned around. As the wagon lurched into motion, my face slammed the wooden slats again. But in the space between, I could see the house. Horses pulled us farther up the street, and I could almost see the window.

"Théo!" I screamed through the slats. But, of course, he couldn't open the shutters. Could he even hear me? I tried again and again: "Théo!"

And then, pain.

Darkness.

How many more prisoners did we collect? How many minutes passed before the door was unlocked and I fell out of the wagon onto the hard cobbles of the prison yard? My temple throbbed with an egg-sized bruise. Had someone hit me? Or did I bump my head? I felt like I was walking in pudding. Everything seemed to happen with unbearable slowness and yet incomprehensible speed.

Was it really just this morning that they brought me here, to this wild place echoing with curses and prayers? Was it only this morning that I looked into the other cells to see bony hands stretching through the bars, pleading, and a man eating a rat, and a girl in green taffeta being sick?

The Abbaye is dark.

I sit in a heap of damp straw prickling with biting insects, scanning the curses and tally marks and names that are etched into my cell walls. I etch a line of my own: my first.

My cellmate faces the opposite wall. If not for her snoring, I'd think she was dead. She slept through my arrival, slept through the screaming episodes down the corridor, and she sleeps now, with her hair in knots wrapped around her fingers. How can anyone sleep here? We hover on the precipice of our graves.

Through the barred slits, I can see a sliver of gray sky, and who knows? Maybe somewhere beyond it is a place where the dead forget the things they've done to each other. Maybe beyond it is a place of forgiveness and light. The funny thing about the earth being round, though, is you can never be sure which way is really up. Is north true? And is heaven there?

Just this morning, I still believed in heaven. I walked in the sunlight with three apples and some cheese, telling myself to listen to my heart.

But every heart has dark corners.

And everything looks different in the dark.

FONTAINE DE GRENELLE SECTION, PARIS
SPRING 1783

"Shhh," Mademoiselle Girard whispered to me, a gloved finger to her lips. "This will be our little secret."

I nodded and winked at her. She returned the wink, her hazel eyes shining with a conspiratorial smile as she took my hand in hers. As usual, wisps of honey-gold hair escaped her loose bun, dancing across her forehead and cheeks in the breeze. We stepped onto the rue de Grenelle, keeping our footsteps soft, as if we were sneaking up on a bird to get a better look at the hue of its feathers.

"There is a whole world, Hélène, a whole world they do not want you to see," she said quietly once we had rounded the corner. The gray waters of the Seine lapped up her words as eagerly as I did.

"Why don't they want me to see it?" I whispered back, my eyes enormous, my curiosity starved.

"Because," said my governess, with her sly smile. "Once you see, once you know, you will never be the same!"

I was ten years old and delighted that she was going to show me something that my parents did not wish for me to see. This would be our secret. And it was lovely to have a secret of my own, for once. Lovely to be the one who knew something, instead of the one with all the questions.

We walked on along the river, my small hand in hers. There were birds and washer women, children and horses. Scents mingled into a disparate perfume—yeasty loaves of bread, burnt coffee, chamber pots dumped in the streets, and horse urine. Paris remained gray, reflecting the sky, even though it had been painted white.

"Where are we going?" I asked, begging mademoiselle for details, but she just gave me one of those maddening smiles and shrugged.

"Do you see anything you would like to sketch yet?" she asked, because we were officially taking this walk as part of my art lessons, an activity of which my father approved.

We were on an unfamiliar street now. A group of children played a ball game beneath laundry lines drooping with dingy blouses and patched up trousers. They were laughing.

I shook my head and we walked on. Those children were like a sunset sky, or a birdsong. Playing happily together, they had something I could never hold onto. Something that would never be mine to keep.

"All right, then," Mademoiselle Girard said. "Why not give your recitation while we walk?"

I bit my lip and looked skyward, as if the low, gray clouds held the words. Mademoiselle never left her books at my home overnight, though at that time, I did not understand why. Every evening, she left me with a few copied lines to commit to memory and then burn. I found the burning terribly exciting—the curling of the pages, the orange turned brown, turned black, then gone. Sometimes it was a line from the *Encyclopédie* or a few verses from a play by Shakespeare or Voltaire. The night before, it had been Plato, and the words made my heart ache in a way I could not explain.

"Come on, now," mademoiselle encouraged. "Let's have it."

"Every heart sings a song, incomplete, until another heart whispers back," I recited. "Those who wish to sing always find a song."

"Beautiful," she said, and handed me a little wrapped chocolate truffle. My reward. "Do you understand what that means, Hélène?"

I shook my head. I only understood incompleteness. I was a piano made of black keys. A violin missing its strings. A lonely girl living in a château of secrets and whispers, always wishing to be someone else.

"It means that human hearts are destined to be *connected*," she said, as we crossed the Pont Neuf. "And if we seek that connection—not a connection simply of the body, but of the mind, heart, and soul—we will find it."

"How?" I whispered, my eyes aching with tears. "How do you find it?"

She stopped walking and took my face in her hands. Smiling tenderly, she pulled me into an embrace.

"Ah, *chérie*," she said, her chin on my head. "There is so much more than what you have seen. Come, we can't be late."

She took me to the Hôtel Britannique, to an upstairs salon filled, to my astonishment, with guests both male and female. When my mother's friends visited, the men fled to smoke cigars or shoot something. My mother's salon was a place for women to gather and delight in the misfortunes of other women. But at the Hôtel Britannique, men sat down on chaise longues beside women and stood side by side talking to them as if they were friends.

"This is a time for socializing. We'll all sit down for more formal conversation soon. Just follow me," mademoiselle said, smiling and taking my hand again, "and do as I do."

We weaved between small conversational groups, and she introduced me to dozens of adults as her "young friend Hélène." She saved Hugo for last. He was dark and dashing, his skin and eyes a shocking contrast to her milky face. I had never seen a man so tall, or a smile so open and warm.

"My dear friend speaks very highly of you," he said in a thickly accented French, glancing at Mademoiselle Girard as he took my gloved hand in his. "But I have one concern."

My eyes grew wide. "Monsieur?"

"She says you are much too serious," he whispered, and laughed a rich velvet laugh that made me giggle too. "Now, that is the sound a child should make."

However, if mademoiselle and Hugo wanted me to laugh, they should not have brought me to this meeting.

When we sat for the formal conversation, Hugo addressed the gathering in the Hôtel Britannique. He had escaped slavery in Saint-Domingue before coming to Paris to advocate for the freedom of blacks in the Caribbean. With a gentle power, he shared stories of his people's sufferings that brought the ladies, and even some of the men, to tears. Filthy slave ships full of illness. Children separated from their parents. Husbands and wives sold separately, never to meet again. Beatings. Humiliations. He lifted the back of his white blouse and showed us deep scars where he had been whipped. My governess had been right: once I knew of such horrors, of such injustices, how could I go home and eat praline?

When Hugo finished, he took his seat beside mademoiselle, and I nearly fell out of my chair when she removed her gloves and took his bare hand in hers. They shared a look of tenderness I had never seen pass between my parents, and I understood their hearts were whispering. She had found her song. Their fingers remained interlaced as other men—and even a few women—spoke about starving Parisian children and the Declaration of the Rights of Man.

I listened carefully, but my eyes kept returning to those hands.

"Are you going to marry Hugo?" I asked on the walk home.

She laughed, but it was bitter. "There are laws against such things," she said.

"But you love him."

She stopped and took my face in her hands again. "Yes, *chérie*. Yes, I do love him. Very much."

"Then the laws must be changed!" I cried.

Mademoiselle smiled. "Only one salon and already you are a Revolutionary. *Très bon!*"

I felt a little chill. A Revolutionary? What did that mean? Was it something the daughter of a marquis could be? Something I wanted to be?

Mademoiselle held a gloved finger to her lips once more. "Our secret," she said and walked me home under peppered darkness.

Fridays were mademoiselle's day off. Lying in the lazy, yellow morning light, I imagined her lips touching Hugo's, their light and dark arms entangled like sweet éclairs. In my imagination, they always recited Plato to one another.

But what did I know of lovers?

I watched our servants polishing silver and chopping vegetables, wondering what Hugo's work had been like as a slave. His stories haunted me. How could one person believe they *owned* another? How could they care so little for the feelings of others?

But what did I know of the plans my family had for me?

I was ten years old and kept plans by the week: Monday was my day for secret meetings with Mademoiselle Girard and her interesting friends. Friday was my day with my father. There were no days with my mother.

No matter the weather, my father took me on walks to the swanky and scandalous Palais-Royal. If it was raining, Gabelle held our umbrellas. If it was snowing, Aimée laced up my boots. But I never stayed home on Fridays, not even when it was cold enough to turn my nose to a dripping faucet and my fingers to icicles, because that was our day. Papa's and mine.

My father rented a flat for "conducting business," or so he told me, above Chevallier's jewelry store, and I often waited for him downstairs with a sketchbook, among the diamonds and pearls. If I was lucky, the jeweler's apprentice, Théo, would come out from the back room to take his break and talk to me about the books in his brother Max's shop or his funniest customers. Théophile Leroux smiled with one dimple and admired my drawings, and I was sure it was Revolutionary to wish to be kissed by a jeweler's apprentice.

On the walk home, my father would buy me sticky-sweet marshmallows, or flowers from bony street girls. He called me *mon bijou*. His jewel. *Ma fille préférée au monde*. His favorite girl in the whole wide world.

But everything changed one Friday in September. The Montgolfier brothers were going to fly their hot-air balloon over Versailles with its first passengers: a sheep, a duck, and a rooster. I begged my father to take me. When he'd suggested that mademoiselle escort me instead, I pouted and batted my eyelashes. "Please, Papa? I want to go with *you*."

He sighed, relenting. "Who could refuse those pretty brown eyes?"

I kissed his dimpled cheek and went upstairs to fetch my bonnet.

Everything about the balloon was dazzling. I wanted to understand its construction, how it floated and flew.

"It's magic," Papa said with a grin, as if I were just a toddler.

"*Papa*," I laughed, rolling my eyes just as a lovely woman in yellow tiptoed up behind him and tapped on his shoulder.

"Jean-Luc d'Aubign?"

His eyes lit up and he turned away from me. "*Mon dieu*, imagine seeing you here!" he cried, and I, his *fille préférée*, suddenly became invisible.

I tugged his hand. "Mademoiselle has been teaching me about scientific theories," I said, and he glanced back at me. "I know hot air rises, but—"

"That's good." He smiled and patted my head before turning back to the lady in yellow, whose smiling lips were the color of wine. She was tall and slender, and her voluminous brown hair was pinned so high it towered above my father's head. She must have washed it in perfume.

"Did you know the sheep's name is Montauciel?" I kept tugging on my father's hand, but he was turned away, bewitched. The woman returned to Paris in our carriage a few hours later.

She stole my seat beside my father and giggled too much, so I picked up my sketchbook and tried to ignore them too.

When the driver stopped behind Chevallier's, my father told me to pick a souvenir while he and the lady went upstairs for a bit. I chose a gold necklace with a miniature hot-air balloon charm and then sat down to sketch while waiting for him to come back downstairs.

The sun went down, and my stomach began to growl. Théo took a break for dinner and shared his bread and cheese. He peeked at my sketchbook and smiled, but I quickly hid it under the table.

"They're good," he said. "Why do you hide them?"

"It's stupid," I said, looking away and taking a bite of cheese.

"No, it's not," he insisted, and reached for the sketches. I handed them over. "Is this what the balloon looked like? At Versailles?"

I shook my head. It was my own design.

"You should be a balloon designer," Théo said, and I laughed.

"I don't know why I even do this. Papa says it's a waste of time."

"Well, he's wrong," Théo said. He flipped through my pages, examining each and every balloon, the ones with roses, and lilies, and rabbits. As he nodded in approval, his wavy, brown hair flopped into his eyes. No boy had a right to such long lashes—especially not a boy I had no right to love.

He begged me to tell him every detail of the afternoon at Versailles, how the animal passengers behaved inside the basket, how the balloon sounded filling up, how it smelled, how big it was and what color and how far it flew. The jewelry store was full of Montgolfier balloon replicas, but he'd never seen the real one.

"Someday," he said, "Let's go up in one. You and me."

I laughed. "Where would we go?"

"Anywhere you say."

"Everywhere, then," I said. "Let's see the whole world."

We talked about India and America and the Swiss Alps until it was time for him to lock up the shop for the night. My stomach was still growling, and Théo was out of cheese. He gave me his last piece of candy, and I finally decided to go upstairs to ask my father if I could just go home.

I trudged up five flights of stairs. Out of the silence of the stairwell, I heard my father groaning loudly. I heard the woman gasping, almost screaming his name. My heart pounding in my ears, I thought for a second to go down and get Théo. Was my father being hurt? Did the business transaction go wrong? I decided there wasn't time for that and widened the crack in the door. I peered in, expecting to find him dying in a pool of blood, the woman standing over him with a knife.

"Papa?" I whispered, my hands shaking, but he didn't hear me. He didn't see me. And he certainly wasn't dying.

I ran back down the steps, hot tears burning my eyes. I wished they would wash away what I'd just seen. At the bottom of the steps, I leaned against the wall and crumpled down in a heap, my forehead on my knees, my hands over my eyes. What exactly was happening, why my father was doing *that* with *her* . . . It was still murky to me. Only the wrongness of it was clear.

Théo sat down on the steps.

"Are you all right?"

I didn't want to uncover my eyes. "I saw my father. And a woman . . ."

"Try to forget about it," he interrupted gently, his cheeks flaming with understanding. "I'll take you home, all right? We'll write him a note that says you weren't feeling well."

I went to sleep dreaming of balloons, of me and Théo chasing the colors of the sunset around the world.

Night would never find us again.

When I told Mademoiselle Girard what I had seen above the jewelry store, she explained it to me. In one little conversation, I grew up.

"That is not love," she announced, arms crossed. "It's rubbish."

I knew what he did was wrong, and that if he could forget about me for so many hours, he'd surely lied when calling me his *fille préférée au monde*. But I also knew my mother didn't giggle or touch his hand or even sit beside him. I knew my father was lonely, just like me.

I asked Mademoiselle Girard if she thought it was possible for my true love to be a jeweler's apprentice.

"Anything is possible when it comes to love," she said with a laugh like a hiccup. She put our lessons aside for the day in favor of walking to the chocolatier. It was sunny, and we laughed and ate too many truffles. Voltaire, she said, could wait until tomorrow, when the clouds came out again.

The next morning, I waited for mademoiselle at my boudoir desk.

I waited for hours.

But when the door finally opened, it was not mademoiselle. It was my father.

"Papa, where is Mademoiselle Girard?" I asked, worried. "Is she ill?"

"Ill?" he laughed derisively, slamming the *Encyclopédie* onto my desk, rattling my trinkets in just the way the book's contributors wished to rattle superstition with science and reason. "If by *ill*, you mean ill-suited to teach my daughter, then yes. Yes, she is very ill indeed. This book is filled with rubbish. *Rubbish!*"

I looked from my fuming father to the book. How could she have left it here for my father to find? And had he actually read it?

"Science and reason are not *rubbish*," I countered, but he scowled. "This book was written by some of the smartest people in the world."

"Your *oncle* will give you lessons from now on," he said, picking up the *Encyclopédie* and tucking it under his arm.

"Oncle . . . Henri?"

My father shook his head slowly. "No, I'm afraid it will take a bishop to undo what has been done."

No. He couldn't possibly mean that my uncle Jean-Marc would give me lessons. Anger bubbled hot in my head. What right did he have to send *me* to catechism after what he'd done with the lady in yellow? What did he know about love, or rubbish, or his own daughter?

"What have you done to mademoiselle?" I demanded, tipping my chin and staring boldly into my father's blue eyes. "Where is she now?"

He stared evenly back at me. "I owe you no further explanation. You'll report to the library at two o'clock for lessons with Oncle Jean-Marc. End of discussion."

I ran outside to the tennis court we shared with my aunt and uncle. Again and again, I pummeled a ball against the wall. It felt good to hit something, imagining the ball as the lady in yellow, then as my father and uncles. I imagined I could smash some sense into the whole unfair world.

My cousin Marie came outside, asking what I was doing and why I was crying.

"My father sent mademoiselle away," I answered, thrashing my racket so hard it whirred in the air.

"It's about time," Marie said lightly, and I froze, clenching my teeth. Marie's governess had been dismissed the year before because her father declared she'd learned all she needed to know. "Now you'll have time for more important things."

Exasperated, I whirled to face her. "What's more important than *learning*?"

"Becoming a lady, of course. You should be happy, Hélène. You're free!" She giggled and patted my shoulder, but I pulled away.

Marie went back inside with a shrug, leaving me stinging and alone. Being just three months apart, we'd been inseparable as little girls, but in the last year, while my mind had been fixed on revolution, Marie's thoughts had begun to revolve around fashion and wealthy young men. Why couldn't she understand the sort of freedom I craved? I felt so far away from her now.

But I felt farther, still, from my father. I could forgive him for his loneliness, but not for taking mademoiselle from me.

Nor could I forgive mademoiselle for being so careless, leaving her books behind for my father to discover. How could she have given our secrets away? How could she have been so cruel as to fill my head with ideas that would *change* me and then leave before I knew what I had become?

My uncle's weekly lessons, however, left no uncertainty about what

I was supposed to become as the daughter of a marquis: a virtuous and proper lady of the court, fit for a rich husband. I nodded my head and recited the scriptures he chose for me. "But I suffer not a woman to teach, nor to usurp authority over the man, but to be in silence."

"The woman is the glory of the man. For the man is not of the woman: but the woman of the man. Neither was the man created for the woman; but the woman for the man."

And then, I sneaked into my father's study late at night to read the newspapers, trying to understand what was happening behind the closed doors of the salons. I sat by the fountain in the Palais-Royal on Fridays, listening to whispers and picking up discarded political pamphlets. I lived on every stolen moment with Théo, daring to hope that maybe, just maybe, the world could be different.

I knew that storm clouds were rolling toward Paris.

I thought the storm was coming to wash it clean.

But what did I know of storms?

||

THE ABBAYE PRISON

AUGUST 13, 1792

There's hot, sour breath in my face as a voice says, "What have *you* done?"

My eyes fly open, yanked out of one nightmare and thrown back into another. The face is an inch away from mine, her tangled hair tickling my face. Her eyes are spooky, too light and too wide.

I blink, and she pokes me.

"I *said*, what have *you* done? What are you here for?"

"Nothing. I don't know."

She laughs, rocking back on her heels. It's disorienting hearing laughter here.

"What about you?" I snap, annoyed. "Why are *you* here?"

"Me? Five years ago I took some money." Something flickers in her eyes as she spreads her mouth into a gapped smile. She can't be much older than I am, but prison has warped her features. "Five years ago the law said it was a crime to steal from a marquis. Now it's patriotic. Heroic even. Ha! All depends on who's making the rules, doesn't it?"

I only dare to shrug, because I don't know who is making the rules now.

"They're going to release me soon," she whispers, like she's telling me a secret. "I'm on the right side now. Who accused you?"

"I told you, I don't know."

"If they've charged you with treason, you'll die here," she says, her sour smile making my skin crawl. "And not of old age."

CHÂTEAU DES CYGNES (40 KM OUTSIDE PARIS)
APRIL 25, 1789

When I was ten, I expected to wake up feeling differently on my birthday—older and wiser, taller and prettier somehow. I began the tradition of rearranging the furniture in my boudoir before breakfast, trying to make it feel as novel and fresh as I hoped my life would be in the upcoming year. But by the time I woke up sixteen, I knew better. Birthdays really just meant a horde of guests would arrive to eat, sleep, hunt, gossip, and generally make my life miserable for three whole days. *Bon anniversaire!*

Still, instead of powdering my nose and trying on dresses, I pushed end tables and wingbacks around the sitting room. I lifted down the heavy gilt frame above my bed to swap out last year's canvas of coral roses with the deep-purple crocuses I'd painted the day before.

Then I hid in the library of our country château with a newspaper I swiped from my father's study. The news was irresistible: the king had summoned the Estates General for the first time in more than 150 years in a desperate attempt to solve our nation's worsening financial crisis. There was talk of a constitution, and of taxing the nobility and clergy. Behind closed doors, my father and uncles were fuming. They didn't know I was listening on the other side.

Apparently, it was going to take hundreds of men converging upon Versailles to comprehend the simple fact that the longstanding and refined traditions of the d'Aubign family did not come cheap. Attending the opera in the latest fashions, meddling in foreign wars, betting on horse races and games of chance, getting drunk on the finest wines, and keeping mistresses all had their price. The sophisticated assumption was always that someone else would foot the bill.

I assumed that these were also the traditions of my mother's family, the du Mauriers, but I'd never met a single one of them. I knew only that they lived in Grasse and didn't speak to my mother, the Marquise Madeleine d'Aubign. Not that I could blame them.

The marquise was currently in the hall, having a tantrum about preparations for the evening's masquerade. "I said *soft pink*, not coral! And where the hell is that boy from Chevallier's with my jewels?"

My heart throbbed. *That boy from Chevallier's.* I wanted to shout through the wall that he had a name. But then she would have known that I was listening. And that I knew his name.

"He's not yet arrived, Madame la Marquise," said our concierge, Gabelle, and I knew his gray head was down, looking at the polished floor.

"If he doesn't get here before the fête starts, I'll have him hung by one of his own gold chains in the Palais-Royal."

My throat tightened, and I looked from the clock to the window. How much longer would I be able to hide here, waiting for the carriage from Chevallier's? The guests would be arriving soon.

My cousin Marie grabbed the doorpost and swung herself into the room.

"Your fête is going to be *fabulous*," she exclaimed as her little pug, Dulcet, trotted into the library to sniff my legs.

I sighed and reached down to pet Dulcet's velvety, wrinkled neck. "Why don't you pretend to be me tonight? The costume would fit."

Marie scooped the dog up and nuzzled her face into her fur. She laughed. "I don't think I could fool your mother."

"But you could dance with Evereaux. Wouldn't that be worth my mother's fury?"

She giggled, considered it, and then shook her head. She'd been gushing about Alexander Evereaux for months, ever since we first met him at the opera and he kissed her gloved hand. "I have a better idea," she said, grinning. My stomach twisted. "Just get someone else to propose to you tonight, so Evereaux can propose to me!"

"Ugh," I groaned. "I'm not going to marry any of our parents' stupid friends."

"Just *try* for once, all right?" she huffed. "You've never even given them a chance." Patting her leg, she signaled Dulcet to follow her out.

I groaned again and stared at the clock, watching the minutes tick away. Marie wasn't the only one annoyed with my lack of interest in the eligible bachelors of Paris. Last Christmas my mother told me that if I hid in my room to avoid another fête, she'd order copies of my key. As the eldest girl in the family by just three months, I was expected to receive (and accept) an offer first, but as far as I was concerned, Marie could have them all, and I would run off with the jeweler's apprentice.

If only he would *ask* me to.

At the sound of approaching hooves and crunching gravel, I jumped up to get a better look. Peering through the slit between yellow brocade curtains, I held my breath. But it wasn't the delivery carriage.

Instead, the one I saw was well built, black, and expensively utilitarian. The gold spokes on the wheels just begged to be stolen, and when the driver swung down to open the door, I could see the prominent pistol on his hip. A gray head poked out to size up the château, and I put a name to the shriveled-up face: the Marquis Esclarmonde de Foix. I'd overheard him speaking to my father at the opera, tracing his bloodline directly to Henry IV. The Foix blood had crossed with the Bourbons' exactly 144 years before Esclarmonde's providential birth.

But just as I was about to turn for the stairs, another carriage approached, this one a creamy white, painted with the golden crest of Chevallier's.

The driver pulled up behind Foix's stopped carriage, and Théo got out. I watched him scan the windows of the château, shielding his dark eyes from the sun with his hand. Parting the yellow brocade, I stepped out of the shadows, willing his eyes toward my pane of glass. But he turned back toward the carriage, reached for an armful of boxes, and then paused to make way for Foix.

The old man straightened his back and approached my house as if it were his own, his entourage laden with valises. Gabelle opened the door and offered refreshments, but the man simply wanted to be shown to his room. I heard the shuffling drag of Gabelle's bad foot, followed by the sharp click of Foix's dress shoes walking away from me.

I poked my head into the hall and, finding it deserted, dashed to the door. I couldn't believe my luck. Théo froze on the step in surprise, but when he met my eyes over the ribbon-wrapped packages, he smiled.

"They've demoted you to *portier*?" he asked, that one dimple pressing into his cheek as he climbed the remaining steps to the door.

"You're about to be demoted to unemployment," I teased back, holding the door open. "You're late."

He sighed. "There were sheep in the road."

"Sheep?" I laughed.

"Yes, sheep." Stepping into the foyer, he set the boxes on an end table and then glanced up at me before untying the ribbon. "A whole herd of sheep that don't give a fig about diamonds or birthdays or jewelers keeping their jobs."

Théo slid a slim, white box from the middle of the stack, which he offered to me with a slight bow. "Your pièce de résistance, Mademoiselle des Cygnes."

I rolled my eyes at the mention of the feathered atrocity my mother had chosen as my costume. I was supposed to be a swan. Ridiculous beyond words, since our country home was called Château des Cygnes—named after the swans that inhabited our lake. My lake. I was sure that, even with a custom-made hairpiece, I'd just look like a stupid, overgrown bird.

But when I lifted the lid, I gasped.

"I just made a spray of pearls and attached them to a comb," he said with a shrug. "I thought you might like it. If you don't, you'll have to come back to Paris for the oyster shell."

I lifted it out of the box and held it up to the light. "I love it. It must have taken forever."

"It's been done for a week," he said, blushing, and I raised an eyebrow. When we were in Paris two days prior, he had said it wasn't finished. But why would he make a special trip to the country just to deliver it?

"Oh, and I brought you a little something," he said before I could ask any questions, pulling from his jacket a slightly dog-eared copy of *Thalia* magazine. He opened it to the second installment of *The Ghost-Seer*. "I read it already. Sorry. Once I started, I just couldn't put it down."

"Max finally got a copy in the shop?" I asked, because it must have been two months since I'd mentioned I was desperate to know what happened next.

"Special order," he said, the corner of his mouth tipping up into a half smile. Though I usually preferred symmetry, this half smile was a remarkable exception.

"Thank you."

He shifted his feet and turned to straighten the stack of boxes. "It was nothing."

Nothing?

"Well, it's getting warm out there, now that the sun is out," he said, tossing his head toward the door. He cleared his throat and straightened the boxes again. "Should be a nice evening for a fête."

I shook my head and lowered my voice. "There is no such thing as a nice evening for this kind of fête."

"Ah, finally!" We jumped at the sound of Gabelle's voice as he shuffled into the hall, grumbling. "Madame la Marquise is growing very impatient. Do you have any idea what a commotion you've caused?"

"Please, forgive me, monsieur," Théo said, dipping his head. "There were sheep—"

"Just give me the boxes," Gabelle interrupted, stretching his arms out, "and get out of here. Not through the front door, idiot! Evereaux just arrived. This way."

With a polite nod, Théo followed him toward the servants' entrance, and I hurried to my boudoir to avoid playing *portier* for Alexander Evereaux.

Château des Cygnes was much bigger than our townhouse in Paris. Heavy double doors opened from one salon to another, each with its own theme: cherubs, a meadow, crystal, birds, and dogs.

I turned down a long corridor and stopped, going up on tiptoe to peek inside the private theater. The doors were always locked, but I could see through the oval windows at the entrance just enough to make out the stage and the heavy velvet curtains. There must have been a hundred empty seats. Shafts of sunlight streamed through the massive side windows, suspending dust and time. The doors had been closed for as long as I could remember, and for just as long, I'd wished they would open and fill the château with music. Why did we attend the opera twice a week when we could have brought the opera to our own home? This, like so many others, was a question my parents refused to answer.

I slipped up two flights of stairs to my boudoir, flopped onto my bed with a sigh, and closed my eyes. Soon, I'd have to receive my guests. Reaching behind my head for the long, smooth rope, I grabbed hold of the tassel without opening my eyes and rang for my maid, Aimée. I'd need to steel myself with a café au lait.

When she opened my door, her fair cheeks were flushed pink, and wisps of blond hair were plastered to her neck with sweat. My mother must have been running her ragged.

"May I help you freshen up, Mademoiselle Hélène?" If Aimée's pretty pink bow of a smile was strained, she didn't show it. She was pure sugar.

"I think my hair is good enough," I said with a shrug as I glanced in the mirror. "Maybe just a café au lait—and bring one for yourself too. You deserve a rest after dealing with my mother all morning."

She suppressed a giggle. "If I may say so, I wouldn't mind visiting the kitchen a bit," she said, then lowered her voice. "That jeweler is here. The boy from Chevallier's. Have you seen him?"

I nodded, suppressing a smile of my own. "Yes, yes, I think so."

"He's *adorable*," she said, glancing in my mirror to tuck some loose hairs into her bun.

"Actually," I said, suddenly tugging at the back of my head to loosen a few strands. "Perhaps we should redo my hair, after all."

"Oh. Yes, of course. It won't take long." The disappointment in her oversized blue eyes almost made me feel guilty. But all too soon she dropped the extra hairpins in my vanity drawer and disappeared to play the coquette in the kitchen.

I sighed, thinking how easy it would be for him to fall in love with a girl like Aimée. A girl without my complications, who didn't need to dress up like a bird to attract a mate.

Touching the tiny pearls on the comb, I thought of Théo's hands, tanned and smooth, strong and careful. The pearls clung to the ends of thin silver spears that would fan lightly across the back of my head at varying heights. Slightly like feathers, without being outlandish. I would have been thrilled to wear it under different circumstances. Pearls were my favorite.

My mother never wore pearls. She was too fair and thought they would blend in with her neck. She was petite, with light hair and light eyes, and actually very pretty. But my skin tanned easily in the sun, and my hair and eyes were nearly black. All of my features—my coloring, my dimples when I smiled or frowned, my slim nose and sturdy frame—were my father's. Except my eyes. Since both of my parents' eyes were blue, I prized the color brown as my own. Being a girl, there wasn't much I could truly call my own, after all.

Lifting the tissue paper in the bottom of the Chevallier's box, I smiled. It was there, just like it always was. I popped the shiny black licorice candy onto my tongue. Surely Théo didn't slip jewels of licorice into all his customers' orders. Surely this was only for me.

But the daughter of a marquis and a jeweler's apprentice? That was the stuff of fairy tales. Stuff poor children made up to dream their hunger away. Stuff you imagined happening in America, where everyone lived happily ever after. It wasn't real life. Not in Paris, anyway.

I wondered, sometimes, if my father guessed at what was in my heart. It was odd that he still let me walk with him to Chevallier's every Friday, even though I was about to turn sixteen and old enough to be married. I was too old for marshmallows, and my mother was the only one who ordered jewelry. But neither of us wanted to be left alone with her for the day. More than once he had caught me whispering or laughing with Théo, but he only gently cleared his throat to alert us to his presence. Neither of us ever spoke a word of it. I liked to believe that he allowed us these moments, but he would not allow them forever.

I listened to the carriages arriving outside my window, the crunch of gravel beneath fine boots, the chatter of glittering women, and the deep-throated, shallow laughter of the men.

All too soon, my licorice dissolved away.

"Well, look who decided to join us," my mother murmured when she saw me, brushing my shoulder as she walked past. My father had headed up a hunting party for the men, and now the women were clustered in the cherub salon, waiting for the afternoon's entertainment. Someone was coming to sketch portraits of the ladies, but the sheep seemed to have held him up too.

The women loudly gossiped and giggled while shooting sideways glances to make sure that whomever they were talking about was turned away, talking about someone else. I clicked my fingernails and crossed and uncrossed my legs. Marie was deep in conversation about the proper placement of velum beauty marks, and I was pretending to listen.

"Don't you think the left is much more feminine, Hélène?" Marie asked as I jerked my eyes away from the window.

"Yes, of course," I agreed vaguely before looking back out the window. I heard her sigh.

Finally, the artist was ushered into the salon and introduced as Monsieur Jacques Bennette from Paris. After bowing ceremoniously, he set up his easel and arranged his pencils.

I watched him carefully. I had asked for art lessons once, after mademoiselle was gone. My father had only laughed.

Being the guest of honor, I was nominated to go first. My cheeks warmed and I looked at the far wall when the young artist's eyes turned toward me, studying me closely enough to reproduce my image. The rest of the ladies turned back to their gossip, and we might as well have been alone.

"If you feel uncomfortable," he said softly with a smile, "it sometimes helps to talk."

I laughed, blushing hotter. "Well, what would you have me talk about?"

"Yourself, of course. It helps me to capture you better."

"Um . . . I don't know what to say."

His shoulders shook with silent laughter as he leaned close to me. "I don't often meet someone of your station who has nothing to say about herself. What are your hobbies?" he asked, turning back to his easel.

"Well, I actually . . . I like to draw. I paint too. Watercolor, usually."

"Interesting. What do you draw?"

"I enjoy . . . nature." I knew how awkward I sounded, and felt my ears burning. I didn't talk to anyone but Théo about my artwork.

Monsieur Bennette nodded, staring at my hair and performing broad, sweeping strokes. "Go on."

"I'm fascinated with light and water."

"That's incredibly fascinating."

My cheeks cooled a little then. "Sometimes, when the sun is setting, I try to capture it before it fades. Especially over the lake, the sky and the reflections of sky. It changes so quickly though, it's always hard to get it right."

"It is. But it's worth the effort when you do. And you know, no one ever knows the difference if you don't."

I laughed. "True."

"What about people? Do you paint people?"

"When I have a model, which isn't too often." I looked up to see my mother twirling a parasol, leading a group of women outside to the rose garden. Only a few remained at the far corner of the salon, hiding their faces behind fans. I assumed they were talking about me.

"You could paint yourself," Bennette said, squinting at my neckline.

I shrugged and laughed again, recalling the most recent deformed sketch I had made of myself. "My nose is my downfall."

"Always begin with the eyes. Noses begin up there. You'd be amazed to find that once you get the eyes, the rest of the face, the rest of the person, comes easily enough." When he said this, he held my gaze, and I caught my breath.

I glanced at him when he looked away from me and back at his work. He was too thin, but his thinness only exaggerated the size of his black eyes and the thickness of his glossy black hair. He blinked slowly, thoughtfully, as his hand fluttered across the easel like a butterfly, quickly visiting the flowers in a rectangular garden.

"I must have sketched my mother a hundred times before getting her right," he said.

"Are your parents artists too?"

"No," he said, without looking up. "No, they were farmers."

"Are they with you in Paris now?" I asked, and he frowned a little.

"I like to think they're in heaven."

"Forgive me," I said, my ears hot again. "I shouldn't have asked."

"It's all right. It's been a long time." He looked up and smiled at me, pausing for a moment before putting his pencil to the paper again. "Do you take lessons?"

I shook my head. "My father thinks it's a waste of time."

"Not everyone can appreciate fine art," he said. Then he sat back from his sketch, nodding in satisfaction. He turned the easel toward me. "There you are, Mademoiselle d'Aubign. It truly doesn't do you justice, but I did my best."

I looked at his drawing and gasped. It was like looking in a mirror.

As he handed the heavy parchment to me, he whispered, "If you need to practice sketching noses, you may attempt mine free of charge. I live in the Bibliothèque, above the Dancing Bear Tavern. I would be honored if you'd come and see me when you're back in Paris."

"I'll try," I promised. My heart swelled at the thought of sneaking into the Bibliothèque alone and climbing the stairs above a tavern for art lessons, but I couldn't imagine how I might get into that neighborhood without anyone noticing. It wasn't exactly the right bank of the river.

"Good," he said. "I'll be on the lookout."

As Aimée helped me into my costume for the masquerade and struggled to fasten the colossal swan wings to my back, I wasn't sure whether to laugh or cry.

"This will really be . . . something . . . Mademoiselle . . . Hélène," she huffed, hefting the wings up to my shoulders and struggling to hold them there while tying the strings under my armpits.

"It's *something*, all right. Here . . . does this help?" I pulled them up by the tips so she could see to fasten them.

"Yes, yes. It does. Almost . . . done . . . There. Now. You look ready to take flight."

I groaned. "Can't I just fly away from here?"

She adjusted the comb in my hair. "Out to your gallants, my lady," she said with an encouraging nod, handing me my mask. I held it up to my eyes in front of the mirror, peering through the two glittering ovals, and felt a shiver run down my feathered spine.

My father knocked at the door. "They're waiting, Hélène. Are you ready?"

"Ready. How do I look?"

He smiled at me with amusement and genuine surprise. "Like a swan," he said, rubbing his chin and offering his arm to me. "It seems Evereaux is quite taken with you."

"Well, I'm not quite taken with him."

"All the ladies are of the opinion that he's rather enjoyable to look at. Don't you think so too?"

"No. I don't like him, Papa."

He laughed gently. "Well, your mother doesn't much like me, either, I suppose. Evereaux is a good match, though. We've made some preliminary agreements."

"Then unmake them," I whispered, digging my nails into his arm.

Loosening my fingers, he patted them. "Hélène, don't be silly. You're not a little girl anymore."

I bit my tongue as he led me outside to the lake, where a wooden promenade bridge had been constructed especially for the occasion. The guests floated in boats among a hundred lit candles bobbing on the water. The lake house was lit and swathed in ribbons, and lanterns hung magically from the trees. An enormous ice sculpture of two swans was illuminated on a table decked with sparkling glasses of champagne.

"Smile, *ma belle*, all eyes are on you," my father whispered, flashing his own magnificent grin at the applauding crowd. We paraded down the middle of the lake, nodding and waving, trying to figure out who was who behind masks, under hats, and beneath face paint. My smile was shaped just like my father's, but the resemblance ended there. I knew it didn't have the same unsinkable confidence and charm behind it.

All the boats were occupied by couples, except for two. In one, my mother waited for my father, a fake smile chiseled onto her face as he kissed her cheek. In the other, a man disguised as a lion waited for me with a silly tail pinned to his rear end and a maned mask hovering over his eyes.

My wings were problematic. Getting into the boat was a ridiculous ordeal that required my father and the masked lion to steady me, holding my arms and back. There was some splashing and a near capsizing, until finally, Monsieur Lion grabbed me by the waist and lifted me down across from him. He bowed and kissed my hand dramatically, to great applause.

I bristled. He should have at least had the decency to remove his mask before grabbing me, and definitely before kissing me.

He shoved off with a long oar, and we floated apart from the crowd under the weeping branches of a willow.

"Well, hello," he said, flipping his mask up onto his forehead and leaning back against the boat. Surprise, surprise—it was Alexander Evereaux. "And happy birthday."

I nodded my thanks, wondering who was rowing Marie across the lake. I could see why she admired Evereaux, with his strong jaw, high cheekbones, sky-blue eyes, and thickly muscled arms. But his obvious admiration of himself spoiled it for me.

"This is a lovely château," he said, exhaling loudly in relaxation and resting the oar as we bobbed at the edge in the shallows.

"I've always liked it. I was born here."

"*That* must be its secret charm." Now his eyes wandered from my eyes and crawled over my breasts and middle.

I looked away, reaching up to touch a low willow branch. "My cousin Marie and I grew up together here. Have you met her?"

"The one with the bad teeth?" he laughed, and I pressed my lips together, not wanting him to see that mine grew straight. "Too bad for her, the eldest cousin took more than her share of the family's beauty."

"Have you seen the other side of the lake?" I asked, desperate to get out to the open water again.

"Why don't you show me?" he said, his eyes bright with the double entendre.

I handed him the oar, then crossed my arms as he reluctantly rowed us out from under the tree. The boat lurched suddenly on a wave, shoving me back into the branches, and I yelped in surprise. He laughed and then reached across the boat to slowly and deliberately pull a leaf from my hair, his fingers lingering near my jawline. We could hear laughter and conversation just a few feet away.

His eyes were unwavering, glowing with want, as he slid down onto his knees, still touching my face with one hand. "Or you could show me here. Just a little something, hmmm?"

I inched backward, but there was only so far to go. He inched forward, his full and handsome lips open. His body hovered over mine under the cover of willow branches. Just as his lips grazed mine and I could taste the cognac and garlic on his mouth, I panicked. "Get away!" I hissed in disgust, and pushed him hard, square in the chest. The shine in his eyes changed from lust to shock, and before he knew what was happening, he was in the water, splashing and flailing and howling one very loud curse that echoed across the lake and drew a crowd.

"I can't swim!" he gulped, before his head slipped under.

Monsieur Foix's boat swiftly glided up beside mine, and I saw that he was Marie's partner for the evening.

"Hurry!" she screamed at Foix, gripping the edge of the boat, her eyes wild with concern. "He'll drown!"

The old man confidently removed his jacket as his boat reached the shore, and Marie began to cry.

"Hurry up!" Marie screamed again, and Foix quickly waded into the water and retrieved a coughing, spluttering Alexander Evereaux.

"What on earth happened?" my father called, his own boat scraping to shore.

"It seems the boy tried to kiss her," Foix said, amused as he dragged Evereaux into the shallows.

Scrambling up the shoreline to applause and laughter, Evereaux glared at me. The other guests gathered around, faking concern while they giggled behind their fans.

"Poor fellow couldn't control his own oar," Foix joked, setting off a round of crude laughter.

"It must not have been long enough," another piped up, and the men roared.

"He'll drown before he gets the chance to steer a vessel!"

Evereaux sat for a moment with his head between his knees, shamefully coughing up lake water. When he stood, leaves clung to his hair, and one of his boots got stuck in the mud as he loped back to the château to change clothes.

Once my father helped me out of my boat, I stepped toward the glittering ice sculpture for a glass of champagne, but my mother grabbed me by the elbow. Pressing her lips to my ear, she hissed, "Inside! Now!" and shoved me in front of her to lead the way.

I strode coolly to the library, my mother's staccato footsteps following me the entire way. I didn't turn around to face her until I sat on the edge of the desk, my arms crossed tightly as I swung my legs.

"What was *that*?" The sharpness of her voice was outsharpened by her eyes.

I shrugged, wobbling my wings. "I don't want to marry him. I won't. You can't make me."

"Can't I?" she stepped unsteadily toward me, close enough that I could smell her musky perfume and the champagne on her breath. Her arms were crossed below the string of black beads hanging around her neck.

I shook my head.

"You'll see what I can make you do! Look around you—all of this! We've given you everything! Jewels, fine clothes, this château and a château in Paris, just as luxurious, to live in! A fabulous birthday fête. And this is what you give us in return? Disobedience? Embarrassment? Shame?"

"I never asked you for any of those things."

"You ungrateful little bitch!" she shouted, and struck me with the back of her hand, hard enough that feathers floated into the air between us. Her emerald ring hit my cheekbone, and it throbbed with pain and heat.

"I want a choice. That's the only thing I want." My voice trembled with the effort to not cry. I wouldn't give her the satisfaction of seeing how much she'd hurt me. I might let her win at tennis and backgammon to avoid a tantrum, but not here, not now.

"You are so stupid and naïve! You think rich women are free to make choices? Free to be happy? We are not even citizens. We are currency, Hélène. The currency of rich men. Currency with a high face value, however." Despite my fury, I sensed the pain of disappointment behind her words. "And your father has debts that need paying."

"How many debts? What do you mean?"

"He's nearly ruined us, Hélène. If someone doesn't help us soon, we'll have to sell the château. Have to sell the artwork, the furniture—everything." *And I've ruined us*, is what she didn't say, *with parties and flowers and gambling and jewels and doctors.*

"So, you prefer to sell me?"

Her eyes narrowed. "You *will* apologize to Evereaux. You *will* obey me, and you *will* do everything in your power to keep him from taking his offer back. Do you understand me?"

I nodded disinterestedly, but I didn't apologize or attend the remainder of my "fabulous" birthday fête.

||

They're coming for me.

Heavy boots pound the corridor, metal toes beating stone.

They're coming for me.

My heart stops in anticipation, unsure how many beats are left. My cellmate watches me with morbid curiosity, a strange smile on her face. Her words echo louder than those feet: *You'll die here. You'll die here. You'll die here.*

A key rattles the lock.

They're coming for me . . .

"Maude Petit. You're being released."

My cellmate stands.

I breathe, weakness enveloping my body like cold water. *She was right. They're letting her go.*

She runs grimy fingers through her ratty hair, readying it for the outside, but there is no readying that hair for anything but shears. Five years of filth won't come out with soap. But she's free. Who cares if she has hair?

"Take this paper to the tribunal," the guard says, and she takes it. I catch the scrawled signature: G. Danton.

Has Georges Jacques Danton taken power? Does he rule Paris now? If he does, I am dead. He is pushing for the murder of anyone who might be a spy, with or without evidence. I curl into a ball, hiding my face in my knees.

CHÂTEAU DES CYGNES

THE NIGHT OF APRIL 25, 1789

When the clock chimed midnight, I was still in the library with the door locked. My father had knocked once, saying the guests were asking for me. "Tell them I'm sick," I shouted, and I could hear him sigh through the door. I'd cut my wings off with a letter opener and curled up on the windowsill, where I perched in silence with my chin on my knees, hugging my legs, watching the night deepen. Finally, I decided to go to bed.

The hall was deserted, and shadows of the wall sconces leapt frantically to the ceiling, as if even they were desperate to escape tonight. I hurried up the stairs toward my room by the shortest possible route. But when I got to the door, I froze. My door was slightly ajar.

I crept vigilantly into the sitting room, where *The Ghost-Seer* lay open to the correct page on my chair, and my slippers were still on the floor where I had kicked them off. I had been nervous about the masquerade, and anxiety bred carelessness, which is why I must have left the door open. Exhaling, I took my shoes off and moved toward my bedchamber.

I curled my fingers around the edge of the door and peered inside. The blanket rustled. Alexander Evereaux lay on my bed with his boots on, his ankles crossed, his head on my pillow. His eyes popped open. He smiled.

"Hello."

"What are you doing here? This is my room."

"Waiting for you," he slurred, grinning and smoothing the back of his ruffled hair. Sitting up, his boots swung to the floor.

"Get out."

He rose and took a step toward me. I backed away into the sitting room, but he followed.

"No one says *no* to Alexander Evereaux."

I backed up, but he matched my steps quickly and trapped me between the wall and his body. He clutched my wrist and yanked me back into my bedroom, slamming the door.

"Stop!" I yelled.

He shoved me hard against the closed door and pressed his body against mine, his hot breath condensing in my ear. The smell of cognac gagged me as his grip tightened on my arm. "Do you know how many women would give their right arm to have an offer from me?"

"I suppose I saved them the pain of an amputation, then," I said, twisting in his grasp and pushing back. I stepped on his foot, but I had no leverage. We weren't in the water. He was a brick wall.

"You're very stubborn," he mumbled, his lips lazy, his fingers tracing my jawline and playing with a stray piece of my hair. "That's not a nice quality in a girl. You embarrassed me and hurt my feelings tonight, you know."

I clenched my teeth as he wrapped my hair too tight around his finger. "You're hurting me now. Let go. We can talk in the morning, but not now. You're drunk."

"No talking. You'll give me what I want, or I'll take it." He pushed me hard, slamming my head against the wall. My feathered skirt was up. He was clutching my thigh.

I opened my mouth to scream, but he was quick with his other hand. He hissed in my ear, "And I'll see to it that you won't be suitable for another."

I closed my eyes and tried harder to scream. Nothing more than a muffled gurgle escaped his hand. I opened my mouth to bite. The pressure of his hand was so firm, my teeth did nothing more than rub against his palm. How was he so strong? Or was I just that weak?

He unclasped my mouth when he couldn't find the hooks between the feathers on the back of my dress with one hand. Grabbing my waist, he spun me around. I hit my head again and my vision blurred.

He shoved me toward my bed, and that's when I screamed without hindrance, my hands flailing for something hard to hit him with, the vase on my nightstand just out of reach as I stumbled past. I landed on my face, on the bed, still screaming, wanting to die before he touched me.

With a jarring bang, the door swung open and hit the wall, and suddenly, Alexander Evereaux was sailing backward away from me.

I rolled over dizzily to see Théo slamming him against the wall.

"Get off of me!" Evereaux shouted, but before he could say anything else, Théo's fist flew toward his stomach.

As Evereaux doubled over, Théo hit him under the jaw. He slumped to the floor, groaning.

Théo turned to me then, leaving Evereaux dribbling blood onto his own white, ruffled collar. "Hélène? Are you all right?" he cried, falling to his knees beside my bed, taking my shaking hands in his.

I nodded, and a wave of nausea washed over me.

"Did he hurt you?"

"I'm fine," I whispered, just as Evereaux shifted, wiping his mouth on his sleeve. He grabbed my nightstand and pulled himself up. Blinking and swaying, he stabbed a finger in the air at Théo. "Who are you? What's your name?"

Théo was on his feet again, but he didn't answer.

"I'll find out," Evereaux mumbled, squinting, just as Théo grabbed him by the collar and shoved him toward the door. From the corridor, I could hear him slur, "I'll find out, and when I do, you'll wish you'd never been born. This . . . isn't . . . over!"

I heard one last dense thud and groan before Théo shut my door. In an instant, he was beside me again, holding my hand.

"What are you doing here?" I whispered.

He squeezed my hand gently and looked at the floor. "I had a bad feeling," he said. "I've heard things about him."

"So you stayed?"

He nodded.

"We need to get out of here," I whispered to Théo. "What if he comes back?"

"He's not going to do anything right now. He can't."

"But you heard what he said," I whispered, just as the urge to vomit overpowered me.

"Here, sit up," he said, gently lifting me from the mess I'd made and glancing around the room. "Where's your wash basin?"

Clutching my stomach, I pushed damp strands of hair from my face. I didn't want him to see me like that. Didn't want him to clean me up. "I'll call for Aimée," I said.

"It's all right," he said, returning with the basin, apparently unfazed at the sight and smell of me. Pulling a handkerchief from his pocket, he wiped my face. When he cupped the back of my head with his palm, I winced in pain. "He did hurt you."

"If you hadn't been here—" Before I could stop myself, I started to cry.

"It's over now," he whispered, placing a gentle, warm hand on my shoulder. But I remembered what Evereaux said.

"No, it's not! He said—"

"You need to tell your father," he interrupted, carefully wiping tears from my throbbing cheek. "And you need to see a doctor."

I nodded, nauseated all over again. What would my father do? Would he believe me? Or would he simply say I had brought it upon myself—that man was not made for woman, but woman for man?

And how could I tell him without disclosing that Théo had stayed on our property without permission? That he had beaten a marquis bloody, then come into my room and held my hand? No, I couldn't tell my father. I couldn't tell anyone.

"Listen, Evereaux doesn't know your name," I whispered. "He didn't recognize you, and nobody else knows you're still here. So you need to get back to Paris. Now."

"You'll tell your father?"

I waved the question off. "If Evereaux finds out who you are, he'll kill you," I said, and decisively rang for Aimée. "You have to go before anyone sees you here."

He didn't want to, but he knew I was right. Aimée was already on her way. I watched as he left my room quickly, looking back at me as he did.

"Oh, Mademoiselle Hélène!" Aimée cried a few minutes later, quickly ringing out a washcloth and cleaning my face. "You're ill."

I nodded and rolled over so she could unclasp the hooks on the back of my feathered gown. If I hadn't been wearing this idiotic costume, if he hadn't had trouble with the clasps, if Théo hadn't heard me scream . . .

"Should I call for the doctor?" Aimée asked, balling up the gown and tossing it on the floor.

"No. I don't need the doctor. Just a drink of water," I said, and for once, I was glad she wasn't allowed to ask questions. Helping me to the indigo wingback in my sitting room, she propped my feet up on an otto-man and put the chamber pot beside me, just in case, then hurried out for water and fresh linens.

"Do you want a hot bath?" she asked, and from the scrunch of her nose, I assumed I smelled awful.

"I think I just want to sleep," I said.

"What about your cheek?" she asked, and I instinctively covered the throbbing bruise my mother had given me.

"I just bumped it. It's fine. Thank you."

"I'll be back to check on you in a bit. All right?"

I nodded, which was dizzying, and she slipped out to scrub herself down. I locked the door and checked it five times, pulling at it with all my weight, again and again, before closing my eyes and pressing my forehead against it. Shakily, I curled up into a ball on my bed.

I felt all my weakness, all my useless fighting against the strength of a man—useless without the help of another man.

If my father knew, what would he say? What would he do? He may have had his lovers, but he wouldn't let someone hurt me. Wouldn't make me marry Evereaux. Would he?

But just the thought of trying to tell him made my stomach churn again.

There were girls who had mothers to tell. Mothers who would have held them close and stroked their hair until they calmed down. I longed for Mademoiselle Girard's comforting embrace and hated my father for taking her away from me. For the thousandth time, I thought about running away.

I didn't come down for breakfast. I was too nauseated to be hungry. My father knocked and I told him to go away.

My thighs wore little round bruises, shaped like Evereaux's fingertips.

Purplish stripes wrapped around my wrist. An ugly red welt puffed up on my cheek, and my head ached and echoed.

Suddenly, a key scraped in the lock.

It couldn't be him. He didn't have a key. No one had a key but Aimée and me. Would Aimée have given him the key?

"Hélène?" Grand-mère d'Aubign's voice was singsongy, like when I was five, and for once, I was happy to hear it. "Are you feeling better?"

"No," I said flatly, my back to her.

"My God, what happened to your face?"

I shook my head and turned away. "Clumsy. I was just clumsy."

"Why don't you come down for a glass of warm milk?"

"I'm not coming down."

"Oh, well. That's all right." She sat down on the edge of my bed and patted my hand. "No one has been missing you. Marie has gotten all the attention this morning."

I turned toward her, self-consciously covering my cheek. "Marie?"

"Evereaux proposed to her. Worked things out with your Oncle Henri. Isn't that marvelous? A July wedding. It will be just what the family needs—we won't lose the château, after all."

Ice shot through my veins, pulsing into my temples. *Nobody says no to Alexander Evereaux.*

I cradled my sore wrist and closed my eyes. I thought about the little girl who swam with me in the lake and played dolls with me in the salon. How we used to make angels in the snow.

"Well, aren't you going to say anything?" my grandmother asked, the wrinkles around her eyes lifting.

"She can't. She can't marry him."

My grandmother rose, laughing. "You've missed your chance, mademoiselle," she said, lifting a scolding eyebrow.

"No—" I said, but her hand was on the door.

"Maybe this will teach you to behave a little better. I'll leave you to think about that."

Each corner of my room felt dangerous. Every shadow on the wall, every scrape and shuffle in the hallway, every close of my eyelids brought

Evereaux back. My bed still smelled sour, and just the sight of it made me shiver. I couldn't stand being in my room. Couldn't stand him knowing where I was. I rang for Aimée.

"How about that bath now?" Aimée asked gently, but I shook my head. I didn't want to be naked. Didn't want her to see my bruises.

"I can't sleep," I told her. "Something is off about my bed. I don't know. I just, I want to sleep in a different room."

"Oh. Well, I think most of them are full with guests, mademoiselle."

"What about the one in the east tower?

"The little one with the violet wallpaper?"

I nodded.

"It's so small, and it's not been cleaned."

"Can you help me carry my things up there? We can take the fresh linens," I said, and began yanking the sheets and blanket off my bed.

She eyed me with cautious concern. "Of course, mademoiselle. But you may want to dress first."

I looked down. I was still in my chemise.

She helped me into a thin muslin dress, one of the ones I liked to wear when playing tennis, and we each carried an armful of my things through the halls and up to the east tower. I clutched my jewelry box, its contents making me feel a little closer to Théo.

The room was dusty and forsaken, far from the shuffling of guest traffic. I snatched the key off the vanity table and squeezed it into my palm.

"Anything else you'd like me to bring up for you, Mademoiselle Hélène?" Aimée asked after she'd finished making my bed, but I shook my head.

"What about your hair? It's still pinned up—"

"I'll do it myself. Really. It's fine."

"Are you sure you're quite all right?"

"Yes. This bed feels much better," I lied, forcing a smile. "I just want to sleep." She nodded and left. Locking the door and checking it with all my weight, I palmed the key and curled up in the lumpy old bed. Exhaustion took over. I slept restlessly through the afternoon, clutching the key to my chest and sweating through nightmares.

It was dusk when I finally got up and looked in the mirror. It was frightening. The welt on my face was purpling and crusting over where my mother's ring had broken my skin. My hair was matted, knotted, and frizzed. Remnants of party makeup were collecting in the corners of my eyes.

A large, tender lump swelled on the back of my scalp. I winced, wiggling the pearl comb out and loosening the hairs entwined around its teeth. No wonder it hurt so much when I hit my head on the wall with that much metal in my hair—the comb, plus at least fifty pins. But when I saw that two of the spears were bent and missing their pearls, I was heartsick.

Exhausted and shaky as I wiggled pin after pin out of my bird's nest of hair, I knocked the comb off the dressing table and onto the floor. It disappeared under the vanity, and I panicked at the thought of losing it. Groaning at the pressure in my head upon bending down, I slid onto my belly, thrusting my hand into clumps of dust.

A disheveled stack of papers was sprawled against the wall as if they had been pushed off the table, and I could feel a piece of jewelry, heavy and smooth, beside the comb. A brooch.

I raked everything toward myself. The dust made my nose burn and my eyes water. Lighting an oil lamp against the falling darkness, I brushed the pages clean and squinted at them. It was handwritten sheet music, entitled "L'Espérance." Hope.

Where the composer's name should have been written were merely the letters VEdM. I hummed softly, following the rise and fall of the notes as I ordered the pages. The melody was delicate and complex, in an achingly sweet minor key. I wanted to take it down to the crystal salon, the one with the piano, but I didn't think to go anywhere by myself, especially looking and smelling the way I did.

Still humming to comfort myself, I turned my attention to the brooch, which was facedown with its pin sticking ominously outward. Picking it up, I held it to the lamp. The stamp of Chevallier's was scrawled across the back, and I skimmed my fingers over the engraving. It matched the engraving on the back of my comb.

When I flipped it over to see the front, I gasped. It was a single eye, brown and rich, painted onto the brooch and framed in diamonds and pearls. It stared into my eyes in dilated silence, and it wouldn't stop looking, wouldn't blink, wouldn't let me go.

The realization crept up on me, and slowly I brought it up to my face in the mirror. It looked just like my own eye. It was as if I were wearing half of a mask and staring blankly through it.

I was simultaneously fascinated and unnerved.

How long had it been there? Was it a man's eye or a woman's? From the look of the thick lashes and the few strands of dark curls visible just above them, I thought it was a woman's. Did that mean the brooch had been made for a man?

"Who are you?" I whispered, turning it over in my hand

And then, I looked at my own eyes in the mirror and asked the same question.

Made for man, my uncle Jean-Marc had taught me, before taking off his priestly robes to sleep with a laundress or nun.

Currency, my mother snapped before she hit me.

You are a Revolutionary! mademoiselle had said, before sneaking off to love a man with scars on his back, a man who had run away to claim his own freedom.

Trembling, I unlocked my jewelry box and tucked the strange brooch inside with the comb. My father had given me this box on the morning of my tenth birthday, and I thought it was the most beautiful one in the world—black enamel painted with a sparkly golden moon and stars. Even the key was gorgeous, delicate and swirling up like a summer cloud. My father had strung the key onto a necklace, and when he reached around to clasp it behind my head, he whispered close to my ear, "Everyone needs a place to keep their secrets."

Before I closed the lid, I whispered mine into the box: *I am a Revolutionary.*

||||

I'm sure my father never imagined that his secrets would someday be locked away in my box. *Impossible*, he would have laughed, his dimples pressing into his tan cheeks.

Just as impossible as his daughter locked away in the Abbaye for four days.

Four days.

And counting . . .

FONTAINE DE GRENELLE SECTION, PARIS

MAY 1789

"I'll come along to Chevallier's," I offered from the doorway of the blue salon. Marie lifted her eyebrows in surprise. The men were at Versailles to supervise the meeting of the Estates General, but the women had come back to Paris to plan a wedding.

"I didn't think you cared about making yourself look nice, Hélène," she'd said over her shoulder as the dressmaker measured the width of her hips. "It's about time you took an interest."

Yes, I thought on the way to my boudoir to fetch a bonnet and the brooch. *It is about time.*

"Good morning, ladies."

It was a girl of about sixteen behind the counter at Chevallier's, a girl I'd never seen before. Lush, dark curls were pinned above her fair face. She looked like a blue-eyed porcelain doll, the kind Marie and I used to make sing and dance and get married.

"Where's Monsieur Chevallier?" demanded my aunt Charlotte, Marie's mother, walking around as if she had the authority to redecorate. "Inform him that Madame d'Aubign is here to work on designs for her daughter."

The girl nodded and slipped through the door to the back room, letting the sound of pounding hammers and the sizzle of molten silver escape into the showroom for just a second. I caught a glimpse of Théo bent over something red-hot.

"Papa?" the girl called into the workshop, and Monsieur Chevallier came out a moment later, wiping his hands on his apron.

"Lucille tells me you have happy news! Which Mademoiselle d'Aubign is joyfully engaged?" Monsieur Chevallier asked, politely looking from me to Marie, who rushed forward with some sort of unintelligible expression of delight. She and Charlotte began conversing in serious tones with the jeweler at the counter.

After fifteen minutes of fidgeting and perusing the shop under Lucille's porcelain watch, I sat down to flip through a newspaper lying on the edge of the counter, but I couldn't concentrate.

How could I recount to Marie what had happened, without telling her Théo had rescued me? And how could I tell the boy who rescued me that I wanted to give him everything Evereaux tried to take?

I wondered what Mademoiselle Girard had said to Hugo. Had she written him a letter? Or had he been brave enough to tell a white woman he would break the law to love her?

The door to the back room creaked, and suddenly Lucille's eyes and mine were on Théo.

I looked away quickly, wondering if it was all over my face. Wondering if the girl behind the counter could see it. From the tilt of her head, I knew she saw.

"Lucille, I wondered if you might be able to get me some fresh water for the gold?" he asked. "Please?"

She nodded and hurried out the back door. He leaned on his elbows over the counter, looking tired. I went to the counter. "I've been worried sick about you," he whispered, and I blushed hot.

"I'm all right. I slept in a different room."

"Did you tell anyone?"

I looked away, down at a scuff on the counter. "Not yet." I saw his hands ball into fists. "It's complicated. He's engaged to my cousin now," I said, tossing my head in her direction while Théo frowned and exhaled forcefully. The thump at the door lifted his gaze.

"I'll set your water at the bench, Théo," Lucille said brightly, opening the door with her back and pushing her way in.

"Thank you," he said, and his eyes were back on mine. His jaw was bulging and his knuckles were white.

"I'll take care of it. I will. But I want to show you something," I whispered, turning my back to my aunt and cousin while carefully opening my handkerchief. "You know how I said I slept in a different room? Well, I found this in the east tower."

He took a step backward, blinking. "What—?"

"I don't know who it belongs to or what it is, but it's marked Chevallier's on the back. Do you think you could find out for me?"

He dropped his hand below the counter to inspect it. "Did you show it to anyone at the fête?"

"No. I've shown it to no one but you."

His face softened and he tucked it in his pocket. "I'll see what I can do. When can I see you alone?"

Alone . . .

As I calculated the staff's and family's bedtimes and mentally mapped out unlocked doors leading to cozy, dim hallways where Théo and I might meet, Monsieur Chevallier excused himself to fetch something from the back room. He pushed the door open, and a splashing sound was followed by a sharp cry.

"Ah, Lucille!" her father exclaimed irritably. "You've ruined all of

Théo's work for the day! Look here, you've soaked his papers too. These are his designs for his master's evaluation."

"I'm sorry, Papa. I'm sorry."

"You'd better apologize to Théo. Do you know how long he's worked on this? How could you be so clumsy?"

Théo raised a finger to excuse himself for a moment. "It's all right," I heard him saying to the girl. "I can draw them again. It's all up here."

"I'm so sorry, Théo," she whimpered.

"It's fine. It was just an accident."

I could hear her sniffling. Monsieur Chevallier sighed audibly before striding back into the showroom to Tante Charlotte and Marie. "I'm sorry for the interruption. Please excuse my daughter. We're busy today, and I thought she might be able to help. What a man wouldn't give for a couple of sons!" he said with a chuckle.

I craned my neck to see Théo helping Lucille mop up the spill around his workbench, lifting dripping pages, assuring her again that it was all right. Their hands touched for a second as she handed him a towel—a second too long.

"Won't you stay for a game of backgammon?" I asked Marie as the carriage neared our conjoined townhouses. The words were climbing up my throat. I was going to say them no matter what—in the middle of the street if I had to.

"Well, all right," she said, and Tante Charlotte went home. Once Marie and I had our game set up in the salon, she sat back in the chair with her arms crossed over her chest. "Well?"

"Well what?"

"I've been waiting for you to congratulate me," she said, eyebrow lifted.

"I've been waiting for a chance to talk to you alone."

She nodded expectantly.

"I'm afraid I'm not going to say what you want me to say, though. You need to break the engagement."

Her mouth fell open. "I can't believe you're jealous. Just because you're older than me."

"No, listen," I said, and the words were burning, clawing at me then. They hurt on the way out. "The night of the masquerade, the night before your engagement, he came up to my room. He tried to . . . to force himself on me, Marie."

She stared at me, openmouthed, for a moment more, squinting, shaking her head. I touched my throat.

"He *tried* to?"

I nodded.

"But he didn't."

I shook my head, trying to find a way to explain what happened without telling her that Théo was there. No one could know he was there.

"Please, Marie. You can't marry him. I don't want you to get hurt—"

She laughed sharply. "Just because you're older than me, you think you can tell me what to do? You think I can't see how jealous you are?"

"*Jealous?* Marie—"

"Listen, I understand that this is embarrassing for you. But that's not my fault. *You* shoved him out of that boat. *You* embarrassed *him*."

"He hurt me!"

Suddenly, she stood, shoving the game pieces toward me. "It's so typical of you to make this all about yourself! Ugh, my mother was right. You're as delusional as your mother."

"No, look—" I started to pull my sleeve up to show her my wrist, but she stomped out to the foyer. "Marie! Wait!" I called from the doorway, but she slammed the front door and marched home.

I knew my cousin well enough to know that once she'd slammed a door, she was the only one who could open it again. So early the next morning, when the knock came, I hoped it would be her, saying she believed me, that she had gotten her father to call off the engagement.

But it was Théo.

Not a complete disappointment.

"Your order is ready, Mademoiselle d'Aubign," he said, bowing politely, but I hadn't placed an order. When Gabelle turned away, he pressed the brooch into my palm, and his fingers curled around my hand. He didn't let go. I caught my breath and hoped Marie wouldn't come knocking quite yet.

"Did you find anything?" I whispered, trying to focus while he was touching me.

"If you want to know, you'll need to meet me later. What are you doing tonight?"

"We're going to the opera. My father and uncles came home from Versailles this morning, and we're all going out together."

"Can you get away for a few minutes?"

"Um . . . yes, yes, I think I could. What time?"

"Whenever you can sneak out. I'll be waiting outside." He spun on his heels before Gabelle could question us. He was gone.

My father was dressed in his finest waistcoat and breeches with a new cravat and his sword dangling at his hip. His red-soled dress shoes tapped and echoed in the foyer. He still hadn't spoken about the incident on the lake. I expected a scolding, but it didn't come.

"It's good to be home," was all he said, offering me his arm.

"How are things at Versailles?"

"Ah, stable. The situation seems to be under control." He scratched his left eyebrow. He always scratched at his eyebrow when he told my mother where he'd been. So, of course, I knew he was lying. I just didn't know how fat that lie really was.

"Is Mère coming tonight?" I asked, knowing he wouldn't tell me anything more about Versailles. I'd try to get a peek at his paper after he went to bed.

"Your mother has declined to attend," he said with a shrug and a little grin. "I suppose we'll have to manage without her."

I breathed with relief. I would find a way to sneak out of the opera no matter what, but it would be much easier without her hawkish eyes.

We arrived at our box before the others. Oncle Henri sat down beside my father, leaving Tante Charlotte gossiping and giggling in the aisle. Marie stiffly lowered herself into the chair next to me, rustling the air with her skirts. I smiled weakly and lifted my fingers in a fan that was almost a wave. She whipped her head forward, staring straight ahead as if I wasn't there, still and silent as a statue until Alexander Evereaux appeared and magically brought her back to life.

He kissed Marie's hand, looking over her shoulder and meeting my eyes before taking the seat beside his fiancée. I felt his eyes on me when he turned to talk to her, and I stared at the stage curtains, squinting and biting the inside of my lip.

Finally, the lights dimmed, hushing the crowd, and the music began. I snuggled under the cover of darkness and music, slouching in my seat and closing my eyes. I remembered where I was going during intermission. And Alexander Evereaux couldn't stop me.

The great opera diva Théroigne de Méricourt stepped out onto the stage, and the theater melted away. I'd heard her once before at Versailles when I was thirteen. She'd been abroad, touring Europe, but now she was back in Paris and even more beautiful than I'd remembered, her tone even more perfect.

Like the end of a lovely dream, the music stopped. The curtain closed. My heart exploded: intermission.

My father excused himself to socialize, and once he was out of sight, I stood.

"I need a bit of air," I said to Marie, who shrugged and splayed her hands with a look that said, *I don't care if you ever have air to breathe again.* Evereaux rose to let me walk past his seat, but I felt his hand graze my hip as I passed.

Stomach burning, I pressed my way out onto the street. Anxiously, I scanned the crowd.

The bells of Notre-Dame rang nine o'clock, and I turned to see Théo walking toward me. My nerves were sizzling.

"Are you all right?" he whispered, concern hooding his sweet eyes.

I nodded. "I never got to thank you properly. For . . . staying."

"If you're all right, that's thanks enough." He smiled, and I sensed we were equally anxious to turn our conversation away from the events of that night. "Let's take a walk."

"Did you find out what it is? The brooch, I mean." I had brought it along, tucked into the pocket of my dress. I felt it staring into the fabric, and even that felt like an intrusion. I wanted to be completely and utterly alone with him.

We took a few steps, but he lifted a finger to his lips and took a quick left onto a quiet, cobbled street. We walked on toward the Seine, a folk song floating in the air from a musical ensemble on the Pont Neuf. Then, slipping into a deserted alleyway, we stopped, leaning into a shadow against the brick wall.

"It was one of a set," he said, and I pulled it out of my pocket. "Someone brought the painted eyes in and asked to have them framed and set as brooches for secret lovers. They would be worn under the lapel, like this," he said, lifting his own jacket. "That way, you could look into your lover's eye any time you had a stolen moment. But even if you got caught, no one would know whose eye it really was. See? For all I can tell, this could be yours." He smiled then and squinted at me, taking it from my palm and holding the brooch in front of my face.

"So . . . whose was it?"

"Monsieur Chevallier wouldn't tell me that. He said our livelihood depends on our ability to keep the secrets of our customers."

"I suppose we all have our secrets," I said slowly, as my hands began to tremble. I was about to tell him mine.

"Well, you know all of my secrets now," he said, nudging me with his elbow and melting me with his half smile before looking out toward the bridge.

"Do I?" I said, nudging him back.

He turned to face me then, his eyes soft and wide, his lips twitching with words he was afraid to say. "Don't you know how I feel about you, Hélène? Don't you know I'd do anything for you, and if anything ever happened to you, I'd never . . . I'd never forgive myself?"

I stared back, feeling like all my words were suddenly sucked away from my lips and right into my heart. He looked down at his feet.

"I know I'll never have a place on a list drawn up by your parents. But if I had a place on yours—"

"You have the only place on mine," I said, and he exhaled and smiled. "The *only*?"

"Don't you pay attention at all?" I teased, and he laughed.

"Oh, I've been paying attention for a very long time," he said, blushing, and shyly brushed his hand against mine. "Since the first day you walked into Chevallier's with your father."

"I didn't *really* start paying attention to you until you finally shaved off that . . ." I squinted one eye and grimaced as I rubbed a finger on my upper lip.

"My mustache? My very debonair mustache?"

I burst out laughing. "Well, yes, once that was gone, I think."

"I grew it for you, you know. To impress you. Good thing I shaved after work today, then, or we might not even be having this conversation."

I reached up to touch his smooth upper lip. "We still would be. I couldn't imagine kissing it, that's all. But I liked you right away."

"Ah, so that's just when you started imagining kissing me?"

I blushed and nodded, shivery with the realization that we were discussing something that was actually about to happen. *Finally.*

"Well, I, being the highly intellectual person that I am, fell in love with you the very first day, and promptly began imagining the kissing."

"And now love at first sight is *intellectual*?" I laughed, but he touched a finger to my lips.

"We sat there talking, when I should have been working, and I thought to myself, 'There are a lot of girls I wouldn't mind looking at for the rest of my life. This is certainly one of them. But I have never met a girl I'd like to *talk* to for the rest of my life. And here she is.'"

I reached around his waist, surprised at how easy it was, breathing in the smell of his shirt, and he rested his chin on top of my head.

In the distance, the lights rippled on the water, the sounds of the evening prattled on—horse hooves pounding ahead of rickety carriage wheels, drunken laughter, a distant argument, a baby crying—and I tried to believe that I was actually there, that the warmth radiating into my body was really coming from his. How could something feel so familiar and so new at the same time?

"*Je t'aime*, Hélène d'Aubign," he said, taking my face in his hands.

I closed my eyes as his lips closed the last inches between us. I had waited so long—one kiss wasn't enough. I pulled him close again, my fingers finally in his soft, dark hair. We whispered these words to one another until the bells of Notre-Dame rang nine thirty.

"We'd better get you back before they realize you're gone," he said, cupping one cheek in his hand while kissing the other. "The first rule of having a secret lover is remaining unseen. But I'm going to get you away from here, Hélène. I'm going to keep you safe. I swear it."

I pulled away dizzily and nodded, my mind suddenly flickering with anxiety. No one could know about this. No one could catch us together. We walked the length of the alley hand in hand, but stopped when we neared the main street.

"When can I see you again?" he asked.

"There's a door along the kitchen that no one watches. It leads out into the courtyard, and the stables. Everyone retires at ten or eleven."

"I'll meet you there at midnight, then," he said. "Tomorrow?"

"Tomorrow."

"I'll be sure to shave," he added with a wink before disappearing into the crowd.

I made my way back to our opera box, ridiculously happy, like a cloud walking on sunbeam legs. When Alexander Evereaux stood to let me pass, I was careful to grind my heel into his toes.

I sat and swirled my fingers over the enameled brooch in my pocket as the music continued for another hour. I felt the dark thrill of a secret now, and I heard nothing but the pounding rhythm of my own heart, tasted nothing but the licorice in his kiss.

While the foyer clock was still striking twelve the next evening, I tiptoed out through the kitchen door. The horses were sleeping under their blankets in the stable, and everything was quiet and dark. I felt Théo's hands on my waist before I could see him, but his lips stopped my screech of surprise and turned it into a laugh.

"How long have you been waiting?" I whispered, wrapping my arms around his neck.

"Too long," he whispered back. "Much, much too long."

The night was still, with only the sound of nightingales and the occasional snort of a horse. The moon gleamed in through a crack above the closed stable door, and the air was cool without being cold. It was perfect.

"So, I've been thinking about America," he said. "What do you think?"

My pulse quickened. "I think it sounds exciting and exotic and…free."

"Well, good, because I have a plan. I'll have my money in September, and once I pass my master's examination, I could get a job most anywhere. I talked to Max."

"Did you tell him about us?" Just calling him and me *us* was delicious.

He shook his head. "Not yet. It's too dangerous to tell anyone."

His oldest brother, Max, was his hero. He'd fought in the American Revolution and then married the American woman who had nursed him back to health after he was shot at Valley Forge. When the war ended, he brought his new wife home to Paris to open a bookshop on the Rue Saint-Honoré.

"I just said I might like to emigrate. He said he would write to some friends and help me secure a position as a jeweler in the States."

I drew a deep breath and nodded. "Are you sure you can leave your family? I mean, are you sure you want to?"

His fingers interlaced with mine. "I've thought about it before yesterday, you know."

"It won't be difficult for me to leave," I said, nodding toward the house with a lump in my throat.

He brought my hand to his lips and kissed my knuckles. "You know I'll come straight home to you every night, Hélène. No secrets."

"I know."

"Just you and me."

I nodded and smiled, hoping I didn't look as ridiculously giddy as I felt. "Just you and me."

He squeezed my hand. "So, how do you feel about Philadelphia? Or maybe Baltimore?"

"I'll brush up on my English."

"You'll have to tutor me. I know about two phrases in English, and they aren't particularly useful ones."

"Tutor? Can an apprentice afford a private tutor?" I teased.

"I have that all worked out too. In return, I plan to tutor *you*."

"You're going to teach me how to make jewelry?"

"No, I'm going to turn you into an optimist."

I laughed. "That will be quite a task."

"You're not a true pessimist, Hélène d'Aubign. You just haven't had much opportunity to believe anything good will happen to you. But I have plenty of time to prove that it will. And a strategy."

"This all sounds a bit calculated."

He nodded. "I've thought of nothing else. I'm going to make you happy enough every day that you'll believe it will always be that way. That you deserve it. Because you do."

"*Je t'aime*," I whispered in his ear. "I . . . love . . . you," I said slowly in English, lifting an instructive finger. "Your first lesson."

He laughed, repeating it carefully and terribly. "Ah . . . looove . . . yuh."

"Well, your English does need work. You'll have to say it a few more times, until you can do it without such a thick accent."

He touched the back of my head and brought my lips to his before trailing them up to my ear and whispering, "And what about this?" I could feel him smile against my neck. "Should we keep working on this as well?"

I brought his lips back to mine. "*Eh bien, le fait de pratiquer nous rend meilleur.*"

HH+

AUGUST 16, 1792

Once upon a time, mademoiselle taught me that some words are the same
in two languages. For example,

En Française: *La surprise*

In English: *Surprise*

En Française: *Le regret*

In English: *Regret*

She did not tell me that some regrets are too deep for words, no
matter how many languages I could say them in.

FONTAINE DE GRENELLE SECTION, PARIS

JUNE 20, 1789

My father was anxious on the way to the opera. He pinched the bridge of
his nose and complained of a headache in the carriage.

Something had happened.

The din of political chatter around the usually noisy Palais-Royal was
frenzied. The air itself seemed agitated, heavy with humidity, ready to
rain. When I snuck out to meet Théo at intermission, the crowd was bois-
terous and celebratory, alive with cheers of *"Vive la nation!"*

Théo was breathless, bursting with news when we met in our alley. After being locked out of the palace, the men representing the common people of France had declared themselves the National Assembly. Inside the king's tennis court, they took an oath not to separate until they had a constitution. Clearly, the game had changed. Power was shifting. It was only a matter of time.

As I edged sideways through the aisles back to my seat, I noticed that a bit more makeup dripped off the marquis' and dukes' foreheads that night, and that the ladies' fans beat more quickly.

But I couldn't focus on politics or the future of France. In just a few months I wouldn't be French. I was going to break French laws and run away with a jeweler, and I wasn't going to feel sorry for it. I held out hope that the Assembly would change my homeland for the better, but I'd be happy to read about it in a paper from somewhere far across the ocean. Evereaux would never touch me again, not even with his eyes.

I was unaccustomed to happiness, to feeling like the world was bright and shiny and good, a place I wanted to live in. The presses ran twenty-four hours a day, and everyone from the girl who sold coffee on the Pont Neuf to my father fretted and hoped and argued, but I hardly noticed.

I was walking in a dream—a good one, for once.

I dipped my fingers in the fountain in our courtyard and watched the little fish zigzagging below the surface, feeling the cool mist on my face. I began to whistle "L'Espérance," painting swirly designs in the water with my fingers.

Then an echo startled me.

I whistled the first few bars again, and a bird whistled back. I realized that one of my mother's pets must have escaped the aviary, and I quickly began scanning the bushes, whistling and following the echo. It was one of the pretty little yellow canaries, and when I held my finger out to her, she hopped on and puffed her soft belly out in song.

"You like that song? Me too," I said, stroking her neck. I hesitated to take her back inside, admiring her courage. But her wings were clipped. She wouldn't have a chance surviving outside.

I put her back in the tall canary cage by the pink-rimmed jasmine plants in my mother's aviary and closed the door apologetically. "It's for your own good," I said. As I turned to go back to the garden, she did her new trick again, and quickly taught it to her sisters.

I waited until midnight to slip back outside.

The evening breeze was soft and fragrant with midsummer roses as I tiptoed, barefoot and carrying my shoes, across the courtyard and to the stable. I glanced again and again at my mother's window. The oil lamp burned bright in her window, as always, and I breathed a sigh of relief when I knew I was out of her possible field of vision.

"I brought something for you to look at. Here," Théo said after I slipped into my shoes. He picked up a dog-eared folder and pulled out several pencil drawings.

"What's this?" I held them up to the sconce on the wall.

"I thought you could tell me which of these you like best. They're different ideas I have for my master's evaluation."

"Théo, they're beautiful."

"Some of them are similar to current fashions. But some of the others are quite new—not like anything else being sold right now. So, I want to know which one of these you would want to wear."

"I don't know if I'm the person to ask about trends," I said, biting my lip.

"I'm not asking you about trends, silly. I'm asking you about what kind of engagement jewelry you'd like."

My eyes must have popped.

"Did you think marquis are the only ones who give gifts to their secret lovers?" he laughed. "Now, the new styles are moving toward simplicity and symmetry, away from excess and decadence. The goal is to emphasize natural beauty—to bring it out, instead of covering it up, which means it suits you perfectly."

"This one is my favorite," I announced finally, handing him the sketch of a short necklace bearing the Greek infinity symbol turned vertically with a single pearl dangling inside the bottom loop.

"Good. Mine too." He smiled and tucked the pages back into the folder and under his arm. "Now, let's go."

"Go?"

"I have a surprise for you. Come on."

He took my hand and led me out onto the street, where we walked for a few blocks, and then down to a small dock where a little wooden boat bobbed on the surface of the Seine.

Reaching under the seat board, he pulled out a stack of blankets, handed them to me, then untied the boat and shoved off. Once we were floating in the middle of the river, he spread the blankets, folded thick and soft, on the bottom of the boat and lay down. Stretching his arm out, he motioned to me, and I rested my head on his shoulder.

We drifted beneath the Pont Royal. A string ensemble was playing a lively folk song, and though it was after midnight, a few people tossed coins, danced, and laughed.

"Read anything interesting lately?" he asked, and I nodded.

"I was reading *Candide* again last night."

"I cannot approve of that," he said, pretending to be serious.

"Oh? So now I require your approval?"

He laughed, throwing his hands in the air defensively. "No. You can read whatever you like. But I don't like *Candide*."

"And why not?"

"Because Voltaire calls optimism madness."

I laughed. "'The madness of maintaining that everything is right when it is wrong.' Sounds like everyone *I'm* related to."

"But optimism is just hope called by another name. It's not crazy to have hope. To believe that life could go right and you could be happy. Maybe it's crazy to believe some things, but not that."

I smiled and slipped my fingers between his. "All right. I approve of your disapproval."

The boat nodded on the river, pressing us together again and again, sending hot currents through me. We watched the moon, full and bright above us, reflecting in ripples on the water. A long, fingerlike cloud stretched itself across the moon, momentarily darkening the river. It slipped out just as quickly, illuminating the night again.

"Should we have a lesson? In English?" he asked.

"All right."

He pointed to the sky. *"Comment dit-on la lune en anglais?"*

"The moon," I answered.

"Et le bateau?"

"Boat."

"Qu'est-ce que c'est?"

I tried to translate while he wrapped a strand of my loose hair around his finger, bringing it to his face and breathing in. "Hair."

"Ah, hair. *Tes cheveux . . . er,* hair, *boucle?"*

"Curly."

"Et doux," he added, propping himself up on his elbow and spreading my hair over my shoulder.

"And . . . soft."

"Et beaux."

"And . . . beautiful," I translated, shaking my head in embarrassment.

"Beautiful," he repeated firmly, touching my warming cheek. "When are you going to believe me?"

I shrugged, smiling.

His fingertips traced the shape of my mouth. *"Et celles-ci?"*

"Lips."

He leaned over me on his elbow, pausing just as his lower lip grazed mine. *"Et qu'est-ce que je fais?"*

"Kissing," I whispered, and I floated on that kiss, on the hundred after it, on the promise just below the surface.

Clouds drifted over the moon and far away, under the cover of the Pont de la Concorde, I allowed my skirt to slowly shift higher.

"Théo, can't we just leave for America now?" I begged.

"Now?"

"What if someone discovers us? What if something happens to you? I just want to go now. Please? I'm scared."

He sighed heavily and rubbed his face. "You know how much I want to do that. But I need to be able to take care of you."

"I don't need expensive things. I don't need anything but you," I said, playing with a flyaway lock of his hair.

"But you need food to eat. You need a place to live. And we need to buy fares so we can get out of here. If we leave now, I'm not even a journeyman—I'm a runaway apprentice."

"But you're a good jeweler!" I protested.

"No one will give me a job. My brother sent the letter already, and they'll be expecting a master craftsman. We just need to try to be patient and careful . . . Two more months. That's all." His lips slid down my neck and skimmed the top of my dress. I couldn't argue.

The boat sloshed tipsily, my hair fell around us like a curtain, and the temperature between us suddenly shifted too. I placed his hands exactly where I wanted them.

"I don't want to hurt you," he whispered breathlessly, his eyes wide with surprise. "I've heard that sometimes, at first—"

"You could never hurt me," I interrupted, because what did I know about pain? If being this close to him would hurt a little, it wouldn't really be pain. The word would change its meaning; I would rewrite the dictionary myself.

"*Je t'aime*," he whispered, kissing my newly exposed skin. "Tell me, and I'll stop—"

But I pulled him closer and prayed he would never stop. It was as if we were melting into each other, fusing irreversibly, as if nothing would ever come between us.

As if nothing could ever pull us apart.

As the first drops of morning lightened the sky, he sighed and said, "We should go back."

"Am I a mess?" I asked, smoothing my hair and straightening my skirt.

He grinned. "A perfect mess," he said, tucking a wild curl behind my ear before tying the boat. When he pulled himself out onto the dock, the side dipped a little, causing a gush of water to pool in the bottom of the boat, just enough to soak the hem of my skirt.

He grabbed my hand to help me out, but pulled me off balance on purpose so I'd stumble against him.

"Sorry," he said, catching me by the curve of my waist and grinning.

"Liar," I laughed, but he took my face in his hands and kissed my lips, deep and slow.

"I'll never lie to you," he whispered. "I love you. And I'll always love you. Come what may."

"Je't'aime. Pour toujours."

Forever.

We intertwined our fingers and started walking. The breeze was picking up, plastering the cold, wet fabric to my shins. We came to the gate of my family's townhouse, still out of the view of all windows and lingered there, not wanting to say goodbye.

A sudden, sharp bark alarmed us from across the strip between my house and Oncle Henri's, and we pulled apart.

"You should go home," I said, hand over my racing heart, laughing at how violently I had started. It was only Dulcet, Marie's little pug, but our secrecy had me on edge. "You need to work tomorrow. I mean, today," I said, glancing up at the fading stars.

He groaned in protest and reached for my hand. "Do I have to?"

"Two months," I said, and kissed him one last time.

I opened the gate and peeked around the corner of the stables, making sure no one was in the courtyard. Dulcet was on the other side of the house, her barks intensifying. I crept across the courtyard, thinking the dog must have gotten the scent of a fox or a rat.

But then I heard a squawk.

The fist of panic grabbed my heart. Was my mother watching me in the dark? How much did she see?

I flattened myself against the cold outer wall, listening. I could see Dulcet from there, her stout little body bouncing up and down as she barked, her shiny black eyes cast upward toward my mother's room. I told myself one of the birds must be out on the balcony, trying to fly free. Who could blame it for that? But then, I could hear a soft voice muttering from above. I peered around the corner, up toward her stone balcony overlooking the river.

Balancing on the thin balcony rail with her arms outstretched, my mother stood with her eyes closed. Bijou, her large white cockatiel, was perched on her shoulder, nuzzling her neck. Her white scarf fluttered in the stiff breeze, gleaming in the cool early light.

"Shhh," I said to Dulcet, crouching down and calling her to my side. She rolled onto her back for a belly rub.

"Mère?" I said from my knees. I said it softly, so softly, afraid of startling her.

"Who's that?" Her eyes flew open. "Who's there?"

"It's Hélène, Mère. What are you doing?"

"What are *you* doing?" she asked irritably, and I stood, holding the dog, so she wouldn't crane her neck to see me.

"I heard you . . . and I came to see . . . Please, please go back inside. I'm afraid you'll fall. Please."

"Maybe I *want* to fall," she said, her voice thin and brittle, the center of her throat hollowed with the force of her breathing. "Did you ever think of that?"

"No! No, Mère, don't do that. Let me come up and help you down."

"I don't want you to come up here with me. I never should have—" She blinked, shook her head, confused. "I didn't want you, not really. You fill me with so much regret . . ." She spoke slowly, dreamily, and I told my bruised heart that she was confused, that she didn't mean it, but I knew she did. Why did it still hurt, after sixteen years?

"Your father wanted a child so much . . . Your *father*—" My mother laughed and wobbled slightly on the balcony rail, jerking my heart against my ribcage.

When I gasped, Dulcet jumped down and began barking again, the bird screeched, and I bolted for the door. My legs were burning as I pounded up the stairs, hoping desperately she wasn't in a twisted heap on the ground. I came to her door, chest heaving, and paused to control my movements. I eased the door open. She was still on the rail, sobs shaking her precariously balanced body.

I tiptoed behind her until she sensed movement and turned.

"Vivienne?" she cried, her eyes flying wide open above her streaky cheeks.

"No, it's me, Mère," I said, as gently and soothingly as possible, tiptoeing closer. "It's Hélène. Your daughter. See? It's all right. It's just . . . me."

I crept toward her, barely knowing what I was going to do next. I could hear Dulcet's toenails scraping against the wooden floor behind me, her sharp bark, and suddenly my arms were around my mother's waist and we were tumbling backward, Bijou screeching and flapping above our heads. Crashing to the stone balcony floor with a cry, pain shot into my hip and elbow.

"What are you doing to me? Let me go!" she screeched, shoving me away and trying to get back up.

"No! No, Mère! Please!" I yelled, tears hotly streaking down my face. "Stop—just, just calm down!" Dulcet growled at her, baring her teeth, ready to bite, but we were moving too fast. I wrestled her down again, and just as she took a fistful of my hair, Gabelle and Aimée rushed in and wrenched her off of me, Aimée prying her fingers open and Gabelle yanking her backward. A few dark strands dangled from her shaking hands.

The house was buzzing with whispers, and the doctor arrived in a flurry, his bag prepared with sleeping pills. They took her to a window-less room and locked the door. My father stood at a distance, chewing on his nails.

"How did you wet your dress, Mademoiselle Hélène?" Aimée asked me within my father's earshot. His eyes darted to my hem, and I scrambled to think of a good reason for still being in my dress too.

"I knocked a pitcher over in my hurry," I said, glancing up at my father to make sure it didn't register as wrong, my stomach twisted with the lie. "I couldn't sleep. Good thing, or I wouldn't have heard her." My father went back to staring into the wallpaper, and I breathed a sigh of relief.

"Monsieur le Marquis?" The doctor peeked into the room and bowed. "A word?"

My father nodded briskly and they conversed in whispers and nods for a moment, until he saw him to the door. The servants went back to bed, and when it was just the two of us, my father pinched the bridge of his nose and shook his head. "You did a good thing tonight, Hélène."

"It was just luck that I heard her. That's all." Guilt stabbed me for deceiving him. But hadn't he been deceiving me all my life? Deceiving her with his "business" above the jewelry store?

His hand grazed my elbow, and I winced. "You've hurt yourself? Why didn't you tell the doctor?"

"It's just a bruise. I'll be fine," I said, rubbing it tentatively, wincing again.

"Well, when he comes back to check on her, I'll see that he looks at you too."

"Thank you, Papa."

"Off to bed now." He kissed my head. "I'll walk you up."

I wondered what he would say when I was gone. Usually, I imagined that he would feel nothing but anger, but now, as he walked me gently to my room, I wondered if he would miss me, if sooner or later I would miss him too.

"Where is the pitcher you upset?" he asked, following me into my boudoir and glancing around.

"Aimée must've cleaned it up already."

"Ah." He walked around my room, picking up sketches and watercolors and putting them back down again.

"I think we ought to go to Des Cygnes for a bit, you and me. It's getting hot, much, much too hot in Paris."

"What about Mère?"

"The doctor ordered her to rest here, under his supervision, until Marie's wedding. By then, it will all have blown over." He sighed and turned to leave. "It always blows over eventually."

"Papa?" I asked quickly, as his hand was on the door. "Has she ever done something like this before?"

"Not exactly like this," he said, cocking his head and inching an eyebrow up. "But she's done her share of oddities. Yes."

"She said she wanted to fall."

"I doubt she would have jumped. She probably just wanted us to find her—just looking for attention."

"But why do you think it happened? Did she . . . did she take something? A new medication, perhaps?"

"It's the way she is." He shrugged helplessly and was gone.

I pulled the covers up over my head, wondering if my mother was ever happy, once upon a time. I tried to imagine her as a child, fair and smiling. Did she play tennis and backgammon happily with brothers and sisters, if she had any? Did she stroll, whistling to birds in the forest, dreaming of happily ever after? I knew no one who knew her then, knew nothing of her past. But I suspected that none of her dreams, whatever they were, had come true.

I lifted my fist to knock on the aviary door and hesitated. I suppose I wanted her to thank me. To say I wasn't such a mistake after all. So I knocked.

When I received no answer, I twisted the key and peered in. My mother sat soaking her feet in a bowl of rose water, staring vacantly at the green-and-gold wallpaper of her aviary. Three sides were glass from floor to ceiling, where exotic palms stretched toward the light. Magenta and white orchids, gaudy gold-and-blue birds of paradise, and gigantic peace lilies were arranged on tables of various heights. The perfume of the flowers mixed with the sweet, earthy scent of birdseed. Molted feathers were scattered on the floor and floated in beams of sunlight.

"Mère? I came to say goodbye."

"Goodbye," she said flatly. The turquoise parakeets pecked at her jewels, one on her shoulder with a gold chain in its beak, another on the side table, examining her ruby ring with a cocked head. Bijou, the large white cockatiel, raised and lowered his head feathers, screaming at his mistress incessantly. It hurt his feelings that she wasn't paying attention to him, and he was beginning to pluck at his own feathers in distress. Bisou, the African gray, swung on his perch by the window, flashing his bright-red tail and repeating his favorite phrases over and over again, interspersed with kissing noises, while the sparrows warbled and twittered incessantly.

"How are you feeling?" I asked tentatively.

"Fine. I'm fine," she said, shrugging and waving her jeweled hand in the air without looking at me.

"Good." I turned to look at the plants and the birds. There, beside the jasmine plant, the canary cage stood empty, the door gaping.

"Mère, the canaries? Have they gotten loose?"

"I tired of them."

"You what?"

"I tired of them. That's all. Yellow is such an unfashionable color these days." She laughed impatiently and clicked her nails in her lap. I slowly walked a few more paces in the room, stopping in front of three yellow feathers on the braided rug in front of the fireplace.

"What did you do with them?" I asked carefully, pretending I didn't see the feathers, pretending a chill wasn't creeping up my spine.

"I sent them away. They're in a better place now," she said, waving the subject away as she lowered her head and narrowed her eyes at me. "But more importantly, what were *you* doing outside last night?"

"I came out when I heard the dog barking."

"Don't you lie to me, Hélène. You were outside—you were fully dressed, and returning from somewhere. You were with someone, weren't you?"

"I was in my room, having trouble sleeping. I heard the dog barking, the bird, and then I saw you. That's all." *Just a little while longer*, I told myself, *and all the lies will be over. They'll know my secret, and they'll be completely unable to do anything about it.*

She smirked at me. "I remember the details of last night with crystal clarity. I saw you."

"You were upset last night, Mère," I insisted, my heart racing. "You were confused."

"I told your father."

"And you think he'll believe you?"

"You'd be surprised what he'll believe," she said, and turned back to Bisou, petting his neck and kissing his head. "Don't think I won't find out."

Fighting panic, I walked to my room. I needed to tell Théo to stay away, not to send me any letters while we were in the country. She was watching. My father was watching.

I paced, wringing my hands, imagining him growing old in a cold cell in the Conciergerie, me growing old alone—or worse, married to someone like Evereaux.

I forced myself to steady my hands to write. Two months. Two impossible months. I was sure I could not survive so long without seeing him. Without kissing him. But I was more certain I'd never survive losing him forever.

I rang for Aimée. After she left, I curled up in a ball on my bed, suddenly crying over the canaries, how the song I'd taught them had been their last.

𝗛𝗛𝗛 𝗜

The key moans in the lock, and wood scrapes stone. My stomach lurches. I close my eyes so tightly; I see spots.

"Hélène?"

"Simonne!" I gasp, and nearly faint with relief at the familiar sound of my dear friend's voice. The guard shuts the door behind her, and Simonne steps into the cell carrying a pillow and wearing a man's red riding uniform, a loaded pistol strapped to her breeches.

"Oh, God, Hélène! Are you all right?" She cups my face in her hands and smooths my ratty hair, her pretty face wrinkled in horror.

I nod, my heart still pounding in my ears. "Have you heard from Jacques? Is he all right?"

"I brought you some things," she says, skirting my question. She opens and unloads the pillowcase, which is stuffed with chocolates, paper and pencils, fresh nightgowns, and a hairbrush—all on top of a real, soft, feather-down pillow.

"What about the bookshop? Is anyone still there?"

Again, she ignores my questions. "Are they feeding you?"

When I shrug, she unwraps a chocolate truffle and puts it into my palm, but it turns my stomach.

"Please just tell me what's going on!" I beg, squeezing the words through my tight throat. "Nobody will even tell me why I'm here. Please. What's happening out there?"

She grimaces, wrapping my fingers around the truffle and holding my hands in hers. "You'd better sit down."

Leading me to the rickety chair shoved against a desk carved ugly with curses, she swears she doesn't know my charges or the identity of my accuser. But the news she brings from outside is more than I can bear.

Holding my swollen, red face in her hands, she asks, "What's your secret, Hélène? Tell me everything, and I'll try to help you."

I close my eyes and consider her offer. There is so much I haven't told Simonne, as much for her protection as for mine. My secrets have become deadly. A threat not only to me, but to everyone I love.

"If I tell you everything, will you promise to believe me?"

She nods. "Of course. Whatever it is, I believe you. I trust you. You're my friend."

I bite my lip. Am I? Has she been more honest with me than I've been with her? Trust is a tricky thing these days, when power and alliances shift overnight, when friends send friends to the blade to save their own necks. If I tell her, she could walk out of my cell and condemn me in one breath. But so many lives are balanced precariously on the fulcrum of my secrets.

"All right." I close my eyes and take a deep breath. "I'll tell you."

CHÂTEAU DES CYGNES
EARLY JULY 1789

Under the shade of a poplar, I took my shoes off and dug my toes into the cool grass. I opened my satchel and pulled out a pencil and water-color paper. I needed to lose myself. I needed to loosen the sick knot in my stomach.

I began with the linden trees, the gigantic horse chestnut, and the trees of heaven, then penciled in the stone path and the château in the background. I sketched the water reflecting the trees, a hawk floating high above it, and the circular white lake house with the early evening light glinting off its copper roof.

It was the worst sketch I'd made in a long time. The perspective was all off.

It had been seven days. A hundred and sixty-eight hours of not knowing what was happening to Théo. And each hour, Marie drew a little closer to marrying that idiotic beast.

My stomach was flattening out. I was light-headed in the heat. Suddenly, all I wanted was to swim. I stepped into the lake house and let my dress fall to my ankles, just as Marie and I had done a hundred times. We used to keep our spare things there, so our mothers wouldn't know we had been swimming. It was our lake house then. Our place for secrets. It was where I told her that I thought the boy from Chevallier's was nice, but she only laughed and said his mustache was silly before changing the subject.

I tossed my clothes on the floor and darted out, naked, toward the lake. Submerged in the cool water, I embraced weightlessness. I did somersaults, dove deep to touch the bottom and burst up again, shaking the water from my ears. Floating on my back, I closed my eyes. The sun flamed blood-red through my lids, and my hair floated lazily around my head as I remembered what we had done in that little boat.

For a minute or two, I think I felt calm. For a minute or two, I think I believed everything was going to be all right. But I could only float so far before reality yanked me back. Panic anchored me to the shore.

Glancing around, I dashed back into the lake house. A warm breeze swept through the open doorway, drying my skin as I squeezed the water out of my hair.

Back in my chemise, I dipped a cup into the lake water. I covered my sorry little sketch with paint, working feverishly to capture it the way I loved it most, with the sun sinking low, the clouds tinged pink and purple and fiery gold, reflecting off the smooth surface of the lake.

It was the last time I would see it that way.

When I returned to the château, my father looked up from his paper and smiled at me. "You are looking well."

"I went out to the lake today."

"Good. It's good for you to get some sun. Your skin browns so nicely."

"It's quite unfashionable, you know," I said with a wry smile, glancing at his browned cheeks.

"Perfectly," he agreed, creasing his paper neatly and setting it down. I was amazed at the difference in him when my mother was away. He stuffed himself with chocolate cake and laughed. I managed a few bites so he wouldn't ask me what was wrong.

"Let's be off to the crystal salon," he suggested, offering me his arm. "Won't you sing to me tonight?"

He hadn't asked me to sing for ages, though he used to ask me all the time. "What would you like to hear?"

"Surprise me," he said jovially, and before I could talk myself out of it, I sat down at the piano and began "L'Espérance."

Glancing up from the sheet music, I observed the rapid evolution of his face—the initial surprise, his eyes looking back and forth and somewhere far away, the bobbing of his Adam's apple. I played the last chord and waited, breathless.

"Where did you, ah, learn that one?"

"I found it."

"Where?" He stroked his chin and down his neck.

"In the room in the east tower. Do you like it?"

"I love it. It's beautiful."

"Who composed it? Papa?"

He hesitated. "The composer? Isn't it written there?"

I shook my head. "Only some sort of initials. See?"

He glanced over my shoulder and stuck his bottom lip out. "Strange. Well, why not play it again, hmmm?" His eyes rimmed pink, and I could have sworn they were wet. He turned quickly then and walked to the window, parting the curtains and staring into the night. The moon, high and full, cast a silvery light on his almost-black hair. He nodded and hummed as I played, and when I finished, he didn't turn around.

"Music is a funny thing," he muttered. "So tied to memory. That was one of my favorite songs, but you couldn't have known that. However, your mother—she doesn't like it. So I wouldn't play it around her."

I stared at my hands on the keys. "She said I was a mistake. That I fill her with regret."

He sighed heavily and turned from the window, coming to put his hand on my shoulder. "I regret many things in my life. Many, many things. I've made mistakes, but you were not one of them."

I spun around on the piano bench, wrapping my arms around his waist. He hugged me then, another thing we hadn't done for ages, and I felt small and warm and important. My papa still loved me. He always had. And I felt sorry—sorry that I was going to have to leave him without explanation. Sorry that I would be leaving him alone with *her*.

"You regret marrying her," I said, as he stroked my hair.

He sighed. "Marriage is a difficult business."

"Did you ever love one another? In the beginning?"

"Ah, *ma belle*, marriage is not a business of love," he said, taking my face in his hands. "Marriage is a thing of necessity, of alliance, of money. Love is a business of secrets. The two must not be confused."

CHÂTEAU DES CYGNES

JULY 12, 1789

Intense mid-July sun streamed through the tall windows of the sultry, packed salon. Heavy with humidity and thirty different perfumes, the air was difficult to breathe. Marie glowed in her white crêpe dress, trimmed with Brussels lace. Fragrant orange blossoms crowned her auburn hair, and her bouquet, tied with blue ribbons, waited. She was beautiful. Too beautiful for him.

My mother rushed to her, exclaiming over her dress. Two weeks of rest had done wonders for my mother's nerves, but had wreaked havoc on mine.

Flushed, I receded toward the back of the salon. I could feel the stares, the glances over whisper-covering gloves—whispers that this should have been my day, that my day would probably never come. I considered standing up and screaming. Grabbing Marie and dragging her outside. Splashing water in her face until she could think straight. But I knew what she would say: *You're as delusional as your mother.*

I stared at my feet.

At one o'clock, the carriages made the procession to the chapel. My parents didn't look at each other or at me. We were silent, and the silence was almost worse than them saying what I knew they were thinking. I wanted to tell my father what happened on my birthday. But what was it he said about marriage? *Money. Alliances. Nothing more.*

People lined the street and gathered to toss flowers on the steps of the chapel. The bells tolled joyously from the spire. Oncle Henri reached up to the carriage to take Marie's hand, and her head poked out from between the heavy damask curtains. Taking her father's arm, she floated toward the altar like a powdery white moth drawn to a flame.

We recited the low mass, Oncle Jean-Marc gave the nuptial benediction, and then there was the customary embracing of the bride by the women of the family. I remained glued to my seat.

The valet de chambre brought a large basket and presented the wedding souvenirs to the guests—sword knots for the men, stuffed with francs, and fans for the ladies. Mine was ivory, with a diamond at the bottom of the handle, and the vellum was painted with nude cupids frolicking in the air above a meadow filled with feasting people. I opened it and flicked my wrist to create a cooling breeze, but it offered minimal relief. I dabbed at my forehead with a handkerchief. The church was becoming an inferno, and the musk and rose water were helpless to cover the rising odor of sweaty bodies.

At four o'clock, to the tolling of bells, we proceeded back to Château des Cygnes for the wedding dinner—trays of fresh oysters and herring, lamb and Gruyère cheese, turkey with truffles, pâté de foie gras, and partridge pâtés.

Just before the guests were dismissed to the crystal salon for a concert, my father clanged a spoon against his wineglass and stood. "I wish to congratulate my niece on her wedding day," he said, grinning his charming grin. "May you live happily and have many healthy children! To the bride and groom!" He raised his glass in a toast. The servants rushed forward silently to refill the glasses as my father continued. "And I would also like to make a happy announcement of my own. My daughter is to be married to Marquis Esclarmonde de Foix. To my daughter and son-in-law!"

A great cheer went up among the already-jovial drunken crowd. Like the time I'd fallen down the grand staircase as a child, the air was suddenly gone from my lungs.

When my father came to kiss my cheek, I jerked away, glaring. I didn't attend the concert. Didn't wait around to let my ancient fiancé kiss my hand. I spent the night in my room, plotting to change the locks and avoid my own wedding.

|||| ||

Footsteps.

A ripple of shrieks and pleas follow the guard—prisoners begging for news. Begging for freedom. For justice.

Seven days have made me bold. My question is ready as the boots draw near: "Has anyone been here to see me?"

"No more visitors," the guard says, without answering my question.

"Can I send a letter? Please?"

"No letters." He tosses me some bread and a new candle through the bars.

"Can you at least tell me why I'm here? Please. Tell me who—"

But the footsteps do not stop for questions.

They echo on and on and on . . .

I slept late and did not come down for breakfast, lunch, or dinner for two days. I had refused to eat until my father broke my engagement, but

Aimée sneaked me some food between meals. Just as I was about to ring for her, Tante Charlotte knocked on my door.

"Hélène? Come down and play backgammon with me. Please?"

I sighed, thinking perhaps I could slip into the kitchen after the game without my father finding out. "All right."

In the cherub salon, my aunt wiped a tear and sniffled at the fact that her *bébé*—the one who had sucked her whole fist and charmed family and strangers alike with her chubby, toothless little grin—was now a married woman on her *voyage de noces*.

I glanced up at the ceiling, painted with pink winged babies. I did not want to think about the probability of Marie returning from the *voyage de noces*, carrying *Bébé Evereaux*. And I refused to think of embarking on such a voyage with "Grand-père" Foix.

Silently, I slid my game pieces while Tante Charlotte moaned and sniffled. I was losing. Badly. But I was too busy thinking about how to ruin my own wedding to care.

Gabelle knocked and entered solemnly, saying, "Monsieur Henri has returned, my lady."

Tante Charlotte stood with a start, upsetting the game board. The pieces clattered and swirled dizzily on the floor, as if they knew that there would be no getting up again. "Already?"

Gabelle nodded and left.

"Something's gone wrong," she said, wringing her hands. "He wasn't supposed to be back for another week."

Pipe smoke curled out into the hall from my father's study in long, wispy fingers, beckoning me. As I lifted my hand to knock on the door, the smoke's sweet bite stung my eyes, and Oncle Henri's agitated voice stopped my hand. I pressed my ear to the door.

My father's voice. "Good God! Are you hurt?"

Oncle Henri answered, his voice so high-pitched I could tell he was sweating. "Just a few scratches. I didn't make it into the city. Carriages and wagons were backed up for a mile, all of us trying to get to the gates.

It was a standstill. Some of the vehicles at the edges were commandeered, but I was hedged in, so they only took my watch and cuff links, smashed the windows in, and ripped the curtains. And then word came back through the line that the people erected barricades, that a mob with guns and cannons were slaughtering officials at the Bastille. I saw Rochefort, and he said that the Prince du Conde was advising the nobility to get out, to join him in Coblenz to devise a strategy. They're calling it a revolution now. Here's the paper."

I could not stand in the hall anymore. I had to see that paper, to see the names of the dead, if they were listed. Théophile Leroux could not be on it. I knocked.

"Yes? Come in."

I blinked through the haze to see my father sitting at his desk with my uncles and Foix, all of them poring over newspapers. Oncle Henri's soft cheek had a two-inch scrape that was beginning to scab over, and he was wiping his head and neck with his kerchief.

Foix stood, the feet of his chair scuffing noisily across the wooden floor. My father just glanced up and down again. "What is it, *ma belle*?"

"What's happened?" I stepped toward them as my fiancé sat back down with a little gray nod.

"Nothing for you to concern your pretty head about," my father said lightly, but he was scratching at his eyebrow.

"It's already concerned, so you might as well tell me."

He tossed his hands up in resignation. "A mob attacked the Bastille. They took off from the Palais-Royal, where some fool made a speech telling them to go to arms."

"The situation is quite under control, mademoiselle," interjected Foix, looking alarmed that I should have heard such an unsavory report. "The guardsmen put down the revolt."

I stepped behind my father and glanced at his paper. Heads of Officials Paraded on Pikes. Mutilated Guards. Violence in the Countryside. He let me see that much before he folded it up and tucked it under his arm. I planned to sneak down for a better look as soon as he was out.

"Foix is right. Everything will be all right. Better be off to bed now, *ma belle*," my father said, and kissed me good night.

I can still feel that kiss on my forehead.

When I opened my eyes, I heard muffled shouting and smelled smoke. An orange glow cast long and frantic shadows where there shouldn't have been any.

I threw my covers off and ran to the window, wiping the condensation off the pane with my palm. The château was surrounded by a ring of blazing torches, and though I couldn't see the faces of those who held them, it was clear: this was violence in the countryside. It would be in the papers in a day or two, with a death toll. They were shouting for my father to show himself. Flames leapt to engulf several bushes. The château was next.

A knock jerked me away from the window. It was Oncle Henri, dripping with perspiration. "We need to get out. Now."

My heart throbbing, I pulled a dressing robe over my nightgown and gripped my starry, black box with trembling hands. Glancing around the room, I wished I had time to gather my paintings and sketches.

In the corridor, my mother waited, fingering a string of rosary beads, her lips moving soundlessly. My grandmother clutched her dressing robe tight at her throat, and Tante Charlotte gripped her arm, colorless. Esclarmonde de Foix stood a few paces apart, shifting his weight uncomfortably, averting his eyes from me in my nightgown. I adjusted the tie on my robe and fell into line.

The six of us raced through the labyrinth of corridors until we reached the heavy doors to the theater. Oncle Henri opened his fist, revealing a large key. He shoved it into the lock with trembling hands. Sweat was pouring down his neck.

"What about my father?" I asked.

"He has a key too."

Under our feet, a banging thrust vibrated the floor. Another impact. A sudden increase in the volume of voices going up in a cheer. A roar.

My uncle looked over his shoulder and drew a sharp breath. "Hurry."

"What about the servants?" I shouted as the key groaned in the lock.

"They've joined the mob."

"But Aimée—"

"It's not her blood they want. It's ours. Come on."

We dashed between rows of violet-cushioned seats, down the aisle to the stage, which was obscured behind red velvet curtains. As Oncle Henri pulled a thick, twisted rope to open them, I expected billowing dust, but they were as clean as the curtains in my room.

Our footsteps were hollow across the empty, wooden stage. We pushed between another set of curtains and into a large room filled with enormous painted sets. For a moment, it felt as if we were in an enchanted forest as jewels on the trees glinted in Oncle Henri's lamplight.

We shoved aside racks of elaborate, old-fashioned costumes, feathered hats, violins, and harps. We slid between the wall and a grand piano toward another doorway. As she stepped over the threshold, my mother screamed.

We all stopped dead in our tracks.

She clasped her head, then put her hand on her heaving chest and laughed weakly. It was only a room filled with full-length mirrors, polished to perfection. We started to run again, but our reflections appeared and disappeared in the corners of our eyes with such unnerving irregularity that we all felt as though intruders were jumping out of the shadows.

We came finally to a small office that smelled like cigars. The walls were made entirely of bookshelves, and from the look of the yellowing papers at the edge of the desk, it had been vacant for as long as the theater. My uncle went directly to the back corner and shoved aside the ladder on wheels. Without hesitation, he grabbed the spine of a thick, gray volume and reached into the opening it left. He wiggled something, and suddenly, the wall began to spin, revealing a narrow, dark passageway behind it. I stood with my mouth open.

"There is only room for us to go down single file. Foix, you lead," Oncle Henri ordered, and my fiancé took the lantern shakily. Once we were all a few steps down, he replaced the book and slid through the doorway. The heavy revolving door thudded closed. Foix held the light high, and I ran my hand along the cool wall, following him as closely as I could.

The passage was made of rough, dirty stone and smelled like damp earth. As we descended, it cooled considerably, and my teeth chattered. Our footsteps echoed, like a great army was descending through this dark passage instead of six frightened people.

How did we keep putting one foot in front of the other? How did we leave my father behind? Fear gives you strength you didn't know you had. It makes you do things you didn't imagine you would ever do.

"Faster," Oncle Henri commanded, and Foix glanced over his shoulder and nodded. My grandmother, directly behind me, wheezed and slowed everyone else as she struggled to keep her footing. I continually glanced over my shoulder to be sure that everyone was together, hoping that at any moment, my father's footsteps would come up behind us.

We trudged on for what must have been half a mile underground until finally coming to a door. Still the passage was only wide enough for one, so we passed the key up, hand to hand, to Foix.

"Where are we?" I asked, taking the lamp from him and lifting it high so he could line up the key to the hole.

"The crypt," my grandmother croaked.

The light danced wildly in my shaking hands.

It took all of Foix's weight to thrust the door open, and as it scraped across the floor to the crypt, the cool mustiness of cellar air flooded the tunnel. I swung the lamp around, illuminating a series of ochre brick archways held up by thick, beautifully scrolled posts. We huddled together as Oncle Henri closed and locked the door.

"Now what?" I asked.

"We wait."

"How long?"

"In the morning I'll go up and take a look, if it's quiet."

"Do we sleep here?" my mother asked, wide-eyed.

"The only ones who *sleep* in here, Madeleine, are those who never wake," my grandmother snapped.

Oncle Henri used the lantern to illuminate the wall torches, then sank onto a stone bench and motioned for Tante Charlotte to sit beside him. Her soft weeping made Foix uncomfortable, and he and the others found their own benches. I was too restless to sit. I wandered around the crypt.

Each archway created an alcove, housing a group of tombs. The names of the d'Aubigns were etched into each, with husbands and wives buried beside one another. I stood reading their names, one after the other. Olivier, died 1587; Perenelle, died 1594; Hubert, died 1618; Robinette, died 1615; Allain, died 1700; Emelisse, died 1703.

A hand on my shoulder made me jump. "Come over here," my grandmother said, and I followed her to another alcove. She extended her hand toward the floor.

"Your grandfather, Jean-Claude d'Aubign." The date of his death was five years before my birth.

"What was he like?"

"He was a good husband," she answered, crossing herself. "God rest his soul."

"You loved him?"

"He gave me three sons. And a daughter."

"A daughter?"

"She died when she was two weeks old. Look, she's buried here," she said, her voice tight. I looked down at a little stone with the name Marguerite Elisabeth d'Aubign.

"I never knew," I said, and put a hand on her shoulder. "I'm sorry."

"I will be lucky to have one child left at sunrise," she said, drawing a shuddery breath and turning back to the others.

I stood above the bodies of my tiny aunt and grandfather, staring into their names, feeling their blood pumping through my pounding heart.

I found my mother dozing, her head lolling backward against the cold wall. The others sat huddled close, the soft murmur of their voices muffled. When I approached, they straightened, silent.

I settled against the wall to endure the long night. Foix looked often at his pocket watch, and Oncle Henri leaned his head back, closing his eyes, but I could tell he was still awake. We sat silently and waited, hearing nothing, seeing nothing, but imagining everything.

Hours later, when we were all so thirsty and restless that we couldn't bear it anymore, the men agreed to go up into the chapel.

They went up cautiously, and I peered at them from the top of the steps, through the barely open door. It was still as death itself. The smell of smoke permeated the air, but nothing seemed to be disturbed. Oncle Henri opened a cabinet and removed the Communion chalices. They went out the back door to the little springhouse, coughing on smoke.

The smoke wafted into the chapel and to the doorway, but I knew that from our vantage point we would not be able to see Château des Cygnes. The hill and strip of woods stood in our way. I prayed for my father. I prayed that he knew of another escape route, that one might have opened miraculously, if that kind of thing ever happened.

"All is clear," Oncle Henri announced when he returned to the crypt with chalices of cold water. We emptied the chalices, and my grandmother asked for more. I insisted on coming with my uncle to the springhouse. I wanted desperately to get above ground, out of the land of the dead.

"Let's have a look out front," he said, and I followed him to the front door of the chapel. He opened it just a crack to peer out, then nodded to me and swung it wide.

That's when we saw them—first their feet, then the rest of them.

Oncle Henri grabbed my shoulders to steer me back inside, but it was too late. I had seen them, seen their terrible faces. Dangling from the bell tower, my father and my uncle Jean-Marc were tied by the neck, back-to-back, their eyes gaping blindly at the sun. Of course no one had bothered to close their eyes. I put my hand up to stifle the scream that bubbled in my throat, welling up from my heart.

I waited alone, shivering in the springhouse, while Foix and Oncle Henri took them down and laid them in the crypt. There was no way to bury them.

After sunset, I ran into the darkening meadow to pick daisies. I felt disconnected from my body as I snapped the stems, completely unreal and un-me as I brought them back to my father, bloody, bruised, and gone. I lifted his cold fingers and tucked the bouquet under them, thinking of my little hand slipped inside of his, his eyes turned away, still so many things I wanted to say.

It was hours and hours of numb silence, tears still trapped in shock, words trapped in our aristocratic throats. We had never spoken of feelings before, and it was too late—too awkward to begin now.

When darkness had settled on the church, the others crept upstairs, but I stayed behind. I hummed my papa one last song, his favorite, and kissed him goodbye.

Tante Charlotte, Oncle Henri, Grand-mère, and my mother slumped on the edge of a row of pews, not speaking, and Foix stood at the open door, his hands clasped behind his back, looking out silently into the night. I wiped my nose on the sleeve of my nightgown and slid in beside my mother.

"We will go to Coblenz," Oncle Henri told my mother and me, leaning forward with his hands folded between his knees. "We've decided it will be best for you two to go to the du Mauriers. They will best know how to . . . You will be more comfortable with them, I'm sure," he stumbled, and I understood that now that my father was dead, my crazy mother was not their problem anymore. Her eyes were wide as she shook her head in protest.

"No! I don't want to go to Grasse. I . . . I can't."

"Madeleine, it is for the best," my grandmother said in a soothing tone, avoiding eye contact with me. "Surely it will be good for you to see them again. Mend some fences, perhaps."

"Mend?" she laughed bitterly. "I don't think there is any time left for that."

"Surely, your sister will allow you to stay with her. We'll send word ahead from an inn. We can travel together until we get to Évry. Then we'll go our separate ways."

"Let us go back into Paris instead of all the way to Grasse, if Mère doesn't want to go. I don't want to go, either. We have a home there, after all," I said, standing up.

"The gates of the city are blockaded. People have gone mad, Hélène. Who knows if we do have homes there anymore? And if we do, we'll be sitting ducks, waiting for this to happen all over again," my uncle said. I sank down again.

"But Hélène's fiancé—surely Monsieur Foix will take us in?" my mother asked, looking pleadingly at his stoic back.

Oncle Henri shook his head and whispered tersely. "He's going to settle his own estate and come to Coblenz, as well."

"So I will go to Grasse alone? Not even allowed to attend my daughter's wedding?"

"Do you think he wants a wife with no dowry? All is lost. We're ruined. The deal is off. Don't you understand that? There was nothing but the house left, thanks to your management," he said with a sharp look at my mother. "Most of what I had, I gave to Evereaux. There's nothing left for us but to flee while we still have our lives."

"What about Marie?" Tante Charlotte interjected, her hand over her mouth.

"We'll send word once we're in Coblenz. She is her husband's responsibility now, but perhaps they will join us."

"How will we get anywhere?" I asked weakly.

"There is a stable out back. I'll drive us to Évry, and then we'll hire drivers from there."

"Should we all travel together?" asked Tante Charlotte. "I mean, it hardly seems safe. Who knows what these people will do next?"

"I'll drive the cart, but I'll change my clothes into something from around here—maybe from the abbot's house. Perhaps there are some cloths you could wrap yourselves in. Hélène and Madeleine could ride in the back."

"The back?" my mother gasped.

"We'll hide you under a blanket . . . or something," Henri said uncomfortably. He rose and began rummaging through cabinets and chests to find something to wear. He stuffed a bag full of as many jewels and cross-shaped valuables as he could find to sell.

The prickly hay was heavy on my back. It smelled like horse manure. Oncle Henri covered my beaded silk nightgown, arranged stray hay around my hair, and told me to breathe at the slat in the back of the wagon.

"Whatever happens, don't move. Don't speak. And ladies," he said gently, lowering his voice, "I'd keep my eyes closed."

If I had previously considered closing my eyes, they were now wide open to see whatever I could through the inch-wide slat. I thought it would be easier that way, to be afraid of one real thing, instead of the hundred scenarios my mind concocted for itself.

Oncle Henri spoke to the horses, and the wagon lurched into motion under the cover of night. I understood why he told us to make no sound, no matter what. Though he padded my belly as best he could with hay and a blanket, every rut in the road was jarringly painful.

As we rattled down the road, the wind changed. Smoke choked me, and the sinister orange glow appeared through the slat. Up on the hill, the château was smoldering. Flames still licked the east tower—destroying the room with violets on the wallpaper. Bonfires danced on the front lawn, crackling with table legs and picture frames.

I settled into the rocking rhythm of the wagon, trying to hear a melody wind itself around the steady beat of the horses' hooves. Spiking my pulse, a carriage rattled by, but no one said anything.

I was still as a stone. I prayed for my father's soul and wished my mother would hold my hand. I wished someone would tell me everything would be all right, that soon I'd be back in Paris, that soon I'd feel Théo's arms around me—

Théo. I squeezed the tears from my eyes, afraid to move an inch to wipe them.

All through the rest of the night in the crowded, dirty inn at Évry, my mother argued bitterly with Oncle Henri and Grand-mère. There was no sleep to be had, between the name-calling, the snoring, the bedbugs, the stink of sweat and animals, and fear. I considered running away to Paris by myself, but I knew that my uncle was right. I wouldn't make it past the gates. All I could do was try to get a letter to Théo as quickly and secretly as possible. He could come for me in Grasse, I told myself. He would. Of course he would. In September everything would still be all right.

At dawn I received stiff kisses on the cheeks from my family. My mother refused to say goodbye or even look at them. We boarded a public coach headed for Grasse, sandwiched between a fat man with a gold pocket watch and a woman with wild feathers on her hat wearing a suffocating amount of rose water. Etiquette seemed to dictate we look at our feet.

"How long will it take?" I whispered in my mother's ear as the driver started the horses.

"Depends on how many stops we make in this . . . this . . . public transportation. Two weeks, perhaps? It's been so long, I don't remember anymore." Her voice was thick. Her knuckles were white.

"It will be all right. Somehow," I whispered, more to myself than to her.

I closed my eyes, but a vision of my father woke me, shook me from the hazy twilight sleep of the carriage. My papa, who wanted me, whose faults were suddenly dwarfed by the fact that I would never see him again. How could his smile fail him? That smile that smoothed everything over, that charmed his debts away. It was gone. It had no power over a debt this size, no power over people who'd been too hungry for too long.

By the third night, we were exhausted with travel and grief, and the coach was at the end of its route. We spent the night in an inn at Chalon-sur-Saône. I grabbed a couple of sous from the drawstring bag Oncle Henri had dropped awkwardly into my hands when we parted. Without waking my mother, I crept downstairs and asked the innkeeper for paper and ink, which he gave me once the coins glinted in the candle-light. I scribbled my letter to Théo at the innkeeper's desk while his narrow eyes looked over my shoulder suspiciously, reading every line.

Our journey took three sweltering, miserable weeks. Twenty-one nights of sleeping either in a carriage, our brains rattling against its hard walls, or in a filthy, bug-infested inn. My skin was covered in itchy welts. My legs were stiff and restless.

There were others like us, fleeing Paris, some with bits of week-old news. I snatched every paper I could, looking for names, details, reassurances.

I found nothing to make me feel better.

As we finally neared Grasse, the landscape changed. The coast came into view, and a stiff breeze carried salt. The road cut a deep groove through fields of thick, soft flowers—jasmine, roses, and bulging rows of lavender, all grown for perfume that would be shipped around the world.

We were about to meet the du Mauriers. The strangers would be strangers no more. Questions could turn into answers, I thought, with a mixture of excitement and dread. My mother dug her nails into her palms. I took a deep breath. Whatever we would find at my mother's childhood home, it had to be an improvement over waiting.

The carriage we had hired at Avignon turned up a steep lane, and we began to rise above the city of Grasse. I looked down at the corrugated copper rooftops of the charming medieval streets, and at the sea lapping at its shore. The hill plateaued, and we stopped in front of an enormous château with open white shutters. Vines thick with magenta flowers climbed the front and sides. The view of the town and sea below was breathtaking.

My mother's jaw tightened, and she rubbed her hands together. A thin, red smear stained her palms.

A servant came out and conversed with her in murmurs. His eyes popped as he nodded sharply and hurried inside. We waited in the carriage for at least an hour, and my legs were screaming to stretch. Finally, we were assigned a cottage at the far corner of the estate. We were told not to come into the château unless instructed to do so. And we were not greeted by any of the family.

THE ABBAYE PRISON
AUGUST 19, 1792

Today my bread comes with a girl. She's shoved in as carelessly as the food, and she smells just as stale. She doesn't say anything. Just cries.

"Come on, you should eat something," I tell her, but she shakes her head. She pushes her crust toward me and continues weeping.

Enough to keep us alive so they can kill us, I think, dipping my bread in some tepid water so it doesn't break my teeth. I take a chocolate truffle out of my pillowcase, then inch closer until my hand is on her shaking shoulders. She looks up at me, and she's so young, so scared.

"It's all right. You're going to be all right."

She quiets down a little and looks from my eyes to the truffle. "I didn't do anything wrong," she whispers, and I nod to show that I believe her.

"I'm Hélène."

"Marielle," she whispers, and eats the chocolate.

GRASSE, FRANCE
AUGUST 1789

The cottage was old, but clean. The brownstone was covered in thick ivy, trimmed carefully away from the open windows, allowing the warm

August breeze to flow freely. The wooden floors creaked, and the plaster walls were completely bare. I breathed a sigh of relief to find that at least I had my own room and bed.

A driving rain pounded the cottage all through our first night, and the wind howled like a wolf in the woods. The lumpy mattress grated on my back as I stared at the flickering candlelight on the ceiling.

The morning broke weakly, all the color washed out of it. Shortly after we'd finished our breakfast of stale croissants and cheese, the first stranger appeared, wet with drizzle.

My aunt Adrienne was shorter than my mother by a good five inches, and had loads of coarse, reddish-brown hair, wide-open green eyes, and even wider hips. I couldn't imagine any pair of sisters more different.

"Madeleine." She set down her umbrella in a swelling puddle. A servant removed her wet cloak and shook it out the front door before retreating to the carriage. Adrienne smoothed her skirts and fluffed her hair before saying, "Welcome home."

My mother stood, her hands clasped in front of her. "Thank you."

The two women looked at each other for a long minute, trying to agree upon the proper form of greeting. A kiss? An embrace? A handshake?

In the end, they settled for, "Won't you sit down?" (as if this were our house to welcome guests into) and, "Yes, thank you. I will."

I stood in the doorway to my room, waiting for instructions. Waiting to be remembered. My aunt's eyes roamed the room until they grabbed hold of me.

"My . . . daughter." My mother said it softly, gesturing toward me. "Hélène. Your tante Adrienne, my sister." I received a nod and then was disregarded again.

"Well, you've had an ordeal." Adrienne brought her hands together and sighed as she settled her considerable girth into a wingback chair.

"A terrible one," my mother whimpered. At the encouragement of a redheaded nod, she retold our entire catastrophe. I pressed my shoulder into the door frame. I didn't want to hear it again, but what did it matter? I couldn't push it out of my mind for a moment anyway. I learned something, hearing it from my mother instead of from myself: the greatest tragedy was the death of her birds.

There were times I blamed my father for her days in bed, her crying spells. And it was probably at least somewhat true. But to hear her retell the story and weep over those stupid parrots and not him, I hated her.

I blamed her for everything.

Everything.

"I'm sorry. I'm so sorry, Madeleine," Adrienne said, and with that, the tension between them broke. My mother reached for her handkerchief and dabbed her eyes, nodding her thanks. They dissolved into an unintelligible conversation of warbly crying. I interlaced my fingers behind my back, wringing out the urge to hurt her.

When they finally straightened up and sniffled, I listened.

"How is Mère?" my mother asked, her lower lip trembling.

"Fragile. She's been unwell for some time now. It's her lungs. Some days are better than others."

"And . . . Père?"

"As he was."

My mother took in a sharp breath, pressed her lips so tightly they turned white, and nodded tersely. Adrienne clasped her sister's hand in both of hers.

"We may have had our differences, Madeleine, but I always believed you in this. I never doubted you. It's all so unfortunate."

A tear slid down my mother's cheek. "Thank you," she whispered, then added, "And Mère? What does she believe?"

"She told you she believed you, and she still does. You should come and see her soon. She'd like to see you, I'm sure of it. I'll have Antoine ensure that Père is properly," she paused, swallowed, and chose her word carefully, "contained."

"All right," my mother said weakly. "Thank you."

Three days passed. We were served meals. A bent-over servant brought us some embroidery in a soft woven basket to keep us occupied and fresh water for washing. There was nothing to do but to think about all we had lost.

On the fourth day, our breakfast came with a note. We were to come to the château at two in the afternoon to see my grandmother. My mother paced circles around the little cottage all morning, wringing her hands and breathing loudly.

When we arrived, Adrienne was conversing with the servants in hushed tones in the foyer, and then Oncle Antoine, my mother's younger brother, came downstairs. He was a tall man with a pleasantly square jaw, a confident and sure step, and glossy black hair tied in a neat ribbon.

"Madeleine," he said, nodding at her. He looked at me and his eyebrows flew up. "And Hélène?"

I nodded, and he broke into a wide smile. "It's been a long time! The last time I saw you, you were this big." He spread his hands the width of a baby and jogged down the remainder of the stairs to awkwardly kiss my cheeks. "Now you're a grown woman. Your grandmother has been praying to Saint Anne for sixteen years that she would see you again. Come up to her room now."

Propped up on the bed was a tiny, frail woman with wildly frizzy white hair that was illuminated like a halo in the afternoon sun. Her nightgown was so loose, she looked merely like its hanger. Her hands were folded gently on the quilt, and her eyes protruded under closed lids. I thought for a moment she was already dead. But then, Tante Adrienne put a hand on her shoulder and softly said, "Mère. Madeleine and Hélène have come."

Her lids parted to reveal the liveliest blue eyes, fixed on my face. Her tight, gray mouth stretched into a toothy, yellowed smile.

My mother rushed to her and fell to her knees, kissing her mother's hand. They spoke softly for a few minutes, and then I saw tears in my grandmother's eyes as she lifted her gaze to meet mine.

"Hélène! Ah, come here." She patted the bed. She took my hands in hers, and I could feel how smooth, how soft and warm they were. She rubbed the top of my hand, smiling.

"You are a vision of loveliness. I am so glad you came."

"Grand-mère . . ." It felt strange to call her this familiar name, for she was truly a stranger. "I am so glad to see you. *You* are lovely."

Grand-mère laughed, and for a moment, she didn't sound like an old woman. But then, her eyes scanned the room, and her expression fell. "Your father—"

"He's dead," my mother said flatly.

Grand-mère frowned resignedly and nodded, rubbing my hand again. She didn't speak, and I wasn't sure if it was emotion draining her or her physical strength waning. My mother left the bedside to converse with Adrienne in hushed tones in the hall. I tried to take advantage of the moment alone with her.

"Grand-mère?"

"Yes?"

"I don't know why . . . why . . . ," I began, in little more than a whisper. *Why I don't know you*, I almost said.

"Don't dwell on the past, *ma chère*. It will only ruin this moment. And this moment is sweet as chocolate on the tongue, the long-awaited dessert after a bitter meal."

Well, what did I expect? After twenty minutes of small talk, my mother motioned to me that it was time to leave.

"Come back tomorrow," my grandmother said with a wink. "Two o'clock."

Apparently, my grandfather took naps at two in the afternoon, like clockwork. When the carriage came at a quarter to two the next day, my mother was still in bed.

"Are you coming?" I asked, but she shook her wild-haired head drowsily. I closed the door and smiled.

I grabbed a charcoal pencil and one small blank page of heavy water-color paper from my box. My last page.

When I arrived, my grandmother was still sleeping, so I sat in a chair in the corner of her room to wait. My eyes wandered over gilt mirrors, perfume bottled in exotic colored glass, pale yellow brocade curtains, and old-style floral paintings.

Finally her eyes opened, and she said my name. We exchanged pleasantries, and then I asked if I might sketch her.

"You draw?"

I nodded.

"Well, you have something in common with your grandfather then. There is so much that I don't know about you. It's so unfortunate," she sighed. "I suppose you can sketch me, if you want the likeness of an old lady," she said with a little laugh.

"I do. I want something to keep—" I stopped, realizing that I was making it sound as if she were going to die, though of course, she was.

"What shall I do while you draw?" she asked, nodding her head in agreement. I suppose she'd accepted this fact already.

"Just lay still . . . and, if you want to, you could tell me . . . a story."

She smiled and leaned back. "Well, which is my good side?"

"They're both your good side," I said, covering her hand with mine and smiling. I meant it. She was beautiful.

I sketched as quickly and carefully as I could. She told me about her girlhood in Pamiers, but none of the information I hoped for. I worked hardest on the eyes, until I got them just right, hoping they would filter down to a perfect nose.

I captured their liveliness and light. And Jacques Bennette was right— the nose worked itself out. It was the best work I had ever done.

When I showed it to her, she laughed aloud.

"Do I look that old? I don't feel any older than you, really!"

"You look beautiful. And I'll treasure this."

"I want to give you more than just a sketch," she said. "Over there, do you see the jewelry armoire? Look, the key is under the ink mat. Go get it."

I slid the inkwell and pen over and lifted the mat, removing a ruby-studded key. She nodded.

"Now, open it up and look through my jewels. I'll give you anything you'd like, to keep. You don't have to wait until I'm dead. If you wait until then, there will be a tug-of-war between my children and you won't get anything."

"Are you sure?"

"Of course. Now, what do you like? Garnet? Emerald? You have your father's complexion, don't you?"

"Pearls," I said softly. "Pearls are my favorite."

"Go into the third drawer, then."

I felt guilty rummaging through the brooches and earrings, but I finally settled on a wrap-style necklace with three tiers, and three drop-pearls. It was the simplest thing in there, which wasn't saying much. "Is this all right?" I ventured, and she nodded and said, "What else do you want?"

I hesitated. "I'd like to be able to go into town. I'd like to go to the church to pray for my father."

"I'll put the driver at your disposal, *ma belle*, as long as you promise to come to see me on your way back."

"I'd love to," I said, perching on the side of the bed again. "Thank you, Grand-mère."

She rang for her maid and gave instructions: It was to be recorded that she had given me the necklace, and the driver was to report to me each Friday morning to take me to church and wherever else I wanted to go. I'd be given an allowance to buy dresses and paper.

Sébastien, the driver, arrived smiling on Friday morning. His face was a friendly map of lines around two calm, bright-blue lakes. He was sixty-five or so, and had been with the family since before my mother was born. He greeted her warmly, but she merely nodded. She had been staying in her room most of the day since we had come to Grasse, but had actually gotten up to eat breakfast that morning. I excused myself for a moment to get the bonnet my grandmother had lent me, a hideously old-fashioned one she hadn't worn in fifteen years. When I returned, my mother abruptly stopped whispering and nodded curtly at him. Sébastien opened the door and helped me up into the carriage.

"You wish to go to church, yes?"

"Yes."

"Very good, mademoiselle. Very good. I'll take you to Notre-Dame-du-Puy. It's a beautiful church, *tu vois*? I'll take you there. It's a good place to pray. It's old, very old. Built in the twelfth century, I think. The seat of the Bishop of Grasse—what was his name, ah, I don't recall his name, but I'll find out for you. I'll tell you next time. Six hundred years! Not much has been around that long, eh? Lots of prayers have gone up from that place, I can assure you. Did you know that Grasse is a medieval town, mademoiselle?"

He went on like that for the entire trip to town, a sweet and simple man who at least tried to be intelligent. He was an eager tour guide, though he got mixed up about his history, dates, and names.

The cathedral was smaller than I thought it would be—nothing like Notre-Dame in Paris, on the *Île de la Cité*. Notre-Dame-du-Puy opened its beautifully carved wooden arms and welcomed me into a sanctuary constructed of white stone. The walls and the pillars stretched upward into a series of curving arches, the vaulted ceiling crisscrossed organically, and the organ glared at me from above the altar like a furrowed brow.

It seemed to know that I hadn't done much praying in my life, least of all for the dead. Putting one foot slowly in front of the other, all I could think of was the last time I was in church, and I shuddered in the cool stillness. Could anyone hear my footsteps? Did anyone care that I was here?

"Mind if I join you, mademoiselle?"

I jumped, but it was just Sébastien.

"Of course not," I said, lowering myself to my knees and trying to find silent words that would float upward.

Sébastien knelt beside me, his lips moving soundlessly, a few tears slipping down his cheeks. After whispering *amen*, he turned to me.

"Now, how can I pray for you?"

My mouth hung open. No one had ever asked me this before. "My father . . . he's dead."

"Oh. Oh my." He stood up from the prayer rail. Motioning to me, he slid into the front pew. "Sit, sit. Now, you tell me what happened." I sat beside him on the edge of the front pew, which was slippery and smelled strongly of polish. The altar loomed before us.

"Do you know what's happening in Paris?"

He nodded. "Yes, yes. I know there is a revolution, yes."

"A few days after the Bastille fell, our home in the country was attacked by a mob of villagers. I escaped with my mother, my aunt and uncle, and my grandmother. But my father wasn't so lucky. I saw him hanging from the bell tower—" I choked on the words, and suddenly this stranger, this sweet old man, hugged me. How could it be that all that time in the crypt, on the carriage, in the cottage, my family never did such a thing? It was a small act of kindness that broke a floodgate inside me, and I wept.

"There, there, there," he murmured, patting my back. "That's it, mademoiselle. You let those tears flow. Tears cleanse the heart of grief, *tu vois*? It's all right now. It's all right."

He gave me a clean, pressed handkerchief. I stood and blew my nose, ashamed of my swollen face. He took my arm gently and led me out to the carriage.

"Where do you want to go next, Mademoiselle Hélène? To the dress shop?"

"Umm, I'd like to post a letter," I said tentatively. "Can you take me to the postmaster?"

The lines on his face suddenly changed, and his bright eyes clouded. "I'm sorry, mademoiselle. I'm sorry, but I've been instructed not to let you post any mail."

"What? Why? By whom?"

"By . . . your mother, mademoiselle," he said, and bowed his head.

"Monsieur, this letter . . . this letter is more important to me than anything. Please? Please?"

He huffed in deliberation and the corners of his mouth tugged downward. "I have orders. And I'm not anxious to disobey Madame d'Aubign."

"Have you ever loved someone, monsieur? I mean, really, truly loved someone? So much that to be without them would be like . . . like being without half of yourself? That you couldn't go on knowing you'd never see them again?"

He inhaled deeply and turned, blinking. Slowly, he nodded his head. "I was married for forty years. She died last year."

"What happened?"

"Ah. She fell and broke her hip in the fall, and died in the spring. It was a long and painful winter. It still feels like winter, even now," he said, looking up at the hot, clear summer sky.

"I'm sorry, monsieur. I'm so sorry to hear that."

"Thank you."

"What was your wife's name?"

"Hyacinthe. And she was an angel."

I nodded, meeting his eyes silently, pleading.

He frowned again and drew a long and labored breath. He fidgeted. "Mademoiselle Hélène?"

"Yes?"

"He's good to you?"

"Yes. Very, very good to me."

He nodded again.

"I don't like to break rules. I only break rules when I'm certain that breaking them is the greater right, *tu vois*? When it would be more wrong to do the right thing than it would be to do the right wrong thing? *Tu vois*?"

I smiled and nodded.

"Just this once, *tu vois*?" I threw my arms around his neck, and he laughed in surprise. "My, my, goodness. Here, now, this will be our little secret."

"Thank you, monsieur. Thank you."

He stopped at the corner of a lovely cobbled street and said, "Now, you get out here, and I won't watch you. You could go to the fourth door on the right to post letters, but I'm not telling you that, *tu vois*? They even have paper and envelopes in there, but you might have figured it out anyway, if you asked the apothecary. I didn't see you go anywhere with any letters, *tu vois*? I don't know a blessed thing. All right, then."

"I'm just going to the apothecary, then. I'll be back shortly."

"Very good, Mademoiselle Hélène. I think I'll doze for a bit."

I knocked on the door, overhung by a basket spilling over with trailing ivy and red and white flowers. The postmaster gave me writing supplies, and with trembling hands I wrote to Théo telling him where I was, that I would be at Notre-Dame-du-Puy every Friday, waiting for him. I kissed the paper before tucking it into an envelope and handing it to the postmaster.

"Is mail coming through to and from Paris?" I asked him cautiously.

"Yes, mademoiselle. Yes, it is," he said with a friendly nod. "Things are settling, a bit."

"Do you have any newspapers?"

"Not today."

"How much for the candy?" I asked, eyeing the jar of black licorice on the counter.

"For you," he said, smiling kindly and putting one in my hand. "Free."

The light breeze of relief blew into my heart as I walked back to the carriage, licorice bursting on my tongue. I removed the dingy old bonnet to let the sun warm my head. Sébastien took me to buy a large pack of watercolor paper, paints, and pencils, and then to the dress shop. I bought a new bonnet and a simple white dress edged with lace that I thought Théo would like. I imagined our meeting at Notre-Dame, his hands on that dress, his arms around it. For the first time in many weeks, I indulged in the luxury of hope.

I visited my grandmother at two o'clock that afternoon as promised, but she was sleeping deeply. I waited half an hour and then left her a note.

I wandered the halls silently until I found what I wanted—the library. I glanced over my shoulder before selecting a few old-smelling volumes of poetry. Tucking them under my arm, I should have turned left to go back to the carriage. But I turned right instead and tiptoed down another corridor lined with closed doors, then rounded a wide corner.

Double doors opened into a room of paneled white damask framed with swirling gold carvings from floor to ceiling. It was clearly a showroom.

I stepped inside.

Two dozen shiny oil portraits hung on the walls, interspersed with ornately framed landscapes and florals. Bronze busts stared vacantly at the walls from carved gilt pedestals.

I looked into the distinguished faces of my ancestors, one at a time. It was difficult to place them chronologically, but I did my best to gauge fashions and styles. Their names meant nothing to me.

I came, finally, to a portrait of a man in a general's uniform, his sword proudly dangling at his side, his dark, curly hair tied with a neat bow. An inscription read, *General du Maurier: The Second Carnatic War, 1749.* He stood in the foreground with an army of slain Indians behind him in the distance, their bleeding, red-turbaned leader clinging to a falling, painted elephant. His eyes were dark and penetrating, his curls springy and smooth. I realized that he must be my grandfather.

And I realized it could have been his eye painted onto the brooch. All that time I had assumed it was a lady's eye, but—his curls, the color—it could have been his. Just as easily as it could have been mine.

I glanced over my shoulder anxiously. How long was my grandfather's afternoon nap? Why was he supposed to be "contained," as Tante Adrienne had said? I all but ran outside and woke Sébastien where he dozed in the carriage.

Back at the cottage, my mother sat facing the fire in a rocking chair with her embroidery. When I'd finished putting my new things away, I came to sit beside her, finding her stitches distractedly uneven.

"Is there something . . . I can do for you, Mère?"

"No." She didn't turn to me, but I heard the wobble in her voice.

"Something I can get you?"

"I miss my birds. But I don't suppose you can get me any of them. They've been fricasseed."

"Perhaps we could buy a new one for the cottage. A little sparrow? Or a parakeet? You always enjoyed teaching them to whistle."

She shrugged and yanked at another crooked stitch. I took a slow, measured breath.

"Will you tell me . . . what happened?"

"Nothing happened. I embroidered while you were gone. That's all."

"You know what I mean. What happened between you and Grand-père. Won't you please tell me why I don't know any of these people— why everything is so strange? I must be the only one who doesn't know. Please?"

She shook her head firmly, and yanked at a stitch so hard, it ripped.

I sighed loudly at her and stared into the fire. The silence between us stretched the evening like wool spinning into yarn, an endless strand that knitted itself into hours, days, weeks.

I opened the carriage curtains to let the cool September air rush over my throbbing head. Sébastien prattled on about the news with his general expert confusion about what was happening in Paris. Once or twice, he asked me if I was all right, and I nodded.

The dark-eyed general was nagging me. Was it his eye staring at the inside of my jewelry box? But how would it have ended up in the room with the violet wallpaper? My eyes stung as I thought about flames reducing those flowers to ash.

Soon, I told myself. Soon Théo would come for me.

But *soon* seemed like the remainder of purgatory, and just as uncertain. What if something had happened to him? Or to my letters? I bounced in the carriage, squeezing my aching eyes closed. His master's evaluation was scheduled for early September. If he left immediately after, he'd arrive before the end of the month.

I had until then to find out what had happened between my mother and her family. I would make someone tell me before I left Grasse.

My grandmother was bright-eyed and smiling when I arrived.

"Tell me how you've been occupying yourself, *ma belle*," she said, and I took my chances.

"I went into the portrait hall the other day," I said carefully, gauging her reaction. She nodded; it was all right. "I got lost for a bit and found myself there. I saw—I think I saw Grand-père. Was he in the navy?"

She sighed, and I was afraid that I'd made a mistake. But then she smiled, her eyes fixed on me again. "He was a general. I hardly knew him early in our marriage because he was always traveling with his men, always fighting here, securing peace there—mostly in India, I think. They said he was a brave man. Brave until the end, when he led his troops into battle and then to their deaths. He almost lost his life too—a bullet went in, but it was his mind that went out. He came back 'retired.' We had plenty of time to get to know each other then, only there wasn't much left to say."

"I'm sorry, Grand-mère. That's very sad. I didn't know."

"Your mother never told you?"

"No. She's never told me anything."

"Ah, Madeleine," she sighed, scratching her white head.

"What happened between him and my mother?" My face tingled with anticipation. Was she actually going to tell me? She shook her head again and threw her hands up in the air.

"What happens when you boil insanity with foolishness, and stir in a bit of crushed sense?" She laughed bitterly. "Forget the past. It's all a muddle of stinking nonsense. Your oncle has agreed to help secure a future for you."

"What do you mean a future?"

"A husband, of course. What else would I mean?"

"Oh. Ah, that's kind of him. But I'm not sure I'm . . . ready."

"Ready? You're practically a spinster. Ready!" she snorted, and I suddenly felt something crack, felt our little friendship trickling away.

"I'm just . . . perhaps in a few months, then I would feel more . . . myself."

"Well, it will take that long for Antoine to convince anyone to get involved with *this* family," she said, and settled into her pillow. Dust puffed into the air, particles suspended in the strong afternoon light. "I'm getting rather tired, *ma belle*. Perhaps we can talk again next week. Yes?"

"All right. Yes. Tell Oncle Antoine I'm grateful for his offer. Thank you."

I found myself in revolt against the cruel tyranny of time as the weeks of September crawled miserably by. Of course, the hands on the clock went round and round at the same speed all the time. Clocks have mechanisms to ensure that they're correct and even, but the heart has different mechanisms that aren't even or measured at all.

And mine was a wreck.

On the first day I had calculated that Théo might possibly arrive, I was in my white dress with my bonnet strings tied at dawn, waiting the impossible hours until nine, when Sébastien finally rattled down the lane to take me to church.

But Théo didn't come.

Sébastien waited with me for hours. My stomach growled and my head ached.

"He might not have been able to leave right away, *tu vois*?" Sébastien conjectured. "Or he might have met some poor weather on the road. The roads can be messy this time of year, you know. He might come any minute, or tomorrow, or the day after. We'll talk to the priest, *tu vois*? We'll tell him to keep an eye out for the boy. I'll go talk to him now. You just rest yourself. Everything will be all right in time, mademoiselle. In time, *tu vois*?"

Frantically, I wrote and sent more letters. Every Friday, I stuffed as many sheets into an envelope as would fit. The postmaster smiled sympathetically at my red eyes and the dark circles hanging under them. I could see that he didn't believe I would receive a reply either.

The diminishing daylight hours and the chill in the air found their way into my heart as November progressed. Alexander Evereaux's threat echoed in my memory. Had he done something to Théo after all? Or had my mother done something—perhaps bribed the postmaster to burn my letters? Or found out about the two of us and sent him to prison out of spite?

As much as I hated looking at bare plaster walls day in and day out, I couldn't bring myself to decorate them—couldn't bring myself to admit that the cottage was anything like a home. December came and went. Winter turned to spring, and still, nothing. I turned seventeen and didn't rearrange a thing.

My grandfather remained "contained" and out of my sight.

Fortunately, my uncle also had no luck in finding a man willing to take in the penniless daughter of a dead man and a mad du Maurier.

⊣⊣⊣ ||||

THE ABBAYE PRISON

AUGUST 20, 1792

Marielle thrashes on the floor. She whimpers, still trying to swat at the bugs that bite her legs and torso at night, tossing and turning upon the mildewed straw.

But this is no place for sleeping. It's a place for itching and stinking, waiting and remembering, hoping and praying.

I try to remember how to pray, but not like Oncle Jean-Marc taught me. I try to pray like Sébastien, with simple words, simple faith, but I have none.

GRASSE, FRANCE

MAY 1790

Someone knocked at the door of the cottage. It was three in the morning.

I rubbed my eyes and peeked out the window, then quickly opened the door.

"A message for you." The footman handed me a folded parchment note from Tante Adrienne, saying that we must come immediately to the château. Grand-mère was worse. She was not expected to live through the night. A carriage awaited us.

I went in to wake my mother, but she rolled over and groaned, waving me off.

"You have to get up, Mère. It's Grand-mère. She's . . . dying."

She waved me off again and pulled the covers over her head. I shook her hard and shouted. "Did you hear me? Your mère is dying. Get up!"

She sat up dizzily, her hair a mess of tangles and her clothes disheveled. I got her a dress and tossed it shakily on the bed. "Here. You can wear this."

She yawned.

"Do you want me to help you with your hair?"

She just shrugged, so I went out to tell the footman it would only be a moment. Finally, my mother stumbled out, muttering something about café au lait.

When we arrived, the priest was saying prayers and the doctor was in the corner, filling a syringe with pain medication.

Not an hour later, my grandmother began to cough.

"Antoine, it's time to get Père," Adrienne said authoritatively from where she knelt beside the bed.

"I must go. Now," my mother said as she sprang to her feet, but Grand-mère shook her head and held up a hand in protest.

"Stay," she wheezed.

Antoine heaved an anxious, irritated sigh and nodded to her, grabbing the doorpost as he hurried out. A few moments later, we heard a loud banging noise from down the hall, two sets of feet shuffling toward us, and heavy breathing, belching, and muttering. There, in the doorway, my grandfather appeared and burst into tears.

"Mère!" he cried, looking toward his wife. "Ma mère is dying! The fever has gotten her at last! No!" He fell to his knees, grabbing fistfuls of his unkempt curls in his hands.

"Father. You are the Marquis Joseph du Maurier," said Adrienne calmly. "It is your wife, Marguerite, who is dying."

He looked around, wide-eyed and confused, brushing dark locks of hair out of his eyes as he swung his head from his daughter to his wife. Finally, recognition settled into his face, and he knelt to take his wife's hand. He muttered to her, stroked her hair through the coughing and gasping.

My aunt leaned close to my ear. "Your mother should have warned you about your grandfather," Adrienne whispered, slipping a thick arm around my shoulder. "He's a bit more confused lately. But he's always been that way, hearing voices, seeing people and things that aren't there. He was never the same after the war."

She hovered over Grand-mère again, but my mother hung back, staring, with her hand over her mouth.

Suddenly, my grandmother was still. She lay back peacefully on her pillow, her eyes sparked as if lighting upon someone familiar, and then she was gone.

The priest swooped in, mumbling in Latin. The doctor slipped his fingers below her jaw, feeling for her pulse. He shook his head—just another day's work. He packed his bag and whispered something to Adrienne before making a quick exit.

My grandfather released her hand and brushed tears from his weathered cheeks. He looked across the room and locked onto my gaze, and suddenly, the storm in his dark eyes calmed.

"Vivienne?" he asked, softly and tenderly, bending forward as if speaking to a child. His mouth opened into a huge smile.

I shook my head no, but barely.

"*Ma chérie*, Vivienne, it's you! Come here and let Papa kiss you."

My questioning glances at Adrienne and my mother received no answer. I walked toward him, uncertain of what else to do and extraordinarily conscious of everyone's eyes on me. Everyone's but Grand-mère's.

Suddenly, his bony arms were around me. He smelled like sweet pipe smoke and sweat. Tears streaming down his cheeks, he ran his trembling, knotted hands down the length of my hair, then kissed the top of my head.

I could see the look of horror in my mother's face. *Vivienne.* I'd been called that name before. The night my mother tried to jump from the balcony.

"Vivienne, Vivienne, Vivienne," he murmured again and again, and no one dared interfere. "I bought you a pretty dolly in Paris!" He turned around to look for it, then his brow furrowed. "I must have left it in the carriage, *ma belle*."

"It's all right," I whispered, and he stepped toward me again and took my face in his hands. As his eyes wandered away from my eyes and over my features, his brow furrowed again as if he couldn't find what he was looking for. He let go of me and took a step backward. Blinking rapidly, he took another handful of his hair.

"No, no, no, no, no. You're not Vivienne. Vivienne is dead." He scanned the room with bloodshot eyes until finding my mother. He shuddered, his entire body overtaken with a sudden rage, then stabbed the air with a shaky index finger. "*You!* You . . . you killed her!"

He lunged toward her with a visceral growl, and it took all of Oncle Antoine's strength to hold him back. My mother shrieked and slipped out the door, her heeled feet clicking frenetically down the hall. I was frozen in place as Antoine and the priest wrestled Grand-père into a chair and Adrienne rang for the butler, who called to the housekeeper to stop the doctor to bring up a sedative, while another maid was asked to call the coroner.

When he was finally subdued in his rooms, we remembered Grand-mère, her thin hands folded on her chest.

She was gone.

How could someone be alive one moment and dead the next? It was surreal. Wrong.

"Do you want Sébastien to take you back to the cottage?" Tante Adrienne asked, but I shook my head. I needed some air. Needed to be alone.

"No, I'd rather walk."

"It's dark."

"I know. I know the way."

She accompanied me to the front door and then paused.

"Are you all right?" she asked.

"I've never watched someone die before. I saw my father—but he was already dead." She embraced me warmly, comfortingly, in a way my mother never had, absorbing the tremble that racked my body.

"Tante Adrienne . . . who is—or was—Vivienne?"

She sighed heavily. "Our half sister. She was an opera singer. And she is, indeed, dead."

"Grand-père loved her very much."

"Too much. In Père's eyes, Vivienne could do no wrong, no matter who she slept with, and she died giving birth to some army officer's child. But Madeleine—well, she was no one's favorite, and admittedly strange. She was an easy target for Josette to blame. Père's mind was fragile enough—it didn't take much for him believe her."

"Josette?"

"Vivienne's older sister. Yes. She was some *theater whore*," she said, as if she were spitting the words into the street. "I think she preferred to call herself a ballerina, but she wasn't a very good one. She told Père that Madeleine *killed* Vivienne, and he believed her. That grasping little bitch destroyed our family."

"Where is Josette now?"

"I don't know. She disappeared."

"Disappeared? What does that mean?"

"If I knew what it meant, I would tell you what happened to her instead of saying she disappeared. I don't know where she is."

"What happened to Vivienne's baby?"

"Didn't live through the birth either. The medical examiner confirmed it—there was nothing amiss, despite what Josette would have us believe. And the child's father never even wrote to find out how they got on. It was scandalously crazy of Père, though, to bury them here on the family land. But then, sanity was never this family's forte."

After a moment, the bitterness of the memory passed, and the sorrow of the moment returned. She dabbed at her eyes. "I'm so sorry you had to witness that awful scene. But I am happy you've gotten to see your grandmother a few times before her passing. I'm sure your mother is distressed. Perhaps you can give her some comfort."

"I doubt she'll take any from me," I said. "But I'll try."

"Hélène? Don't tell her that I've told you. I wouldn't bring it up at all if I were you, all right?"

Of course I wasn't going to tell her. I finally knew something.

VEdM—the initials I had seen on the sheet music. They stood for Vivienne E. du Maurier.

"L'Espérance" was her creation.

And that bit of information was mine.

We were not invited to my grandmother's funeral. In fact, Tante Adrienne sent a note ordering us to stay away. They planned to inter her in the walls of the church on Saturday.

On Friday, Sébastien came as usual. Solemnly, he removed his hat at the door.

"To church, *ma chérie*?" he asked, and I nodded.

He was quiet on the road. I thought he must have cared a great deal for my grandmother. We went all the way into the village without a word passing between us.

I still felt the rush of anticipation entering Notre-Dame-du-Puy, hoping against hope that Théo would be standing there, waiting for me. I couldn't get used to the disappointment. Where was he? Prison? Purgatory?

I went to the postmaster, as usual, sheepishly handing him a stuffed envelope. Still Sébastien said nothing. As we were nearing the château, he turned down an unfamiliar lane. He sighed. And then, he finally spoke.

"You've learned of Mademoiselle Vivienne."

I nodded. "Did you know her?"

"Of course I did. Yes. We all knew her."

"My aunt said she was well liked."

"Liked? She was adored. Loved! She was like a daughter to me—to everyone who knew her. When she died, it was as if all the birds had up and flown away in the middle of summer, *tu vois*? I couldn't believe it."

"And she died . . . in childbirth?"

"So they say."

"Did she live here, with the family?"

"Ah! I'll show you where she lived when she was in Grasse. Her mother's cottage—your grandfather gave it to Donatienne—it's just around this bend. No one has been in there for a long time, I think. When Vivi . . . passed, they brought her things back by the carriage load and filled the cottage with them. After Donatienne, her mother, passed away, it was just locked up, in case Josette came back, I suppose. Ha! What a joke that was. God only knows what they've done to Josette."

"So Vivienne didn't live here?"

"She lived in Paris most of the time, *tu vois*, because she sang at the opera house there at the, oh, what do they call it? *Château Royale* or something like that? The place of the Duc du, ah, ah . . . ?"

"The Palais-Royal. Yes, the Duc d'Orlèans runs it."

"Yes, that's it. She sang there, and sometimes she went to the real palace too. Sang to the king and queen. She was good. Excellent. A prodigy."

"So, she died in Paris?"

"I think so. But I don't know. It was all hush-hush. She wasn't here, I know that for sure. And they brought her things and filled her mère's cottage with them. All those instruments, all those dresses, and no Vivienne to make them sing, to make them dance."

He slowed the carriage to a stop in front of a large cottage, larger than ours. "That's it."

We sat in silence, staring at it. He sighed, and said, "Tomorrow, they're burying your grandmother, *tu vois*?"

I nodded.

"Tomorrow, everyone will be gone, *tu vois*?"

I nodded again.

"Tomorrow, if you come back here, you might find the back door open. But I didn't tell you that, *tu vois*? You could walk here yourself,and try the door and waltz right in. The lock could've rotted out, and the door just opened up for you. Or a window could've broken. Someone could've left a key carelessly under the mat, or right in the door. But I wouldn't know about it. If you took a walk and happened upon it, well, that wouldn't be breaking any rules, *tu vois*? And nobody would know."

He drove me slowly back to my cottage, reminding me of where to turn between the lush hedges of lavender, a small lake, and tall, scraggly pines so that I could walk back the next day.

Dawn didn't really break on Saturday morning. A swirling fog obscured the line of woods behind our cottage, a fog so dense I could barely see the lane. They were already preparing to take my grandmother to the church. I dressed and sipped at café au lait, hoping it would clear enough outside that I wouldn't get lost—although it wasn't as if anyone would miss me if I didn't return.

At ten o'clock, I heard the bells chiming for Grand-mère. They were in the church. Wrapping myself in a cloak and grabbing an umbrella for good measure, I looked in to see that my mother was still sleeping. Slipping out the front door, I rehearsed Sébastien's directions. The sun was making minimal progress, but I could see where the lane turned, the lake at the bend, and the row of pines. The cottage popped out of the ethereal fog like a dream.

I felt exhilaratingly clandestine as I walked around the back and tried the knob. It opened with a sorrowful moan, and I found myself in a dim sitting room overflowing with musical instruments. A grand piano. An enormous gilt harp with ivory inlay and a carved cherub on top. Stacks of violin cases, topped with a pile of bows and a small, colorfully enameled compact of rosin. A harpsichord. Flutes and recorders in strange shapes and colors that must have come from abroad. A pochette—the little miniature violin so small it could fit in a pocket. Stacks and stacks of sheet music.

Three canvasses stood on easels, covered with cloths. I peeked under the first and found an oil of a much younger, smiling Grand-père. His eyes were clear. His face was smooth, and his hair was combed. He looked happy.

Behind another cloth was a small still life of curvaceous perfume bottles and jasmine. The third stopped my heart mid-beat.

It was my lake.

The little, round lake house, the swans, the perfect colors of sunset, Château des Cygnes in the background, the edge of the rose garden visible at the far corner. I flung the cloth completely off of it and stepped back, covering my mouth with my hand.

I glanced up at it again and again as I explored the rest of the room. Two jewelry armoires were placed haphazardly between wingback chairs, and I turned the key that stood poised in the lock. Pearls and diamonds. That's what she liked. The drawers were packed with necklaces, earrings, brooches, tiaras, and bracelets.

A small trunk filled with papers sat open on the floor beside the armoires. There were sketches of ballerinas in various positions. Sketches of officers in the Royal Army and Navy, all posed the same way: one hand in a jacket pocket, the other on the sword. I flipped through, wondering which of them might've been the father of Vivienne's child. Beneath them was a group of sketches of a middle-aged woman with kind eyes sitting at a harp, whom I took to be Donatienne. Sketch after sketch of a baby's face, a baby's hand grasping a large finger, baby feet. Emotion stung my eyes and tightened my throat. My little cousin.

But Tante Adrienne said she hadn't lived through the birth.

Underneath the sketches were two letters with the royal seal and numerous other envelopes with the return addresses of men with noble and military titles. I was sliding an ardently admiring letter from a duke back into its envelope when a gentle voice froze me in place.

"You've come."

I looked over my shoulder, my blood rushing like a caught thief's. It was Grand-père.

"I-I'm . . . I'm sorry," I stuttered, "I shouldn't be here."

My grandfather looked at me, and his deep brown eyes were clear. He smiled. "Stay. I know who you are," he said. "You're my granddaughter."

"Yes," I said softly. "I am your granddaughter."

"Hélène."

"Yes."

"Vivienne's child."

I pressed my lips together and didn't speak to validate or argue with this statement.

"There are times when I am . . . confused. But right now, I am not confused. My mind is as clear as it was when I was a young man—a young man in love." He closed the door behind him, and I noticed that the knees of his trousers were wet.

"We buried my wife today. But this, this is my home. The woman who lived here, she was my life—she was my love. Donatienne. She loved me, even when I was confused. She loved me even when my head hurt from that damned bullet. And Vivi, she would sing, she would play flutes and mandolins and any instrument I bought for her. What a gift she had with music! She would sing to me, and I would know where I was again—I was home. I would know who I was. I was her papa. I loved her. And Josette. But she's gone too.

"Josette, she would dance, and she would say such funny, clever things to make me laugh. She doesn't come to me here, not like Vivi and Dona."

"They come to you . . . here?"

"Yes. Yes. I ask Vivienne, 'When is your sister coming?' 'I don't know, Papa. I don't know. She wants to see you, but she can't get away from Paris. She sends her love.' That's what Vivi tells me. Ah, I would give anything to hear her voice again."

"I'm so sorry, Grand-père."

"I taught them to draw and paint, you know," he said, gesturing toward the uncovered canvas.

"I . . . I . . . draw and paint too."

He broke into a smile and nodded his approval. "Of course you do. Yes, that is good. You sing too?"

"Yes."

He walked around the room, running his fingers carelessly over harp strings and playing dissonant chords on the piano. He blew into one of the recorders and with thick, unsteady fingers tried unsuccessfully to pick out a tune. Shaking his head, he reached for a small trinket box painted with delicate violets.

"For you," he said, offering it to me, then motioned that I follow him outside while I was still saying thank you. I followed him to the edge of the wood. Under the dripping arms of branches, three gravestones stuck up out of the grass, surrounded by fresh-cut flowers. He must have laid them there before coming inside. I could see the pile of wilted, discarded flowers in the woods. Yesterday's.

He ran his fingers over the stone he knelt before, not caring if his pants were soaked and muddy, and I saw the name "Donatienne du Maurier" under his gentle, trembling touch. He turned to the stone beside it, marked "Vivienne Elisabeth du Maurier," and finally to a tiny one beside that, reading "Petite Fille du Maurier."

"If you stay a bit, they'll come."

A raindrop fell from a branch and slid down the back of my dress. I shivered.

"I . . . ah . . . I told my mother I would be back soon. I can't stay . . . I . . . shouldn't be here now."

"Madeleine. Yes, you don't want to make her angry. We both know what she does when she's angry."

I didn't move or breathe. He crouched, both hands gripping the stone of his lover, pressing his forehead against her name for a long time. I hugged the little trinket box to my chest and looked over my shoulder. His servant hung back about twenty paces, but I wasn't sure if this made me feel better or worse. Grand-père looked up, the pattern of the engraved letters pressed into his forehead. Our eyes—our same eyes—stared into each other's.

"You don't know the truth."

I shook my head.

"Everyone lies. Everyone lies. Everyone thinks I'm too old and confused, and perhaps I am most of the time. But I know that you are my granddaughter. And your father was a clever man." He laughed softly, as if this were some sort of joke I was supposed to understand.

"Was he?" I asked, leaning closer.

"He may have been an utter fool when it came to women, but he was clever when he named you. He left you a clue, *Hélène*. Madeleine was ready to name you Thérèse, up to the day of your christening, but then your father surprised everyone. He said, 'Hélène. Her name is Hélène.' And she was furious."

"Why? What does it mean?" I whispered, just inches from him.

"It was Hercules—no, Zeus—Heracles?—who disguised himself as a . . . a . . . a bird of some kind. I think . . . I think, it was a goose." He stopped to chew his thumbnail, and he began drumming the fingers of his other hand on his soaked knee. "What *was* the bird? The bird . . . was it the lady who turned into a bird? Leda, I think. No . . . the bird . . . She hatched out of an egg. I know that much."

"Grand-père, do you mean Helen of Troy?"

"Of course, yes." Now he drummed his fingers on his cheek and shook his head. "A swan, perhaps? No, that isn't right. That isn't right. No . . . no . . . there was Paris and Aphrodite and a great horse—war and death. Paris? Paris . . . Paris. Wars are terrible. Terrible . . . People do bad things, Hélène! People lie . . . everyone lies . . ."

He drifted into a sad and silent confusion, his eyes clouding like the mud he knelt in, and my heart sank. I could see that it was useless, that the truth was buried somewhere six feet beneath me, and that my grandfather was somewhere much farther away than that.

Watching him slip away, I was stung with the realization that here, there were people who loved me. There were people who looked like me, who sang and painted, who lived in the sunshine, surrounded by flowers, and I was never allowed to know them.

A few droplets spattered us from the sky, and I began to hum. If Vivienne could help him know who and where he was, could I? I hummed the first few bars of "L'Espérance."

He cocked his head and his eyes flew open with such alarm, I stopped, certain I'd made a terrible mistake. But he whispered, "Go on."

I knelt in the mud beside him and finished the first verse. He whispered again, "Go on. Please, don't stop." Tears began to stream down his face, but he kept nodding, smiling, not bothering to wipe them as they mixed with quickening droplets from the sky. When I finally finished, he wrapped his arms around me, the sweet scent of his pipe mixing with rain, and said, "Thank you. Thank you, *ma chérie*."

The servant stepped forward, shooting me irate glances.

"We must hurry back. They'll be waiting on you for the dinner," the man said, and gently encouraged him toward the carriage. Grand-père nodded and took his arm, his brow furrowed, muttering to himself. But then he looked up and locked my gaze once more, saying only one word: Nemesis.

As the carriage and Grand-père's waving hand disappeared into the fog, the clouds unleashed a stinging rain. I darted for the cottage to grab my umbrella, but the wind whipped it inside-out as soon as I set foot on the front step. I folded the umbrella and glanced back at the graves uneasily.

Nemesis. Nemesis.

Lightning crackled as it dove into the woods.

I had to wait it out.

After leaving my muddy shoes on the doorstep, I settled at the cluttered desk to open my gift from Grand-père. Drawing an eager breath, I glanced around at Vivienne's other lavish belongings.

Why this?

As I turned it around to admire the painted flowers on all sides, I heard something move inside it. Above the lock, a golden leaf handle invited me in. I tried to pop it up, but it wouldn't budge. I wiggled it, dug my nails between the gold-rimmed top and bottom and tried to pry it open, but it was no use. The box was locked.

As the rain hammered the roof and puddles widened outside, I rummaged through drawers and checked the corners of the trunk for a key. I opened creaky instrument cases and peeked under musty clothes in the bedroom bureaus. The scent of rain mingled with dust and long-unwashed fabric as I looked under pillows and inside delicately embroidered silk slippers. No key.

I went to work again on the fruitless task of prying it open with my nails, then with a silver-handled letter opener I found on the desk. I shook it and held it to my ear as something metallic rattled inside the ceramic box, torturing my curiosity.

Resting my chin on my fist and staring at it, I knew there would be no opening it except to shatter it. But the box itself was beautiful. I couldn't break it. It was a gift. Besides, for all I could tell from shaking it, there was nothing of value but a metal button inside.

Perhaps Grand-père had the key. Perhaps I could meet him here again tomorrow, and he would bring it. I could sing to him again. Maybe his mind would clear again and he would tell me something, something that made sense.

Nemesis. Nemesis. What did that have to do with me—with my name? He was confused. His brain was damaged. It was nothing. Nonsense.

I distractedly read some sheet music, trying to pick out the tune amid the hundred mismatched melodies and rhythms pounding in my head. There had to be something there. Something that made sense.

When the storm finally passed, whipped away by a still-strong wind, I sloshed back through the mud to my cottage. My skirt was soaked and spattered brown. My shoes were sludgy and disgusting. Fortunately, my mother was still in her room. After closing the door soundlessly, I tiptoed into my room and wedged a wooden chair against the door to lock it before undressing, wondering what I was going to do with my clothes.

More importantly, what was I going to do with the box? I wouldn't let my mother find it. It was mine.

I rearranged my things to fit Vivienne's trinket box inside of my own box, blinking away the image of my father that came to me. I tried to see him smiling, instead, giving me my beautiful starry box. Rubbing his hands together as he asked me if I liked it. Hanging the key around my neck. Kissing me on the top of my head. I traced a tiny violet on the cool ceramic lid of Vivienne's box before locking it safely away in my own, wishing there was a lid for my aching heart, a key to lock it away.

The next morning, my mother and I ate breakfast to the sound of another pounding rainstorm. We didn't notice the knock at the door and both started when Adrienne strode in dripping, leaving muddy footprints behind her.

"Well, it seems Hélène has paid her grandfather a little visit."

"Hélène?" my mother gasped.

"Now he's terribly upset. You've made him worse, Hélène. It was a very bad thing to do."

"I'm sorry . . . It was an accident. I was taking a walk and so was he—"

"Weren't you told to stay inside yesterday?"

"No," I snapped. "I wasn't told to stay inside. I was told not to attend the funeral."

"Why did you let her out, Madeleine?"

"I . . . I didn't. I was sleeping. I didn't know she'd left the house."

Tante Adrienne laughed a silent, mocking laugh and shook her head. "He says he can't tolerate you on the property anymore, Madeleine. He's been smashing things. You should see his room, it's a disaster. God help us if he makes it into the dining room. He's a strong man, despite his age."

She leaned her shoulder against the window frame and stared out at the thick, moist sky. Her wiry, red curls bounced as she shook her head.

"How was the service?" my mother ventured, a weak attempt at a subject change.

"Lovely. It was lovely, of course. Everything Mère deserved."

"And . . . the will? Has it been read?"

"The will?" Adrienne whirled to face us, squinting.

"Yes. What did she leave us? I mean . . . I mean . . . what do we get?"

"What did she leave you? What do you get?" Adrienne repeated, her green eyes flashing.

"Yes, that's what I asked you, Sister. I want what's mine."

"Don't you recall the size of your dowry?"

"That was a long time ago," my mother said bitterly.

Adrienne closed her eyes and took a deep breath. "Antoine and I have discussed it at length—we'll fund your trip to Coblenz. Both of you."

"Me?" I blurted. "Why, me?"

"You've upset him, Hélène. I don't think you understand the gravity of the situation or how very fragile his mind is."

"But he's not upset with me. I could stay. I could take care of him. I could . . . could sing to him. He likes that. I want to take care of him. Mère could go to Coblenz, and I could stay here."

"Your grandfather cannot look at you without seeing Vivienne. If you stay, he'll never be at peace," she said, shaking her head firmly. "The decision has already been made. You'll leave in the morning. You'd best pack your things."

My mother's mouth hung open, but no sound came out.

Théo. His name throbbed through me with every beat of my heart. Before dawn, I was sitting on the step, waiting.

At the approach of the carriage, I ran down the lane and stuck my head in the window as Sébastien reined in the horses. "I need you to take me to Paris. Not Coblenz."

He deflated. "Mademoiselle Hélène. *Ma chérie.*"

"Please?"

"I cannot disobey orders. Not this time. Not when she would know, *tu vois*?"

"But what if he comes here looking for me? This is where I told him I would be. Something has held him up, but he's coming. I know he's coming. I have to stay here or go to Paris. Please? Please, Sébastien?" Tears streamed unashamedly down my cheeks as I gripped the window frame of the carriage.

"*Ma chérie.* He's not coming."

"Then I have to go and find him. What if he's in prison?"

"Then you cannot help him."

My head fell onto my white-knuckled hands.

"Paris is a mad city, *tu vois*? They want blood—your blood, Mademoiselle Hélène—and I'm surely not going to deliver it to them."

"I don't care about that. I don't care. I need to get back. I don't care," I sobbed.

He bowed his head and frowned. "I care about you, whether you care about yourself or not. You're young with a whole life ahead of you, *tu vois*? We'll go back to Notre-Dame, *tu vois*? You leave a note there with the priest for this boy. Tell him where you're going. If he comes this far, he'll follow you there too."

I nodded, swallowing my defeat. I dragged my feet and wiped my face with the back of my hand as he coaxed the horses up a bit and hopped down to help us with our luggage. My mother poked her head out of her room, and for the first time in many months, her eyes were bright and large.

"Sébastien! Here are my things. Let's be off, then. The sooner we leave, the sooner we arrive, yes?" She brushed her hands off and nodded briskly.

"As you wish, madame. As you wish," he muttered, and avoided my gaze.

As we approached the church, he slowed, and my mother furrowed her brow, her eyes darting nervously around. "What's this? Why are we stopping?"

"Mademoiselle Hélène asked me to let her pray once more before we go on. I think that's a fair enough request, madame."

"And just when did you become so devout?" she asked, but I hurried out before she could stop me, the letter burning my breast beneath my dress. I rushed through the doors, looking for the priest. I wandered under echoing alcoves until I finally found him at the Communion cabinet, rearranging jewel-studded chalices.

"Excuse me," I said softly, and he turned. "Could I leave a letter with you? I need to leave Grasse . . . suddenly. But my fiancé will be looking for me here. Could you give this to a Monsieur Leroux when he arrives? Please?"

The old priest examined my letter and nodded. "I'll give this to him if he comes."

If.

"Thank you," I whispered, leaving the letter in his wrinkled, unsteady hands, feeling like I was leaving a part of myself there with him. Would he lose it? Would he forget? Would Théo ever even come?

The sun flashed blindingly into my eyes as I opened the cathedral doors. Shaking my head and trying to blink the spots away, I moved toward the carriage. I stumbled up and heaved myself onto the cushioned seat, then nodded silently at Sébastien.

"Everything all right, Mademoiselle Hélène?"

I nodded.

My mother said nothing, but I could feel her watching me, her eyes darting, birdlike, from the window to my face and back again.

‖‖‖ ‖‖‖

THE ABBAYE PRISON

AUGUST 21, 1792

"Do you think I'll go to hell?" Marielle whispers into the darkness. Neither of us can sleep with thoughts like this keeping us awake.

"The tribunal doesn't decide that."

"I'm not a royalist!" She is vehement. Honest. But then, her voice breaks. "I'm just a whore. And whores go to hell, don't they?"

"Says who?"

"Priests! The Bible! I'm a bad person, and I—"

"No. Sometimes people do bad things for good reasons. Or even good things for bad reasons. But you're *not* a bad person."

This brings her to tears, as if I've just absolved her. "I didn't know who he was. All I knew was that he could pay, and I was hungry. The police came, bashed in the door, and said he was some marquis wanted for treason. But I didn't know!"

"The judges will understand." I hold her gaze steady, willing it to be true. "God will understand too."

So she tells me her story. How, at sixteen, she's already been abused by more men than she can count, just trying to survive. She's already spent four years in hell, as a prostitute in the Palais-Royal.

"Not all men are like that," I promise her, my heart breaking for both of us. "Some men are gentle. And good."

"Is he still alive?" she asks, sniffling. "This man who's been good to you?"

And suddenly, our roles are reversed. She is the one comforting me as I say, "I don't know . . ."

COBLENZ, GERMANY

JUNE 1790

"Madeleine. Hélène. What *are* you doing here?"

My grandmother sat in an overstuffed chair with a fat calico cat snoozing in her lap. She leaned forward, her expression a mixture of shock and amusement.

"We've missed you so! Hélène just couldn't stand to be away from her dear Grand-mère. So we've come back," my mother exclaimed jauntily as she rushed toward Grand-mère to embrace her. She fell to her knees and startled the cat, which hissed at her and jumped down to slink under a side table. Grand-mère stared at me over my mother's shoulder, her eyes bulging in their sockets.

"Is that so?" she asked, slowly and deliberately patting my mother's shoulder, a bushy, gray eyebrow raised at me.

I shrugged and forced a smile. "How are you, Grand-mère?"

She sighed dramatically, letting go of my mother and taking hold of the cane that rested against her chair. She tapped it on the wooden floor a few times. "I've started using this, since the doctor can't seem to do a thing about my bunion. And my back hurts. I'm not getting around so well as I used to, you see. But I'm comfortable otherwise. Thank God for Evereaux. He's saved us."

"Has he?" I surveyed the small but beautifully furnished salon, suddenly feeling cold. She nodded.

"I knew he was a good man," my mother said, shooting a smirk at me. I shivered.

"So, now that you're here, where are you staying?"

who was sick, dead, or nearly so. I finally breathed when she told me that Alexander Evereaux was in Paris, advising the king on behalf of the émigrés of Coblenz. I was then graced with visual evidence of her stubborn bunion, the obligatory details about her chamber pot usage, and the appropriate alterations in her diet.

Finally, she stopped to suck on her teeth, sitting back in her chair with her hands folded on her plump belly. The cat brushed against my legs, its tail twitching.

"Now," she said, with a little nod. "Your mother's explanations would flatter me if I thought they might be true. But you and I both know you didn't come to Coblenz because you missed me. So, what happened?" She looked like Marie's little pug when she wanted a treat.

"I don't know what happened."

She laughed. "You are many things, Hélène, but you're not stupid. You know. Now, come on, tell me."

I crossed my arms. "Some old argument was reignited, and we were told to leave. And I can see now that my father was tricked. Wasn't he? He didn't know what he was getting himself into. He didn't know he was marrying someone like her, did he?"

She rolled her eyes. "No, he didn't know. But he got what he expected. And that was enough."

"What he expected?"

"The money. He had debts, Hélène. Many debts."

"But Mère—"

"Life, ma chérie, is a matter of expectations. If you have reasonable, realistic expectations, you will be happy, for they will be met. If you have unreasonable, idealistic expectations, you will find that you're never happy. The idealist never gets what he wants. He's a dreamer, so in love with a world he wants to be true, he never lives in the one he has. But to be a realist is to be alive—to truly live the life we are meant for."

"And what are we meant for?"

She smiled. "Luxury. And children. That's what I expected, and that's what I got. I didn't ask your grandfather to stay home every night, to

My mother laughed nervously. "Any room will do."

"*Any room will do*. Yes. Any room will do," she sighed, drumming her fingers on the crook of her cane. With another heavy sigh, she pushed herself up. "Well. I'll talk to Henri. Make yourselves . . . comfortable," Grand-mère grumbled as she hobbled out.

My mother began walking around the room, picking up trinkets and setting them down, touching the curtains, sitting in all the chairs. I watched her from a damask wingback covered in cat hair, surprised that I could still be surprised by her.

Oncle Henri cleared his throat, and she set down a porcelain dog with a clatter on a glass-topped table. His head was shining and his shoulders were rounded and raised with agitation.

"Well," he said, looking like he was experiencing a sudden bout of indigestion. "This is a surprise."

Tante Charlotte followed, her arms outstretched. "Hélène! Oh, it's so good to see you again! And Madeleine!" She turned and kissed my mother on each cheek. "Now I'll have a tennis partner again. I can't get Henri to play with me, and Marie is pregnant. Did she tell you we have a court?"

"That's wonderful!"

"Marie is pregnant? How is she?" I asked.

Tante Charlotte's smile weakened a little. "She's fine. A bit tired. But fine. Well, you get settled in. Some rooms are ready. They're nothing much—we don't have the space we were accustomed to. Oh, I'm just so happy to see you both again! I have so much to tell you!"

We were given tiny guest rooms near the servants' quarters and didn't complain. I felt a small satisfaction that my room was larger and prettier than my mother's, but it didn't erase the truth that we were once again unwelcome guests. The key became my new best friend. I just hoped Evereaux didn't have copies.

The following afternoon, I was summoned to meet with Grand-mère.

Over chocolates and café au lait, my grandmother relentlessly doled out details of who had emigrated to Coblenz, who was cheating on his wife and who was sneaking around behind her husband's back, who was pregnant and who was looking for a husband for their daughter, and shower me with some sort of affection beyond our duty to one another. I had all that I needed, all that I set out looking for, and so, I was happy. In fact, I still am. All this Revolutionary nonsense, jealousy and greed of all kinds—it's all because no one will simply have appropriate expectations. Just look at your cousin."

"Marie?"

Grand-mère leaned toward me, the skin around her mouth crinkling into a frown, her eyes lighting upon what I knew was about to be a juicy bit of information. She clucked with her tongue and said, "She's been acting so unreasonably, I should think she'd taken a lesson from you." Her mouth wrinkled up into half a smile.

"She's . . . unhappy?"

"Oh, yes. Yes, she's unhappy. But it's entirely her own fault. Look at this place. It's lovely, isn't it? And their house is twice as nice. He's saved us from ruin. He's been good to the family. He's even gotten her with child. What more does he owe her?"

I shrugged.

"Well, this wasn't supposed to be about Marie, was it?"

"I told you, I don't know what happened. Something happened a long time ago, but you knew that, didn't you?"

"I knew there was a row, yes."

"And you sent us back, knowing that?"

She shrugged, lifting her hands. "Desperate times. It wasn't my fault Foix didn't want to keep up his end of the bargain. Without Evereaux's help, we'd all be ruined. Oh, that reminds me, did I tell you Foix has married the widow of Henry Blakeford? That Englishman had more money than any of us, and it's all secured in Child's Bank!"

"Yes, you did."

"Ah, well, anyway, it's time for us to dress for dinner. Have you seen Marie yet? No? Well, wait until you see her tonight at dinner. You'll be surprised by how much weight she's gained already. It's all gone to her face, poor thing. But she does eat too much. And she still has three months to go!"

We had traveled so long to get there, to lovely Coblenz, where the rivers and émigrés met. I was jittery and clumsy, bumping into things and stubbing my toes and drifting off along my own rivers of thought.

Théo was nowhere to be found. Marie was unhappy. Vivienne was dead. Josette was missing. My mother was wide awake. And I was scared.

As I slipped into the simple, white dress I'd bought in Grasse and did my own hair, I thought of Aimée and Gabelle, and all the others in the château that night. I had hoped, perhaps, that some of them would be here in Coblenz with the family, but I saw no familiar faces among the service. I couldn't blame them for leaving the family. I just hoped they were alive.

I twisted some of my hair up into a little bun, fastened it with the pearl comb, and slipped a string of pearls around my neck. I hadn't dressed for dinner in nearly a year, and I'd never done it all by myself. Staring into my reflection, I imagined my grandmother remarking that I looked terribly *bourgeoise*. That, at least, made me smile.

The dining room wasn't enormous, but it was big enough for about thirty people, and I was surprised to find every seat filled. Dukes and princes and *comtes* milled about with their wives, and I was presented to each of them. When Foix and his rich widow-wife arrived, I slipped out to the foyer and pressed my back against the textured wallpaper until Grand-mère came looking for me. She pointed to the chair between my mother and Marie, who sat with her hands on her large belly, staring into her lap.

"Hello," I whispered as I pulled my chair close to the table.

"Hello, Hélène."

Marie didn't speak again throughout the long dinner of roast beef and artichokes, salad, and various pâtés. Her shoulders, her eyes, her hair, her belly—everything about her looked like it was being pulled downward by some invisible force. The Comte de Brionne kept my mother and me busy with a hundred questions about Grasse, which my mother readily obliged. She was flirting with him, and he seemed to be encouraging her. How was I still surprised by her? How?

After a decadent cake, Oncle Henri announced that the men would retire to play cards.

"Would you like to see my house?" Marie whispered, grabbing my wrist under the table.

"Yes, sure. When?"

"Now?"

I nodded. "Let's go."

She whispered something to Tante Charlotte, who nodded and smiled at me, and then I followed her through the foyer and out into the street.

"It's just over there," she said, pointing to the charming, half-timbered house across the street that was nearly twice the size of ours. Now that she was facing me, I could see that Grand-mère was right about her weight, and she walked with an uncomfortable waddle, always holding her belly.

"Congratulations," I said, touching her shoulder as she twisted the key in her door. "About the baby, I mean."

She smiled dimly, her eyes flat, and said, "This way."

We walked through a huge foyer and down a shadowy hallway hung with artwork: portraits of the Evereaux patriarchs, landscapes, and a curly-haired maiden swinging in a meadow, kicking one foot above her head to give her gentleman friend a look up her skirt.

"The dining room," she said, opening a door and waving her hand. It was stunning, with a wall-sized pastoral, seats for at least sixty, and a glittering crystal chandelier.

"It's beautiful," I said, but she shrugged and motioned that I follow her through two lavish sitting rooms, then back into the foyer.

"Come upstairs. I'll show you my boudoir."

We ascended the marble staircase, holding onto a swirling rail, to an open balcony that gave a view of the foyer, its floor inlaid with a pattern of fleurs-de-lis. "He special ordered the floor," she said. "He said it looked too German before. But I liked it the way it was. My room is here."

As she pushed the door open, she waved me into a small sitting room with side-by-side upholstered chairs and a pretty, sky-blue desk. Dulcet's bark startled me, and she came running to sniff my feet and lick my hands, rolling on the floor for a belly rub. Marie sank into one of the chairs like she had just run a marathon and said, "Do you mind if I take my shoes off?"

"Of course not. It's your room."

As she bent to remove them, Dulcet scurried over and took each one for her, then deposited them at the foot of her bed, which was through an open doorway. When she'd finished helping her mistress, she hopped up into her lap, and Marie kissed the dog's head before turning to me.

"Sit down. Please. If you want, you can take your shoes off too."

"I'm fine. Thank you," I said, laughing a little, then noticing how swollen her feet and ankles were.

"So, how do you like living with Grand-mère?"

I laughed sarcastically. "I'm well-informed."

She laughed silently and clicked her nails in her lap. Dulcet nudged her hand, and she went back to stroking the dog's back. "So, what has she told you about me?"

I shrugged. "Not much."

"Well, tell me what she said."

"I don't believe half of her gossip."

"Don't I have a right to know what she's saying? What everyone in Coblenz thinks about me?"

I leaned back in my chair and sighed, staring at the ceiling. "She said you're unhappy. That you had . . . unreasonable expectations for your husband. There. That's all."

A tear trickled down her cheek. "Hélène. I'm a fool."

I pressed my lips together. I couldn't exactly say she wasn't.

"I should have listened to you. I thought . . . I thought somehow things would be different. I wanted it to be different so badly. Can you forgive me for the things I said to you? I said so many bad things to you. I'm sorry."

I slid my chair closer and touched her arm. "It's all right."

"No, nothing's all right. Why am I so stupid?" she wailed, pounding the heel of her hand into her forehead. Dulcet whimpered and nudged her arm.

"You believed the best in someone. That's more than I can say I've ever done."

She sighed and went back to petting Dulcet. "You want to know what happened?"

I nodded.

"Our *voyage de noces* was wonderful. He was . . . attentive and romantic. Then we got back and Paris was a mess, so we settled some financial matters and came to Coblenz to help the family. He bought the houses and took care of everything. Then I told him I was going to have the baby. He was so happy, Hélène. I thought I'd proved you completely wrong. We had a big fête to meet everyone in Coblenz—all the émigrés, even the king's brother. Alexander slipped out for a bit, and I went looking for him. Do you know where I found him? In bed with Madame d'Rocheforte.

"I made a big scene, Hélène. I yelled and screamed; it was terrible. I felt like I was watching myself do it. He slapped me hard and left for Paris the next morning. He said he was going to advise the king, and he took letters and petitions from the men here. It's been four months, and I've had no word from him. My father's had a few letters about politics, but he's sent me nothing."

"Nothing?"

"Nothing. I don't know if he'll ever come back. I mean, he might have just abandoned me! Who knows what he's doing, who he's with—" She bit her lip and looked into her lap.

"It hasn't been *that* long," I said softly, thinking of the last year. "He's probably just trying to prove a point. He'll come back to see the baby. And you. I know it."

She shook her head again. "If it's a boy, he might forgive me then. He'll stay if he has a son."

"Is that what you want? You want him back?"

"Yes. Yes, it is what I want. Of course it is. I still—this is what makes me such a fool, Hélène. I still love him. Still want him to love me. You're lucky to never have been in love. It's not like the fairy tales."

I hesitated. But I needed to tell someone. I needed us to be Marie and Hélène again—the girls who told secrets in the lake house. The lake house may have been turned to ash, but there was still hope for us. There had to be. I took a breath.

"I've been keeping a secret from you. I was in love. I still am."

"Is that why you came to Coblenz? Is he here?"

"No, it's no one here. He's in Paris."

"Who? Who is it?"

"Do you remember when I told you I thought the apprentice at Chevallier's was nice?"

Her eyebrows shot up. "You and the jeweler?"

I nodded.

"The apprentice?"

I nodded, and she laughed, leaning back in her chair.

"When did you tell me about him? We must have been ten."

"We were."

"That was back when he had that silly mustache and his ears stuck out."

I laughed. "Yes."

"Well, he improved a lot since then."

"He did, didn't he?"

"And he seemed . . . nice. You deserve nice, Hélène.

"So do you, Marie."

She shook her head, waving my words away. "So, is he coming here for you? Or what? I'm so confused."

"I don't know. I sent letters after . . . after the château burned. But I haven't heard anything."

"Maybe your letters didn't go through?"

"Maybe."

"Well, I should have known you would do something like this," she said, shaking her head in amazement. "Was it romantic, having a secret affair?"

I smiled and swallowed away the tightness in my throat. "Of course it was. We planned to go to America together last September, once he'd finished his apprenticeship. We were going to get married and he was going to work there."

"You were going to leave France and not even tell anyone? It was the real thing—true love?"

My eyes started to prickle. "Yes."

‖‖ ‖‖ |

"Has anyone been here to see me?" I call to the hand that throws bread at me.

"No visitors."

"No visitors *allowed*? Or no visitors have *come*?"

I watch through the bars, waiting for an answer, but he doesn't look back. He just throws bread at prisoner after prisoner after prisoner, because we are only faces to him, not *people* aching for the people we love on the outside. We are only mouths eating bread, not lips missing the lips we used to kiss. We are just hearts waiting to be paraded on the tip of a pike, hearts with no business beating or breaking.

"I've seen them turning visitors away," the man in the cell across from me says through his own set of bars. His eyes are soft when they meet mine. His accent is strange. I can't place it. "My window, it faces the entrance."

When he tilts his head toward the outside wall, toward the turret window, I can see his uniform. He's a Swiss Guard.

They imprison the Guard now?

If so, what hope is there for me?

COBLENZ, GERMANY

JULY 1790

"The master has returned," Grand-mère announced with a raised eyebrow, looking at me across raspberry breakfast pastries and fresh pink roses.

"Oh?"

She nodded and sucked her teeth. "We're invited to dinner and welcome-home festivities with Marquis and Marquise Evereaux tonight. You must dress in your finest, though I doubt that will be enough to help you to fit in. Unfortunately, there's not time to buy you anything new, so you'll have to make do. Everyone will be there. This will be interesting, for sure," she said, and my stomach tied itself into a knot.

That night, the dining room was jam-packed with people and loud with gossip, laughter, and arguments. My grandmother introduced me to the people I hadn't met at our house, and reintroduced me to the ones she forgot she'd already introduced me to. There were questions about Grasse, but my mother deflected them all with her overly cheery demeanor and explanations of how I couldn't bear to be away from the d'Aubigns. My stomach tied itself tighter.

Finally, the "master" arrived with his wife on his arm, a huge smile taking over her face like it did on her wedding day. He kissed her on the cheek before holding her chair out at the foot of the table. When he pushed her in with extra care, checking on her belly and patting it for good measure, the guests laughed good-heartedly. As he took his own seat at the head of the table, our eyes met and he winked at me. I lost my appetite.

"So good to see you again, Cousin Hélène!" he said merrily. I squinted at him and then looked to Marie, who shivered a little and pointed at her neck to show me a new necklace, an early anniversary gift from the prodigal husband. I smiled hopefully at her, but as my eyes settled on the piece of jewelry, my heart stopped. Time stopped. The room went quiet, and I could hear nothing but the blood rushing in my ears.

It was a Greek infinity symbol turned vertically with a single pearl dangling inside the bottom loop.

Théo's design.

My food just sat there getting cold. I was frozen, staring at it until everyone else finished eating and retired to the grand salon for a string quartet concert. The buffet at the back was spread with a hundred glasses of champagne.

From where I stood sipping at my drink, I saw Evereaux's profile moving closer. Instinctively I took a step away, but then he stopped in front of his father, who stretched out a hand and looked him up and down.

"How are things in Paris, son?"

"Oh, very much changed," he answered, shaking his father's hand. "You'd hardly recognize it."

His father grumbled in disgust. "Yes, your letters said as much."

My heart surged. Letters were coming through to Paris. Letters *were* coming through.

"Are you pleased with me now, Father?" Evereaux asked, his voice at once small and smug. I glanced at the elder Evereaux.

"All you've done is talk, Alexander," he said, shaking his gray head slowly. "I will be pleased with you if you accomplish something—someday."

"Isn't advising the king on behalf of these great men something? Aren't words with kings worth something?"

"Only if they bear fruit. Words alone never did anyone any good. You must be a man of action. Action against this filthy Revolution. Action is all that will get us our property and money back."

"I'll get it back, Father. I swear it."

"Words—still just words," he said, and clattered an empty glass on the footman's tray. For a flickering instant, I pitied Alexander Evereaux.

But then, his eyes met mine over the buffet. He spoke to his father, but he looked meaningfully at me. "You know I always keep my word. I always finish my business."

Without another word, he blended into the crowd. I stood at the buffet, the pounding of my heart drowning out the gossip and laughter around me.

I couldn't think about it all, couldn't sort out what it meant or what

I should do. When the men retired to talk politics in the study and the women gathered around Marie to *ooh* and *aah* over her new jewelry, I grabbed one last glass of champagne for the walk home and excused myself on account of an imaginary headache. Soon enough I had a real one.

"Your breakfast, mademoiselle," I heard the servant say.

"Just leave it outside the door, please. I'm . . . not dressed."

"Of course, mademoiselle."

"Thank you," I croaked, and waited a moment to be sure he was gone before creeping over to the door and lifting the tray. My stomach was queasy, but I hoped some coffee and a bite of sweet bread might stop the throbbing in my head.

All I could think of was the worst: Théo must be dead, and Monsieur Chevallier must have used his designs anyway. I held the pearl comb so tightly, it made red, sore impressions in my skin.

As I finally put it back into my box, beside the little trinket box from Grand-père du Maurier, a thought struck me, and I froze. I flipped both boxes upside down. The mark was the same: *Du Barry's*. I pulled up the key to my own box, the one my father had strung around my neck so many years ago. I looked at the key and looked at the lock on Vivienne's box.

It was too simple. Too easy. Too obvious.

But it fit.

I caught my breath. Would it really turn too? I expected it to stick, to keep shutting me out, but it turned. The lid popped, and breathlessly, I lifted it.

"Papa." I whispered it into my palm. A blue eye with a dark brow. I could see his smile in it.

I scrambled for the other eye, frantically and clumsily untangling it from necklace cords and rings. I cradled one in each of my palms—two eerie, faceless eyes gazing up at me silently. Knowingly.

They were identically framed, rimmed in pearls and diamonds on a backing of gold. The stamp of Chevallier's was again imprinted below the pin. But this one had an inscription above the pin: *Forever*.

"Hélène?"

"Yes, Mère? What is it?" I snapped, shoving the two eyes quickly into the trinket box and snapping both lids closed. How long had I been sitting there?

"I'm so bored! Come and play tennis with me! Charlotte has a headache," she said through the door.

"I'll be there in ten minutes. I need to dress," I said through gritted teeth. It was all falling into place. My head was clearing. The music my father loved and my mother hated. My father bought both boxes at Du Barry's. I had the key all along.

I took off my dress from the night before and changed into a thin cotton one for tennis. My brain was on fire with theories and questions, but finally, at least one answer: my father and Vivienne—the set of lover's eyes were theirs.

Vivienne. My grandfather's favorite child. Everyone's darling. My father's lover. My mother's nemesis. She hated Vivienne—but did she hate her so much that when she found out, she killed her? Or was Tante Adrienne right? Did Josette make it up? It would have been easy to make up. Easy to believe.

Ten minutes had passed already, and I hopped out of my room on one foot, still tugging at my shoe. I didn't know what I was going to do, what I was going to say, but one thing was certain: I wasn't going to let her win this game.

"Well, your game has certainly improved," she said with a tight smile as we finished the first set.

"No, actually, it hasn't improved." I squared my shoulders and smiled back at her.

"Oh?"

"I've just gotten tired of letting you win."

Her lips parted and she snorted, her eyes hot. She bounced the ball and wound up to serve, but missed completely. Flustered, she tried again and hit it directly to me for an easy return. I put a fierce backhanded spin on it, and she ran in the wrong direction.

"I've gotten tired of a lot of things, actually."

She laughed. "Is that so?" She served into the net and had to come up against my side of the court to pick the ball up, but I beat her to it.

She was only a foot away from me when I said, "Why won't you tell me anything?"

"There's nothing to tell."

"What about Vivienne? Was Papa in love with her?"

"Love? I don't think they ever called it *that*. He was *in love* with every woman he could get his hands on. Except for me."

"Is that why you wouldn't tell me? Because it's true?"

She laughed mockingly, but took a step backward. "You're going to believe a madman?"

"I don't know who to believe. So I'm asking you. Did you do it?"

I bounced the ball hard to make noise on the floor and caught it again. *Bounce, catch, bounce, catch.* I stared into her pale eyes, unwavering. She took another step backward.

"How dare you ask me that? How dare you!"

"I understand how you could hate her for it. I'm not too impressed, myself." *Bounce, catch, bounce, catch.*

"Was I jealous? Of course. You father never wanted me—just my money. She was nobody—a spoiled opera singer. Was I sorry when she died? No. But I always thought *he* did it. It doesn't take a genius to shove a woman down the stairs."

"Papa?"

She laughed. "Oh, did he fool you with that smile of his too? He was such a charmer, always above suspicion."

"I don't believe you."

"Nobody ever believes me. But I wasn't sorry to see *him* dead, either. I was glad he was gone. Relieved. But you don't have to kill someone yourself to be glad they're dead—glad they finally got what they deserved."

"No wonder he didn't love you," I said before I could stop myself, almost regretting it. Almost. "You're cold . . . and heartless."

"You think I'm cold and heartless?" Her voice went high and brittle as her eyes caught fire. "Maybe you're right, because I wouldn't be sorry to see you dead, either. And if you think I'm a killer, if that's what you really think, then perhaps you shouldn't be making me angry. Perhaps you're not speaking wisely. Did you ever think of that?"

"So you admit it?" I said in barely more than a whisper, dropping the ball and backing away from her and toward the door.

"I don't need to admit or deny anything to *you*. You!" She picked up the ball and threw it at me. I ducked. She began bashing her racket against the wall, each crash echoing into the next, until it was smashed and splintered, and the strings stuck out, crooked and limp. She hurled what was left of it at me, screaming, "Who are you to ask me questions? What do you know, you little whore? You and your secret lover, sneaking around in the stable. Did he give you pretty things? Did he make you promises? Well, where is he now? They all like to give us pretty things and tell us *forever* until they get what they want. Then they find other pretty things to make promises to."

Until they get what they want. Images of that little boat on the Seine flashed into my mind. Surely, he wanted me for more than that. He *loved* me . . .

"I hate you," I told my mother, my voice breaking. "I hate this whole family. I hate that I belong to any of you."

She leaned close to my face, her sleepless eyes terrifying. "Then at least, for once, we agree on something."

I scrambled to my room, banging my elbow on the doorframe, and started throwing my things into a pile on the bed.

Where is he now? Where is he now?

I sloppily shoved everything, which wasn't much, into my valise. Fumbling shakily with the latches, I told myself what to do. I would find Théo. I'd prove to her that he didn't find someone else, that he loved me, that he was alive, and that we would have the life we wanted. The life we chose. I would do anything but stay there with them. I wasn't going to be my mother's next victim. I was sure she had done it.

My father wasn't a killer. He wouldn't hurt someone. Would he? No, no, he wouldn't. But she would.

Still, I couldn't comprehend what any of this had to do with me. What had I ever done to her? Why did she hate me so much?

Chest heaving, I stumbled down the stairs with a hastily scribbled note announcing that I was going to stay with Marie for a few days to help prepare for the baby. I handed it to the doorman, valise trembling in my hands, and glanced one last time at the foyer, the staircase, the chandelier, and up toward my mother's room. The door thudded behind me, and I breathed goodbye.

Jogging across the street, I felt the thrill of escaping and the terror of not knowing. I knocked furiously on Marie's door, and when it opened, I was breathless.

"I need to see Madame Evereaux, please."

"She's not feeling well. She doesn't want any visitors today."

"Please, it's urgent."

"I'm sorry, she said no visitors."

"Would you tell her it's me? Please, tell her it's an emergency. Please?"

Frowning impatiently, the doorman shut the door in my face, but after a moment, he swung it open and motioned for me to come in.

I tried to compose myself on the way up the stairs. The door to her boudoir was ajar. "Marie?"

"Come in," she called, her voice raspy. "Close the door behind you." The curtains were drawn and the lamps were dark. She sat in a chair with Dulcet in her lap, her head down.

"I'm sorry to hear you're not feeling well," I said, trying to catch her eye.

"I'm fine. It's nothing. What's your emergency?"

I drew in a shaky breath and sat down, glancing at the door. "I'm leaving. Now."

She looked up at me then, and I gasped at her bruised eye and the crust of blood around her nose. I fell on my knees at her feet, startling the dog.

"He did this to you?"

She looked at the floor.

"What can I do to help you? Are you all right? The baby—?"

"I'm fine. It's fine." She rubbed her belly and smiled weakly, nodding. "Still kicking me in the ribs all day and night. Why are you leaving right now? What happened?"

I put my hand on her belly and wished I could take them both with me to Paris, to safety. But was anywhere safe? "Your necklace . . . the one he brought back from Paris . . . it's Théo's design."

"Oh, God," she whispered. "His design? You're sure?"

I nodded.

"But what if—what if he's not there?"

"I have to find out."

"You'll never see my baby," she wailed, taking my hand. "Oh, Hélène, I'll never see you again!"

I swallowed hard and looked from my feet to her face. "Do you want to come with me? Run away? I'll take care of you. I promise."

She was quiet for a moment, and I thought she might actually say yes. But she shook her head. "No. No, I'm not brave, Hélène. I'm going to learn to keep my mouth shut. I'll be all right. Just follow Grand-mère's advice—*set my expectations correctly*," she warbled, imitating her voice.

"You're braver than you think."

"If you still have hope—a chance for something good—then you have to go."

$$\text{IIII IIII II}$$

THE ABBAYE PRISON

AUGUST 23, 1792

Pretty little spy.

Funny how some words stay with you, while the billions of others you hear and think every day run out of your mind like water. I hear them in my sleep, always when I'm awake.

They pound in the rhythm of boots, in the scrape of the locks, in the cries of the prisoners at night.

Always, I fear it will be the last thing I will be called, the last words I will ever hear.

There are things I want to know before I die, things I want to do and hear and feel and see. I want to know the secrets of the past, of love, of the future. I don't want to become a part of the past. Not yet.

EN ROUTE TO PARIS

JULY 1790

I had just crossed the border. For once, Alexander Evereaux wasn't lying. Things *had* changed.

I was in a public coach full of citizen-soldiers from the provinces, traveling together to Paris for what I learned was to be the "Fête de la

Fédération," a celebration of the fall of the Bastille. Thousands of other men like my coach-mates were making their pilgrimage to Paris from all over the provinces, calling themselves *fédérés*. They all wore red, white, and blue rosettes of fabric on their lapels—patriotic cockades.

The fédéré across from me, willow-branch thin and just barely a man, squinted at me and adjusted the cockade on his uniform jacket. "What is a pretty German girl like you doing on her way to Paris?"

"I'm not German. I'm French," I said, warming as all their eyes turned to me.

"But you're coming from Coblenz."

"Yes." I stared out the window, as if by looking away I could turn their eyes away too. They were half drunk with celebration already, and I was the only female in the coach.

"Then you must be a spy. A pretty little spy." He licked his lips. "Why don't you try getting some information out of me?"

"I'm not a spy. I'm going to Paris to meet my fiancé," I said, too conscious of whether or not it looked like I was telling the truth.

"And is he a Royalist like you?" interjected another, staring at me suspiciously.

"I'm not a Royalist, monsieur," I managed, shaking my head, knowing I looked and sounded on the brink of tears, wondering what would happen to me if they didn't believe me. Wondering what would happen to me even if they did.

A round of laughter went up in the coach, but the tall, middle-aged man beside me suddenly shouted over their laughter, clapping his hands to silence them. He was clearly in charge.

"That's enough, Didier. Don't bother her, any of you. There will be plenty of girls for you in Paris—see this?" he said, and handed over a pamphlet that distracted the others from me for a while. It was a directory of the ladies of the Palais-Royal.

"Ignore them," he said softly, turning to me as the others whistled and jabbed at each other with their elbows, reading names, descriptions, and prices aloud. "I'm Citizen Petit. Have you been away from Paris a long time?"

"A year. And not by my choice."

"Then, here. You'll need this," he said, and unpinned a red, white, and blue cockade from his lapel. He nodded toward my dress. "Don't be seen without it. Things have changed, citizeness. No more 'monsieur.' No more 'mademoiselle.' We are *citizens* now—all equal."

I nodded, pinning it on my dress obediently.

"As soon as you can, you should get a red cap. And a striped skirt. But this white dress will do for the Fête," he said, pointing his chin toward the dress I was wearing, the one I'd bought in Grasse. "All the ladies will be wearing white for that. But don't wear any lace, it's been outlawed."

"Thank you, citizen," I said, suddenly terrified of a Paris so changed it didn't allow lace.

"Do you sing, spy?" Didier asked after pocketing the pamphlet and producing a flask.

I nodded.

"Then you'll lead us in the 'Ça ira'! Our singing is terrible," he said, wiping his mouth and waving the flask in the air triumphantly.

"I . . . I don't know it."

Another round of laughter went up.

"Then we teach the pretty little spy to be a good patriot!" he laughed, and began singing horribly off key. The others joined in, Petit loudest and worst of all. It was an anthem to optimism, filled with joy at the promise of better days ahead.

> *Ah! Ça ira, ça ira, ça ira*
> *Réjouissons-nous, le bon temps viendra!*

"You're right," I said, stifling a smile. "Your singing *is* terrible." And they all laughed again. After three rounds of the song, I joined in too, and they applauded my singing and patriotism, offering me sips from their flasks. I politely declined, but kept on singing with them until they fell asleep.

Two of them snored. They all stank. Petit's head lolled onto my shoulder. It was going to be a long ride.

"You never did tell us your name, pretty spy," Didier said the next morning, smiling sleepily at me. "How will I find you later? Eh? Once we're in the city?" The toe of his boot played at my feet, and I jerked them back under the bench.

"I thought you had a pocket full of girls."

The others laughed and jabbed him, reaching in his pocket for the pamphlet, which he clutched protectively. When the ensuing wrestling match had ended and Didier was again in possession of the pamphlet, he looked at me, grinning.

"Well?"

"My name is Hélène. And I'm not a spy, all right?"

"But what's your last name, Hélène?"

I looked down at my feet and out the window and up at the ceiling of the carriage. Citizen Petit put a hand on my arm.

"You don't have to tell them the truth, you know," he whispered, smiling wryly.

"Leroux," I said, tasting the sweetness of it on my tongue. "Citizeness Leroux."

As we finally neared the gates of the city on the thirteenth of July, coaches were backed up for a mile. Travel was at a standstill for hours. The excitement of the Fête and of being so close to the end of our journey was almost unbearable. All around, Fédérés were jumping out of carriages and hopping up on top, banging on the sides, hooting and singing, and playing cards in the road. Word was passed down the rows of coaches that there were some problems with paperwork at the gates. Not everyone was being allowed back in.

Didier insisted I lead the crowd in song in the grass, and I soon had thirty men and a handful of women around me, arms around one another, tears streaming down their faces as they sang and swayed back and forth. They tossed red caps in the air, embraced and shook hands, calling one another *brother*. Those who had flasks lifted them in a toast to the French nation.

"Do you have the time?" I asked Petit, anxiously glancing at the angle of the sun. It was taking forever.

Citizen Petit pulled a watch from his vest pocket and smiled wistfully. "Do you know what we did a year ago tomorrow?"

I nodded. "The Bastille, yes." Of course I knew.

"After the fall of the Bastille, we took our clocks out and stopped them. Then we started them again. The world began anew that day—in Paris, and all across the provinces," he said, still smiling, and breathed on the glass face of the watch before rubbing it on his coat. "It's a quarter to four. We'll be inside the city gates before darkness falls. I'm sure of it." He patted my shoulder, then took up a game of cards.

Soon after, word came back again that the holdup had been carted off to prison along with his family of spies. My stomach lurched with the carriage as we started moving toward the gates. I barely breathed as a man with a red cap and a clay pipe took our papers for inspection. He didn't return with mine for nearly half an hour, and when he did, he blew smoke in my face.

"Coblenz," he said, squeezing the word out between the teeth that clenched his pipe. "Why were you in Coblenz?"

"I'm running away from my family, citizen. From my Royalist family. I've come back to Paris to be a good citizen."

"Hmph," he grunted, looking at my papers sourly.

"A word, honorable citizen?" Petit said, leaning out the window into the smoke cloud. Citizen Petit vouched for my character and patriotism, promised on his honor as a Frenchman that I was with them, and then, to my surprise, Didier and the others put their hands on their hearts and swore the same.

They let me through.

As we neared the center of the city on the thirteenth of July, I noticed that the shops were closed and hastily scribbled signs hung on front doors. I squinted at a watchmaker's shop and made out his neat handwriting:

Helping our great nation by completing the amphitheater to welcome our most distinguished brothers from the provinces. *Vive la Nation!*

The men were all at the Champ-de-Mars, lending their muscle to build a stadium for the Fête. It was a *journée des brouettes*, a day for moving earth together with wheelbarrows and shovels and bare hands.

Meanwhile, women wearing red caps were hanging lamps in the trees, ready to be lit the following day for the Fête, and even the children playing in the street wore cockades and red, white, and blue. Several buildings were boarded up—the wigmaker's, a pâtisserie, a small parish.

Citizen Petit and his men were let off at a hotel on the rue de l'Égalité. We were only three streets from the Palais-Royal, then two, then one. My heart was pounding so hard I thought I might die. The driver pulled the horses to a stop in front of Chevallier's, where a sign of *"Vive la Nation*—Closed" hung on the door.

"Your stop, citizeness."

Down the street, I could hear drums, the boom of a cannon, people singing, music starting and stopping as musicians rehearsed, and the general commotion of preparing for a celebration. Fédérés were pouring into the city from all directions, a sea of men in uniform embracing and singing. Wagons full of filthy, laughing people were returning from working on the amphitheater.

I walked slowly up to the door and cupped my hands around my eyes to peer into the dark, empty shop. The jewelry cases were festooned with red, white, and blue ribbons. I could see necklaces, bracelets, and brooches shaped like the Bastille in the nearest case.

Where is he now? Where is he now?

And then, the door to the back room opened. It was him—alive and whole, cradling something shiny in his palm. This was it. The moment I'd been waiting for. The moment when everything was going to be all right.

I smoothed my hair. Cupped my hand in front of my mouth to check my breath, which was pure coffee. *At least he likes coffee*, I thought. *Black with a spoon of sugar.*

I turned the knob and the little bell above the door jangled. His head shot up and he froze. He squinted at me, then blinked, shaking his head, and looked again. "Hélène?"

I was a fountain of tears as I ran to the counter, and he scooped me up into his arms and lifted me off the floor. "You're alive," I whispered. "You're all right."

He set my feet on the floor again and nodded, a strange panic spreading across his face. "Hélène? It's really you?"

I nodded, lifting my lips toward his, but he stopped me with his shaking index finger. "But you were—where have you been?"

I opened my mouth to answer, but stopped as he looked around anxiously. "Come back here," he said. "Before someone sees."

He opened the door to the back room with shaky hands and locked it behind us. He pressed his body against it, staring at me like I was there to rob him or worse. "Hélène?" he whispered.

"When you didn't come, I was so scared . . . so scared something happened to you." I took a step toward him, but he stared at me, stiff and wide-eyed.

"Where was I supposed to come? What address was I supposed to write to? Where were you, Hélène?"

"You didn't get my letters?"

"Letters? No. I didn't get any letters!"

"I sent dozens. I tried—"

"Where were you?"

"I was in Grasse with my mother's family, and then I was in Coblenz with my father's family. I wrote to you every week, every Friday. They said mail was coming through. Something had to have come through!"

He shook his head. Had my mother bribed the postmaster?

"You're all right," I whispered. "That's what matters. You're here. We're together." I took another step toward him, but he sighed and raked his fingers through his hair, turning away from me and pressing his forehead against the door, whispering, "Oh God, no. Oh God. Oh God."

"What? What is it? You didn't want to see me?"

He kept his face pressed against the door, then slowly raised his fist and pounded it. "I tried to find you, Hélène. I tried so hard to find you. The papers said you all died in the fire. They said no one survived."

I wanted him to take me in his arms so much it hurt, and I wrapped my arms around myself to ward off the tremor radiating through my body. Something was wrong, so wrong, and suddenly I knew that nothing was ever going to be all right again.

"I was sick, Hélène. Sick, all right?" He turned to me, and the anguish in his eyes washed over me in a tidal wave of panic. Why wasn't he touching me? His words tumbled out, frazzled and disjointed. "I couldn't eat, couldn't sleep, couldn't think straight. All I could think of was that you couldn't be gone forever. I went to your château—what was left of it. I asked people in the village, but nobody knew anything about what happened to you. 'Nobody got out,' they said. Everybody said that. I told them I was looking for your father because he owed me money, hoping they'd tell me the truth. But nobody had seen you."

"There are tunnels," I whispered.

"I'm sorry! I'm so sorry." His face was in his hands. Tears ran between his fingers.

"What did you do?"

"I . . . I married Lucille."

"You *what*?" I felt my heart stopping, everything inside of me grinding to a halt, breaking. He sank into a chair, his head falling into his hands. The moments of silence between us were suspended into an eternity, as if time would never start again.

But then the front door swung open, jangling the bell. Lucille's sweet, singsong voice floated into the back room. "Théo?"

"I need to go," I whispered, squeezing the words through my thick throat, digging my nails into my palms so I could focus.

"Théo?"

"Yeah. Just a minute," he answered gruffly and then lowered his voice to me. "I'll pay for an inn. Or you could stay with my brother until we . . . sort things out. They have a vacant room."

"I have some money. You don't have to do that."

"Yes," he said, stopping my hand from reaching for my valise. "Yes, I do."

"What will you tell her?" I whispered, nodding toward the door.

He took a shaky breath. "I'll take care of it."

"What are you doing in there, *mon cher*?" she called, her footsteps coming closer to the door, hollow and sharp on the wood floor. Before she could try the locked door, he flicked the latch and opened it.

Lucille froze. "What's this?"

Our eyes met momentarily, one of her delicate, dark eyebrows lifting.

"She needs a place to stay," he said. "I'm taking her over to Max's. Lucille, close the shop for me? Please? I'll be home for dinner."

Lucille nodded, her mouth tight.

Théo helped me up into his cart, his fingers lingering against mine. The buzzing celebration of the Palais-Royal was a blur.

"My mother must have found a way. She must have found a way to take my letters," I whispered.

The cart was uncovered and the street was crowded, making conversation impossible. But I couldn't find words anyway. I wanted to say everything and nothing. I wanted to scream at him, to kiss him, to never see him again, to run away together and never look back.

He reined the horses in behind a three-story building on the Rue Saint-Honoré in the Vendôme district, with a bookshop on the ground floor. It was only a few blocks down the street from the Palais-Royal, and the National Assembly was visible just south of it, bordering the Tuileries Garden. Squeals of laughter and a baby's cries drifted from the second-floor window. Men and women came in and out the door in a constant stream, some carrying books or papers or pamphlets, most empty-handed. He helped me down, and I followed him into the smell of ink and paper and tobacco. It was easy to see that the man behind the counter was Théo's brother.

Max was thinner and ten years older, and when Théo waved at him, he brightened and excused himself from the counter to embrace his brother. I thought it peculiar that he should be open while all the other shops were closed for the *journée des brouettes*. But then I noticed his limp and the slow heaviness of his left arm, and I remembered Théo telling me he'd been shot in the war.

Théo whispered in his ear, and his eyes widened and fastened on me with pity and grief.

Max closed the shop. He shooed the customers out and flipped around the sign on the door. "Elisabeth? Could you come down, *chérie?*" he called up the stairwell. He turned to me, his mouth and brow tight. "You'll stay with us."

"I . . . I don't want to impose. I have money," I said, bending to open my valise, but he stopped me with a gentle hand.

A petite woman with frizzy black hair came down the stairs, her full red, white, and blue skirt bustling behind her, and glanced from Max, to Théo, to me. Max whispered in her ear and her thin lips parted into a gasp as she rushed to embrace me, crying, "Oh, dear Lord, have mercy!"

The attic was sweltering, with one small dormer window, a squeaky bed, a desk, and a bureau painted white with little pink flowers on the drawers. Elisabeth stood in the doorway, looking at Théo. He didn't move.

"Well," she said, taking a sharp breath. "I'll be back with some dinner." And then she left us alone.

The question was swelling in my chest, threatening to explode. I took a breath. Tried to control my voice. Tried not to scream it. "What happened?"

He rubbed his face. His eyes were rimmed red and circled dark. "I didn't take my master's evaluation in September," he said slowly, sinking onto the edge of the bed. "I put it off until after Christmas. I didn't go to work for a month, and then only sometimes. My mother called five different doctors. Lucille started looking in on me, trying to get me to eat something. She convinced Monsieur Chevallier I was sick, that I needed some time, to hold my job.

"I finally told my brother. Max knew some of the border-patrol guards from when he was in the army, and he said that a lot of your people had been going to Coblenz with the Prince du Conde. So he asked around, wrote some letters, and found that your uncle, aunt, and grandmother had all crossed the border. Foix crossed the border with them, but you and your mother didn't. We found out that your cousin and her husband crossed the border later too. But still, no trace of you. I waited for letters. I prayed. I begged. I promised God anything if he just brought you back to me. But there was nothing.

"Finally, in April, my brother said I had to accept the fact that you were gone. Lucille was waiting. She was there day after day, filling orders and making deliveries when I was too sick to work, bringing me food and newspapers after work. Monsieur Chevallier was gracious enough to let me keep my job. Max said I should try to move on, that it was what you would have wanted—"

I let out a bitter puff of air and turned away from him. "What I would have wanted," I repeated, shaking my head, then whirled back to face him. "It hadn't even been a year!"

He wiped his swelling, red eyes and took me by the shoulders. "I want to get fares and go to America with you. I want so badly to go, just like I promised, and keep you safe."

"But you've made other promises."

He nodded, squeezing his eyes shut.

"How could you do this? How could you do it?

"I'm sorry. I—"

"You never really loved me!" I cried, pushing at his chest. Shoving him away. Trying to shove my mother's words away too. "You lied to me! You never loved me!"

"How could you even think that?"

"No, how could *you*? You just—you got what you wanted, and then you found someone else—"

"No!" he cried and then lowered his voice. "No. I didn't get what I wanted. I only ever wanted you."

"Do you love her?" I asked, the words choking me, but he didn't answer me. Not really.

"I never stopped wishing it was you, not for a single day, not a single hour, Hélène." He stepped closer, and I didn't push him away. He dried my cheek with his thumb. I let him hold my face in his hands. I let him wrap his arms around me one last time. "Can you forgive me?" he whispered.

My tears soaked into his shirt as I closed my eyes. I couldn't say anything. I couldn't comprehend forgiving, only hurting. Only *impossible*.

"I want to take you away from here more than anything. I want to be with *you*, Hélène."

"But you can't," I whispered, my voice breaking. "It would be wrong."

He nodded. "It's not her fault, and I—"

"I know. It's my mother's fault. I know."

"Can you forgive me? Can you at least forgive me and not hate me?"

"I don't hate you. I could never hate you. I—" I started to say *I love you*, but stopped myself. We couldn't say those words to each other anymore. They were wrong now. "You should go. You said you would be home for dinner."

"I don't want to go," he said, his voice cracking. "*Je t'aime.*"

Elisabeth knocked, and I jumped.

"I'll put some dinner out here for you," she said through the crack in the door.

"It's all right, Elisabeth," he said, letting go and running the back of his hand down my cheek. "I need to go. I promised to make it home for dinner."

He promised.

I was given hot food, a cool bath, and fresh sheets.

"Do you need anything else?" Elisabeth asked, handing me a cup of water and fluffing my pillow.

"I'm fine. Thank you. This is so kind of you."

"I hope the children won't wake you. We have five of them, all adopted. And Adèle . . . she has nightmares. She doesn't speak, but she can surely scream. God knows what that child has seen. And the baby, she doesn't sleep well yet, either."

"I'll be fine. Please, don't worry about me."

"Well, of course I am worried about you. So let me know what I can do."

I nodded, and when the door closed, I collapsed onto the bed. I wept until there was nothing left inside of me. Until my eyes were swollen shut.

I must have slept, because a howling scream woke me in the hot darkness. Disoriented and alarmed, I bolted upright. Where was I? Then, everything came crashing back to me against the chaotic crying and footsteps downstairs.

I didn't want to be awake. Ever again.

It had rained all morning and through the early afternoon. A heavy, soaking, warm rain that was turning to steam in the newly arrived sunlight. I sat slicing an apple mechanically into wedges, carving out the seeds and dropping the peels into an unruly pile on the smooth, worn tabletop. My vision was as unsteady as my hands, and I slipped, slicing my palm.

Slowly, I turned the blade so that it caught the sudden sunlight, blurred in my wet eyes. The red steel matched a swelling line on my hand. My breath caught in my throat. I closed my eyes and wished nothing more than to not have to open them again, squeezing my hand tight, feeling the sticky, warm wetness.

My mother had been right. She had won.

A red pool grew drip by drip beside a pool of tears, bulging until they met and suddenly widened on the dark wood. I didn't move, tried to not feel anything but the burning sensation in my palm. I could fathom that. There were words for it.

Sounds of laughter rattled through the latched window somehow, up from the street, where Max's children smacked a ball back and forth between them. The air was stagnant and thick. I thought to open the window, but didn't move.

Elisabeth called to the children, and when they ignored her, Max's voice, loud and sharp, got their attention.

"Listen to your mère! Time to go." The bounce of the ball stopped, but their laughter didn't. Together, their footsteps faded away from the street outside the bookshop. The whole of Paris, the whole world, seemed to be moving away from me to the fédérés' celebration in a happy chatter, swelling with rounds of patriotic songs—"Ça ira" again and again. I shut my eyes and saw swirls of red.

Their voices died down, and the last wisp of laughter quietly drifted away like the smoke of an extinguished candle. My crimson palm turned to a rusty, creased map. Shadows widened, but the hot little room did not cool, and the sun slipped away.

Puncturing the darkness, fractured red light lit the room for an instant. The thick air was alive with a fizzy crackling. At the first of the rockets, I moved to the window and sat on the peeling sill, watching the sky catch fire, my hot forehead pressed against the cool pane. The sky above the city was filled with a rainbow of pyrotechnics, reflected brokenly in puddles on the street.

Théo came before the sun, tiptoeing upstairs and whispering my name through the door. He carried an armful of sketches and watercolors.

"I took them from your house," he said. "I broke down the side door, the one close to the stable. I took what I could . . . for you."

I started to reach for them, but drew my crusty, bloody hand back self-consciously. He took it in his, his brow knitted in concern, then jogged downstairs to ask Elisabeth for a bandage.

He silently washed my hand with a cloth and cool water. Gently winding gauze around my hand, he knelt on the floor in front of the bed. Once he'd finished, he brought my bandaged palm to his lips.

"You can't keep coming here," I whispered.

"I know."

I stood up, staring out the window instead of into his eyes.

"Where will you go, Hélène? Is anyone left?"

I shook my head and shrugged.

"You could stay here," he said, but I puffed a dark and silent laugh.

"I'm not going to let you just go out on your own and get killed. I promised to take care of you—"

"I can take care of myself," I said, and it came out sharper than I wanted. "Just . . . just go. I'll figure something out. I can't see you anymore."

He rose to leave, sighing heavily and shaking his head. "I'm . . . I'm so sorry."

"Théo?"

"Yes?"

I wanted to stop him. I wanted to say I loved him and would run away with him if he asked. I'd leave and never look back, never care if some poor girl's life was ruined. But I couldn't say those things. I couldn't turn him into my father. All I could do was figure out where to go next. How to stay alive. "Can you . . . can you help me find my aunt?"

He exhaled loudly and nodded. "What's her name?"

"Josette. Josette du Maurier. I just need an address."

"I'd do anything for you, Hélène."

He closed the door, and I opened the sketchbook, my fingers numb.

Théo.

He'd saved my hot-air balloons.

||||| ||||| |||

Un, deux, troix, quatre, cinc, six, sept, huit, neuf, dix, onze, douze, treize.
Thirteen.
I count my etched lines again, because there must be thirteen thousand.
But it's only been thirteen days.
Each day, the ache in my head intensifies. I think my heart is reaching up to stab me in the brain.

I stared at the crumpled note in my palm in Théo's handwriting: *Josette du Maurier, 7501 rue d'Enfer (as of January 1770). The best I could do.*

The fading number painted on the cracked, once-white plaster above the door read *7501*. It was in the Theater District, and as my eyes followed the windows up to the sagging roof, the twin rectangular towers of Notre-Dame were visible through the watery morning haze. I took a step toward it and then a step back. What was I going to say if she were there? I was Madeleine's daughter. Nobody's favorite.

I wanted to offer some sort of apology. I wanted to know what to apologize for. I wanted to tell Josette that her father, my grandfather, loved her. Knowing something like that could make all the difference, even if it didn't change anything.

Would she hate me? Would she try to hurt me? Or would she tell me the truth? Would she take me in, say it wasn't my fault—whatever *it* was? No matter how terrible the truth was, I wanted it. I needed it.

"Can I help you?" The voice of a bespectacled middle-aged man sticking his shining, bald head through the open window startled me.

"Um, yes, I'm wondering if a woman named Josette du Maurier still lives here?"

"Josette du Maurier?" he echoed, his bushy eyebrows raised. I nodded, and he leaned farther out the window toward me, squinting. "She hasn't lived here in a good twenty years. Why would you be looking for her? Eh?"

"I, um, I just wanted to talk to her. Do you know where she lives now?"

"If I knew that, I'd have her last month's rent. The last time I saw her, she was going out with a man in the middle of the night—nothing unusual for *her*. But she never came back. Left her things, left everything behind but her rent money. Just never came back. Disappeared from God's green earth, as far as I can tell."

"I'm sorry to have bothered you."

"No bother. But if you find her, let me know. I could use a few livres."

"Right. Good day, citizen," I said, and trudged back through the sizzling, stinking streets of Paris to the bookshop.

As I neared the door, I stopped and listened.

"It's dangerous to keep her here is all I'm saying." It was a tense, shrill female voice. One I didn't recognize.

"I understand your concern," said Elisabeth. "But we'll do as we see fit."

"What if she's a *spy*? Have you considered that?"

"She's not a spy, Lucille," Elisabeth said. A plate clattered onto the table with extra force. And then another. And another.

"How do you know? She's one of *them*—her parents were Théo's customers before the Revolution! What does anyone even know about this girl, really?"

"She needs a place to stay, and for now, she's staying here."

"Fine," Lucille snapped. "But don't expect me to come around while she's here."

"Lucille?" Elisabeth asked, her voice steady.

"What?" she snapped.

"What has Théo told you about her?"

"Just that she was a customer," Lucille said. I exhaled, feeling as if I were shrinking. All the air was being sucked out of my lungs. "Apparently, he made jewelry for her a few times, and now she thinks she can take advantage of his whole family. She's just taking advantage of how gullible he is!" Lucille said.

Anger tingled my ears. *Gullible?* Théo was *not* gullible. He was honorable and intelligent, artistic and brave and—

"This girl is not simply staying for free," Elisabeth said, her voice steady and stern. "She's here to work, and if an aristocratic young lady is willing to work for her own food and live like a regular person, I think that's admirable. *Revolutionary*, in fact. So, are you staying for dinner, or not?"

"I can cook for my own husband, thank you," Lucille snapped. When she slammed the door, the shutters rattled and the baby wailed.

She didn't turn to the left, or she would have seen me. She marched down the street to the right and didn't look back.

My attic room was hotter than the street. I lay under a thin sheet, drenched with sweat.

Days slid into each other, and my thoughts were an unraveling spool of thread I didn't try to catch. I didn't know why it mattered.

I held the knife in my hands again and again, and looked at my wrist. Who was I?

The child of murderers, liars, cheaters, lunatics, and thieves.

Unwanted, forgotten, and never good enough.

I belonged nowhere and to no one.

There was no way out.

The ideals I thought would make me free now held me prisoner.

I pressed the side of the knife against my fingertip, thinking about my blood.

And then, I thought about hers.

I thought about how it would look pooling beneath Lucille Leroux's head, her pretty eyes blank.

"Citizeness . . . Hélène?" The small, sweet voice made me feel naked. I shoved the knife into the desk drawer.

"Yes?"

"It's Sophie."

I rubbed my face and smoothed my hair before opening the door for Max and Elisabeth's eldest adopted daughter, who was shyly carrying something behind her back. Her big brown eyes met mine, and she thrust a handkerchief into my hands.

"What's this?"

"I made it for you. See? It has an *H*. Maman helped me. I can't read yet."

"It's beautiful," I said, smiling at the crooked pink stitches forming the jagged first letter of my name. "No one's ever made something like this for me before. Thank you."

"I thought you needed it. I could tell from your eyes that you cry a lot. I could tell you're sad."

I nodded, and she wrapped her arms around my waist. "Maman says I cried all the time when they first got me too. But then I got happy. So will you stay with us?"

"I . . . I don't know."

"I want you to stay," she said shyly, and tugged at my hand. "You're friends with Oncle Théo, and I like Oncle Théo. But I don't like Tante Lucille."

"Oh?"

"Maman says she just pretends to be nice," she said, but immediately clapped her hand over her mouth, her brown eyes huge. "Oops! I wasn't supposed to repeat that."

"I won't tell anyone," I promised, going down on my knees and hugging her, my resolve bent and ready to break. "I'm good at secrets."

She smiled. "Maman says it's almost time for dinner. Will you come downstairs to eat with us today? Please?"

"Um, all right."

"You should probably brush your hair."

"It's pretty bad, huh?"

She made a funny face and nodded, giggling, then bounded downstairs.

I looked out the window and into the street, pressing my forehead against the damp pane. I saw my own reflection dimly and stared through it, as if I was looking through my own ghost at the spluttering rain. *I don't know this person*, I thought. *I don't want to.* And then I realized that I did.

For the first time, I saw Madeleine d'Aubign in my face.

I set my jaw. I washed my face, brushed my hair, and went downstairs to dinner.

After weeks of being the ghost in the attic, I was introduced to the entire family properly.

Max and Elisabeth had five adopted children and one ugly, long-haired orange cat named Monsieur Malodorant, who rubbed my legs under the table and mewed for scraps.

"We've tried changing his name to Citizen Malodorant, but he just couldn't get used to it," Max said, smiling wryly. "So now we just call him Mal. We've tried to get rid of him a few times, but it was no use. Adèle keeps feeding him."

He winked at the little girl beside him, who smiled faintly back as she pulled her hand up from under the table. Adèle was willowy and silent. Her hair was stick-straight and stringy, and above her high, freckled cheeks, intensely green eyes followed my every move. Elisabeth whispered to me that she didn't speak at all, though she was five years old. An orphan of the Revolution, she'd been with them a year, but they didn't know if she'd ever spoken or if she had simply stopped.

Étienne was also five, skinny and sun-browned, and, his mother told me, the best stick-ball player to be found in the Vendôme. He grinned at me and shrugged. He knew it was true.

Sophie, their oldest child, was six, missing her two front teeth, and always pushing wildly curly blond hair out of her brown eyes.

Pierre was a little man of convictions. Two years old, redheaded, and religiously opposed to wearing clothing or sitting still long enough to finish a meal, he had three jokes memorized, and he expected (and got) a round of laughter from his brother and sisters and parents every time.

And the baby, Victoire, had become Max and Elisabeth's after her parents, their neighbors, both died of tuberculosis.

"So, are we going to adopt you?" Sophie asked as she took a piece of bread and passed the basket to me.

"I think I'm too old to be adopted," I said, laughing weakly.

"Are your parents dead, or didn't they want you?"

"Sophie!" Elisabeth exclaimed, her face shining with sweat and burning with embarrassment. She shook her head and put a finger over her lips.

"It's all right," I assured her, and turned to Sophie. "My papa is dead. And my mère didn't want me."

Elisabeth scrubbed around the rim of a large soup pot, humming. I carried a stack of bowls to the counter with a clatter, attempting to be helpful.

"Can I do anything else?"

She turned and smiled, shaking her head. "I'm glad you came down for dinner."

I smiled weakly and picked up a rag to wipe the counters.

"You can leave that for Max," she said over her shoulder. "Now, Théo mentioned an aunt . . . do you have family you want to stay with?"

"She doesn't live in Paris anymore. None of my family does."

She set the pot down, wiping her hands on her apron. "You're welcome to stay with us. We *want* you to stay. But if you can't, if it's too much, then we'll help you find another place where you'll be safe. And happy."

"Théo said . . . you needed help in the bookshop? That the flat was for a shop girl?"

"Yes, but you can have it. It's yours for as long as you need or want it. None of this was your fault, and we can't help but feel responsible—"

"I'll take the job," I said, and she nodded and embraced me.

"Good. Very good. When you're ready, and not before."

And so, I became Citizeness Hélène Michel, a cousin of Elisabeth's from Dijon. My parents were dead. I had no siblings. That was the story we'd tell if anyone asked. And everyone asked.

If Château des Cygnes was a house of secrets, the Vendôme was a place of none. Everyone's business was hung out as freely as their laundry, their arguments and private moments stretching across the narrow alleyways and into other open windows. Most of them at least attempted to get drunk on watered-down wine. Few of them tried to be beautiful. They were too busy trying to stay alive.

I gave Max and Elisabeth my real story the way they gave me theirs, in bits and pieces while Elisabeth taught me to cook and hem a dress and when things were slow in the shop and Max pulled a chair up beside me. Elisabeth talked about the small town in Pennsylvania where she grew up and the parents she loved and lost to fever. She told me about the day she found Max shot and left for dead, brought him home, bandaged him up, and fell in love with him. Max never told war stories, but he liked to talk about ideas. It was the question, not the answer, that fascinated him. He asked for my thoughts, for my feelings. He liked to talk about the children.

Little by little, I trusted them with my father's sordid life and death, my grandfather's madness, the canary feathers, and the eyes. When I told Elisabeth about my mother, there were tears in her eyes. She hugged me.

We never talked about the piece of licorice on the bookshop counter, though. It was there every Friday morning, waiting for me. Not even little Pierre touched it.

PART II

Tribulation first makes one realize what one is.
                                        —Marie Antoinette

卌 卌 IIII

When you do not know what I am, then I am something.

But when you do know what I am, then I am nothing.

What am I?

That stupid riddle won't leave my mind today. It makes me think of Mademoiselle Girard, my governess. My friend. She used to give me riddles to work out, but she wouldn't give me the answer. Ever. Sometimes it took me hours or days or weeks, but this one was easy.

A secret.

Could mademoiselle be here, somewhere, in this prison with me? On another floor, in another cell? Worn beyond recognition? The realization that my father might have sent her here sickens me. I hope she ran away with Hugo and never looked back. I hope she found another family to work for, another child to teach Voltaire and riddles.

When you do not know what I am, then I am something.

But when you do know what I am, then I am nothing.

What am I?

These days, another child might answer:

An aristocrat.

PARIS

1791

In Max's bookshop, I was allowed to read whatever I wanted for free, no sneaking required. I sold the wrap-style necklace from Grand-mère du Maurier, bought an overstuffed blue chair and an easel, and squeezed them both in beside the window of my flat. It was a hot room in the summer and cold in winter, but it was mine. On my eighteenth birthday, I rearranged the furniture. I worked and paid for it, and it felt more like home than anywhere else I'd ever lived.

The royal family also made their home in Paris in those days, but not by choice. A mob had stormed Versailles and insisted that Louis bring his family to the capitol, to live in the broken-down and drafty Tuileries Palace. He put on a red cap, toasted the nation, and told the people they had no better friend than he. But one summer night in 1791, he and his family were caught near the Austrian border, fleeing like thieves in the night. His little charade was unmasked: He wanted to get out. He wanted help from Marie Antoinette's family. He wanted to stop the Revolution.

The Jacobin Club prepared a petition to depose him, and put it on an altar to Liberty in the Champ-de-Mars. The people of Paris were asked to sign it.

"Our names must be on that petition." Elisabeth's dark eyes flickered with intensity as she stared at Max, who sat rubbing his chin, distractedly fanning the pages of the book that lay open in his lap.

"But you realize what it means? How dangerous it is?"

"The children can stay with your mother. We need to do this."

Max sighed heavily and closed his eyes. I sat silently at the table, and Elisabeth glanced from him, to me, and back again.

"Max, if he's given his way, it will be war. You know that. We must finish what we've started. He can't stay. He can't be allowed to escape again, or keep asking Austria and Prussia for help. What will become of us then? What will become of our children? We have to think of them, of the future. Of our grandchildren, of—"

"All right," Max said with resignation, flipping the book closed and rising to kiss her on the cheek. "If you believe so strongly, then we'll go."

She nodded, but I could tell she wasn't satisfied. She wanted him to agree with her. They rarely fought. But when they did, Max always gave in to her. She followed him up the stairs.

"You do believe it's the right thing, don't you? Max? To make France free like America?"

"We'll go."

Her feet drummed back down the stairs and she peeked at me over the bannister. "You'll come too, Hélène?"

I nodded. I wanted to go too. The last thing I wanted was for things to go back to the way they were. That would mean victory for Alexander Evereaux and all his friends in Coblenz. Victory for the past.

I stood in line with Max and Elisabeth, the children happily at Madame Leroux's house just five doors down from the bookshop. The spirit of brotherhood was strong with easy chatter and open laughter, and smiles were bright like Christmas morning that morning in July. The atmosphere was so sunny no one thought anything bad could happen that day. No one, it seemed, but Max.

As we moved slowly up the steps to the altar of Liberty, I sensed Max's discomfort growing. The fact that it was an altar to Liberty unsettled him. He rubbed the back of his neck, looked right and left and over his shoulder.

The man in front of us couldn't write. His forehead beaded with sweat as he shifted from foot to foot and finally scrawled an unintelligible scribble before passing the pen to me. I nodded encouragingly, saying "Thank you, citizen," and signed my own name with a flourish. Except I didn't sign my own name. I felt like a liar, like a coward, as Elisabeth Leroux signed her name beneath mine, large and dark. I was hiding. I was still hiding.

As we made our way down the steps to the platform and onto the grass, a murmur went up from the crowd behind us. I spun around to see a woman pointing insistently at something under the platform steps. A cluster of men moved in to investigate, crouching down low. Two men were dragged out by their ankles, and women covered their mouths in surprise.

Someone shouted, "Spies!" igniting imaginations in the crowd.

"They're going to set fire to the altar!"

"The king sent them to burn it up!"

"Bastards!"

"Spies!"

"Traitors!"

They were hauled away, their protests swallowed by the roar of the hissing, booing, spitting crowd.

"How did they know they were spies?" I shouted into Max's ear.

"They don't know." He grabbed me by the arm. "It's time to go home."

Against the grain of a thickening crowd, we pushed between sweaty bodies and dodged grimy elbows. Every muscle in our bodies alert and tense, we pressed on. As a cheer went up behind us, I looked over my shoulder. The accused spies were dangling from a lamppost, still kicking.

"Dear God!" Elizabeth cried, clasping her hand over her mouth.

"Come on, keep moving," Max ordered, firmly steering us both onward.

I was in a dizzy panic as we struggled through the deafening mess. The disorienting rhythm of boots and hooves reached my ears just before I saw the blood-red flag straight ahead. General Lafayette and Mayor Bailly were on horseback, leading ranks of National Guardsmen in formation, weapons ready.

The people were supposed to be afraid. They were supposed to stop their fussing and go home like naughty children, but they didn't. They booed their mayor and the Guard, and catcalls rang out. Then, a shocking volley of stones went up, striking a few of the guardsmen. I knew in the pit of my stomach what was going to happen next. I wanted to close my eyes, but I couldn't. I wanted to close my ears, but it wouldn't have mattered.

I covered my head as Lafayette's hand went up, ducking as a few bullets exploded into the sky: a warning.

The crowd scattered for an instant, but there was no containing them. Men and women scrambled for more stones as Lafayette tried to shout above them, "Disperse! Return to your homes immediately!"

No one moved, except to pick up more stones.

"Fire!" Lafayette yelled, and a great spray of hot lead whistled past us. I screamed.

I felt as if Max might yank my arm off as we took off running. We were pushed and stepped on and swept along by hysterical people, some of them dripping with blood, some of them weeping and shrieking the names of those who had fallen.

We couldn't stop without being trampled, and so we kept running, running, until the mob ahead of us began to thin. The rapid fire had slowed to a random popping, and we slipped into a side alley to catch our breath. Then we walked, panting and sweaty and shaky, not speaking a word until we finally reached the door of the bookshop. My dress was torn, my feet were throbbing, and my ears were ringing.

Elisabeth sobbed against Max's shoulder. "I'm sorry, I'm sorry! We shouldn't have gone!"

He kissed her head. "We're all right."

She turned to me, sniffling. "Hélène, I'm sorry."

I put a hand on her back and said, "I wanted to go. I would have gone without you. It's all right." I went to bed, praying that Théo was all right and tempted to pray that Lucille wasn't.

We learned that Citizeness Channel had been shot at the Champ-de-Mars. A National Guardsman's bullet ripped through her calf. She was our neighbor two houses down, a nineteen-year-old girl with three small children who sold coffee on the streets to feed them. They didn't know if she would ever walk again.

Elisabeth brought her fresh bandages, cooked for her family, and sat with her through the night to get her through the pain.

Meanwhile, Max was left to put his own five children to bed. He bumbled through the children's routines, and Sophie proudly pointed out his every oversight.

Pierre hid, naked and screaming, behind the corner chair while Max cleaned up a puddle on the floor.

"Why are you crying? Come on, now, Pierre," Max coaxed, wiping his forehead with the back of his hand.

"Papa," Sophie said, rolling her big brown eyes as she teased him. "Pierre needs his glass of water. He's only asked you five times."

"Oh. Right. The water."

"This is why girls are mothers."

"Well, you've got to settle for me for just one night," he grumbled from his hands and knees. He rose to catch Pierre, clean nightclothes in hand, but immediately the little boy took off, running upstairs. Étienne kicked a ball around the salon. Victoire toddled over and clutched Max's leg, nearly tripping him. I laughed and picked her up before she fell.

"Why can't Hélène be our mother tonight?" Sophie asked, her eyes bright with the wonderfulness of the idea. "Hélène, you're a girl. You're old enough to be a mother. Aren't you?"

I laughed. "Yes, I suppose I am."

Somehow, we managed to get all five of them to sleep before midnight. Finally, it was down to me and Mal, who curled up contentedly at Adèle's feet and closed his yellow eyes too. I crawled into my own bed, exhausted, waiting for the inevitable.

As usual, the screams rang out at two. I reached for my robe, shivering and disoriented, then hurried downstairs just as Max was opening the children's door. Adèle was kicking and screaming and punching the air, oblivious to everyone else in the room. Max puffed a sigh and said, "Elisabeth picks her up. I'll try that."

I began rocking and patting Victoire in the kitchen, and Sophie and Étienne huddled sleepily beside me, their hands clenched over their ears. Pierre found a far corner and began clanging his blocks together. Mal paced back and forth, his tail held high and twitching, wanting to go near Adèle, but afraid.

After half an hour of intensifying screams, Sophie shouted at my ear, "Maman sings sometimes."

I passed Victoire to Sophie and tapped Max on the shoulder. "I'll try."

He laid the hysterical child on her bed and looked at me tentatively, rubbing the eye she'd just unknowingly punched him in. "Are you sure?"

I nodded and sat on the floor beside the bed, just far enough from her flailing limbs. "Adèle, it's me. It's Hélène. Everything's all right," I shouted, but she arched her back and screamed again. I put my hand on her back. I hummed "L'Espérance."

I hummed over the screaming, over the baby's crying, the crashing blocks, and slowly, her body softened. Her crying slowed and quieted. She looked at me, her eyes like green puddles so deep, none of us knew what was beneath them. Then she let me hold her, still trembling, the remnants of sobs hitching in her throat. I kept singing softly, rubbing her back, until she was still.

"It's all right," I whispered in her ear as I laid her head on the pillow, brushing the damp strands of hair from her cheek and tucking them behind her ears. I pulled the blanket up to her chin. "I have bad dreams too. But you're here now, see? You're safe. It's over." I kissed her forehead, and her arms shot out from under the blanket to hug me around the neck. She pressed her lips against my cheek forcefully, then clung to me silently, her face in the curve of my neck, before resting back against the pillow and falling asleep.

We tucked the other four children in, whispered good night, and tiptoed into the kitchen.

"Thank you," Max said with a wink. "Boys are not very good mothers, are we?"

I smiled. "You make up for it by being a good father, at least."

"You'll be a good mother yourself, one of these days."

I laughed bitterly and shook my head.

"It's not the end for you, Hélène. It's not the end."

"No? Then what is it?" I didn't think about finding someone else. It was enough of a miracle that one person had loved me. I couldn't imagine it happening again.

"I don't know, exactly. I don't know. But your life is not over. Of that, I'm sure."

|||| |||| ||||

I think about the things I've done.

The things I almost did.

The things I wanted to do.

Here, in the dark, in the cold, it's hard to remember which is which.

PARIS

SEPTEMBER 1791

The leaves crisped gold, the air chilled, and I was convinced that both my life and the Revolution were over.

The king accepted the Constitution, and with his signature, France became a constitutional monarchy. The political clubs were being shut down, and the French émigrés had been ordered by the National Assembly to return to France within a month or face dire consequences. No more counterrevolutionaries plotting with foreign powers in Coblenz. No more violence and riots at home. No more noisy debates.

It was over.

Complètement.

The d'Aubigns and the Evereauxs might live on the Seine again in a few weeks, and I knew that if I wanted to find out what was left of my old house, there wasn't much time to do it. It wasn't like I could walk back into the salon and say, "Good morning, Mère, just wondering if I had a tube of blue paint lying around upstairs. Give Cousin Alexander a kiss for me. I'm off to work."

But, it still wasn't clear whose power would tip the balance, the king's or the National Assembly's. I knew my family wouldn't come back defeated with their tails between their legs. Hopefully, they wouldn't come back at all.

We didn't yet know that the king would use what little power he had left to veto the Assembly, that we were actually headed toward war, and that that war would change everything. So, we celebrated with the rest of Paris, waiting for a hot-air balloon to take flight over the Champs-Élysées, happy for anything that meant peace.

"Papa, it is so *slow*!" Sophie whined, shifting from foot to foot as the balloon slowly filled. "This is taking forever!"

Max laughed and squatted down to face her. "You wouldn't think so if you were up in it, now would you? Do you think you'd like to go up in the clouds, my Sophie? Wouldn't that be exciting?"

"No," she said, pouting. "It would be too high, with just a little basket to sit in. I'd like to be a princess in a soft, fancy carriage instead, with pretty dresses and chocolates. Could we go get a lemonade? Please, Papa? Maybe a marshmallow too?"

Max laughed again and patted her head. "Soon. Have patience. Your brothers and sisters are enjoying it."

As the balloon lifted off, trailing tricolor ribbons, Étienne and Pierre jumped up and down, cheering with excitement. Little Victoire pointed a chubby finger from Elisabeth's arms and squealed, but Adèle just stood there holding my hand, her freckled face to the clouds, her lips parted and her green eyes wide with wonder.

"It's amazing, isn't it?" I whispered to Adèle, and she nodded without looking at me.

"Do you want to look at the art at the Louvre Palace, Sophie?" Max asked, as the balloon finally disappeared.

"Yes! But I want a lemonade first. I'm thirsty. Can we stop and see Oncle Théo too? I want to see if he's made any new bracelets!"

Max glanced at me and shook his head. "Not today, *ma belle*. Not today."

Strolling along the Seine, we all bought lemonades and marshmallows. Elisabeth tried to rub the crusty white sugar off the children's little lips and cheeks with her handkerchief before entering the Louvre, which was open to the public for the Salon of 1791. As we meandered through the display, every few minutes Elisabeth had to grab Pierre's hand, shrieking, "Don't touch!" After he touched the knee of Pajou's marble sculpture of Psyche, she finally carried him back to the cart ahead of us.

That year's exhibit was dedicated to the Revolution. I stared into Jacques-Louis David's enormous and epic rendering of the Tennis Court Oath. There was a portrait of Robespierre, the thin-faced young lawyer and assemblyman who championed the people. Well-formed, muscular Roman and Grecian heroes stared into the crowd, reminding us of the glory and virtue of a republic.

And then, there was a familiar name—Jacques Bennette—below the portrait of Helen of Troy. She was draped in iridescent white and turned away, staring out of a lofty bedroom window at the destruction of Troy.

Of course, it wasn't unusual for him to paint a mythological character. They were all around me, hanging on the walls, striking poses on pedestals. But I couldn't help feeling like it meant something, maybe more than one thing. Was it supposed to be the nobility, looking out on the destruction of the past? All of us watching our beautiful homes looted and burned to the ground? I closed my eyes and saw the flames, saw Jacques Bennette's face, his dark eyes, like onyx set in porcelain.

I couldn't help hoping, for just a second, that when his brush touched the canvas, he had thought of me.

Victoire was draped limply over Max's shoulder, dozing as we walked back to the cart, and Pierre was napping with his head on Elisabeth's lap when we reached them. Max drove back with a smile on his face as we chattered about the paintings and sculptures, and the children giggled about how incredibly naked they were.

As we neared the Pont Royal, I finally made my request. "Could you turn here? Please?"

Max turned and lifted an eyebrow at me.

"I wondered if I could see my house. I haven't since I came back. I won't be long."

He furrowed his brow and nodded. "Of course, Hélène. Of course." He turned the horse and we crossed the bridge into the Fontaine-de-Grenelle.

It was empty. My house on the Seine was nothing but walls and broken bits of wood and glass.

My furniture was smashed, my bed was gone, and my clothing was stolen. Someone had taken my paints, and where my bed had been, the word *blood* was painted in crude capital letters by a finger, the scarlet drips now dried where they had slid down the wall.

At my window, where threads of shredded velvet dangled in the late-afternoon light, I peered between spears of shattered glass at the Seine. The deep windowsill was frosted with two years of dust, and spiders had made themselves at home. This was no longer my room, no longer my home. No one saw *me* here. They saw nothing but our wealth, and they hated everything it symbolized.

They didn't know I hated it too.

And what about Vivienne? What would she see if she looked at me? Would she see my grandfather, her own father? Would she see my father in me and love me or hate me? Or would she only see my mother? Only the guilt, only the hatred? Would she hate me because I was the child who survived, when hers was lost?

Passing through the ghostly, echoing halls, I couldn't stop looking over my shoulder. My father's study was covered in shards of glass. There wasn't a trace of his desk or his newspapers or his pipe. My mother's aviary was a mess of seeds, smashed cages, and scattered dried-up flowers and leaves. In front of the cold ashes of the hearth, a little yellow feather remained on the rug, its quill caught in a loose thread.

I didn't want to see any more. I didn't want anything that was left in this house. I didn't want any of it to belong to me, ever again. I hurried out to the courtyard, past the cracked fountain, stopping for a moment to touch the splintering stable door. *Théo.*

It was a mistake to come.

I ran back to Max's cart, afraid of how easy it is to hear the wrongs of the past in the present. How easy it is to hear wishes for the future like so many singing birds, but how impossible for anyone to know what lies in wait for tomorrow.

"Can you draw us a picture?"

"Can you tell us a story?"

"Please?" the children begged.

As Elisabeth measured and mixed ingredients in the kitchen and Max sat scribbling at his desk, the children followed me upstairs with scraps of paper, jumping up and down, pulling at my shawl. I sat cross-legged on my bed, leaning against a pillow, digging my nails into my palms. I blinked away the shattered glass, the yellow feather, the BLOOD on the wall, the stable door. And Théo.

"What kind of story?" I asked wearily.

"A princess story!" Sophie squealed, her hands clasped together under her chin.

"An adventure," Étienne ordered, his browned arms folded across his chest.

"A *love* story."

"Dragons."

"Pixies."

"Ghosts!"

"All right, enough! I'll tell you a story with a princess and a pixie and a ghost. How about that?" I jumped up, unlocked my box, and concealed something in my still-trembling fist. I glanced from Adèle to my Montgolfier balloon necklace before closing the lid.

"What's that?" Sophie asked, up on her tiptoes and trying to pry my fist open.

"You'll see. At the end of the story."

"Is it a scary story?" Sophie whispered, flopping onto her stomach.

"A little."

"Is it kissy?" Pierre asked, scrunching his nose.

"Not so much."

Étienne grinned. Pierre came to sit in my lap. Adèle stayed cross-legged on the floor, Mal curled up in her lap. I started my story.

"Once upon a time, there was a beautiful dark-haired maiden who sang at the prince's castle. Every instrument she touched came to life and filled the castle theater with lovely music. Everyone adored her: the people of the kingdom, her carriage driver, her parents, her sister, the handsome prince. Everyone but the jealous princess.

"One night, the princess climbed a craggy mountain overlooking the sea, all the way to the enchantress's black castle. She promised the enchantress anything, anything, if only she would take the maiden away so that the prince's heart could be hers.

"'All things have their price,' the enchantress said, tapping her long fingernails against her lips.

"'I'll give you anything—my jewels, my clothes, all of the coins in the castle!'

"'Not everything can be paid for with coins or jewels,' the enchantress said. 'But, if you truly want to be rid of the maiden, take this,' she said, handing the princess a silver locket painted with the image of a swan. 'Capture two of her tears, and when you close the locket, she will be your prisoner.'

"'And the prince's heart will be mine?' the Princess asked.

"'Oh, I can't give you that,' the enchantress said. 'Love cannot be stolen—only given.'

"The princess ignored this and raced back to the castle, where the maiden was singing on stage. The princess hid behind the curtain, waiting, with the locket open and ready. She thought of a story, a story that would surely make the maiden cry. As soon as the maiden finished her song and stepped behind the curtain, the princess took her aside.

"'Ma chérie, something terrible has happened to your beloved prince,' she lied. 'I'm afraid he's gone, gone forever!'

"It worked. Big, sparkling tears rolled down the maiden's cheeks, and as soon as the princess clamped the locket closed, the maiden turned into a swan!

"The princess locked the swan maiden in a cage in the castle aviary. She announced to the kingdom that the maiden was gone, dead, never to return. Everyone cried and wore black, except for the princess, who smiled and wore yellow. Music disappeared from the kingdom. Every theater door was locked, and every stage was darkened. The prince walked right past the cage and didn't know that it was his beloved. Finally, she died of a broken heart, and all that was left of the swan maiden was a pile of soft, white feathers.

"Time passed, and the prince and princess were married. The princess thought she had won, but the prince didn't love her the way he had loved the maiden. In fact, he didn't love her at all. And the princess was not happy.

"One night, many, many years later, when the prince and princess were wrinkled and white-haired and walked with canes, a mischievous little pixie fluttered through the halls of the castle. She happened upon the princess's room, and sneaked in unnoticed. There, she found the locket.

"When the curious pixie opened the locket with her tiny fingers, she found the maiden's tears, still wet. Suddenly, in a flash of light, the swan cage opened! Soft feathers swirled into the air, and two swans flew out of the open window.

"The old princess looked around in alarm, realizing that her prince had vanished—that he had become the second swan! She looked down at her own hands, and found them covered in black feathers. She had been changed into an ugly raven, and was locked away in the maiden's cage.

"The locket lay on the floor of the cage at the raven princess's feet. She looked down in horror to see that the image of the maiden's dark eye was imprinted on one side, and the image of the prince's blue eye was imprinted on the other. Just. Like . . . This . . ."

The brown and blue eyes stared up at the children from my palm.

They gasped and squealed.

"To watch her forever!" Étienne exclaimed, shivering with creepy delight.

I nodded. "Forever. To this day, the swans still swim on the lake of the castle, which was named Château des Cygnes in their honor."

"Where did you get those?" Sophie cried, clenching my blanket in her fists.

"I found them."

"Is it the maiden's eye? Really?" Étienne asked, raising a skeptical eyebrow.

I smiled slyly and shrugged. "Maybe."

Sophie grabbed my hand, and I glanced down to see that even Adèle was staring at me. "Is it real? Is it a true story?"

"They were all ghosts," Étienne whispered, wiggling his eyebrows up and down.

"Maybe."

"Did they really live forever as swans?"

"I don't know." I got up to put the eyes back in my box and brushed my index finger against the blue one, my father's. "I hope so," I said, slowly closing the lid.

"Was it real? I mean, the eyes, the princess, the ghosts? Was it a *real* story?" Sophie demanded, her eyes enormous.

I took a deep breath and smiled, shaking my head. "It was just a story."

"Do you believe in ghosts, Hélène?" Étienne whispered.

"Do you?"

"Yes! Absolutely!" he exclaimed.

Sophie shook her head adamantly. "*Non!* It's superstitious!"

I laughed. "Yes, it is *superstitious*. And that's a very big word. Where did you learn that?"

"From you!" she giggled. "So, is it time for our lesson? Please?"

"Yes, it is. No more silly ghost stories," I said, moving toward the door and grabbing a stack of papers from my dresser, taking another deep breath. "It's time to read. Facts only."

They followed me down to the salon and clustered around a side table on their knees. Elisabeth's written French wasn't nearly as good as her written English, having grown up in America. So, I had made a reader for Sophie and Étienne like the one Mademoiselle Girard had made for me, with pictures for each letter sound and basic grammar. Sometimes I wrote little stories in simple words featuring the children—the girls as pixies and princesses, Étienne as a Viking or knight, Pierre as a dragon so he didn't have to wear clothes.

Adèle watched silently over my shoulder as Mal purred uproariously in her arms. I suspected she could already read, even though she didn't speak. The look in her eyes was always one of intelligence, intelligence and fear. As the others practiced writing their letters, I folded a small piece of paper and wrote "Come back up to my room. I have a present for you," and passed it to Adèle. I watched her eyes follow the script and her lips move into a faint smile. She met my eyes and nodded.

I clasped the Montgolfier balloon necklace around her neck, gently pulling strands of her dark hair up and over the chain. I don't think I'd ever realized how sad it made me until I saw how happy it made her. It had always meant an ending to me—the realization of who my father really was, what he did, and that I wasn't really the most important girl in the world to him. But now, as Adèle's mouth spread into the first toothy smile I'd ever seen on her face, it meant something else. It was a beginning.

As the aroma of warm bread and fish made our stomachs growl, Sophie and Étienne read together, word by word, small sentence by small sentence. Elisabeth poked her head in and out of the room, smiling and encouraging them. Max finished his work and clapped his hands, applauding their progress.

"Papa!" they squealed, and ran to hug and kiss him, nearly knocking him over in their excitement. "We want to read to you. Come, will you listen?"

He laughed and sat with three children on his lap and a cat at his ankles. When they had finished, he squeezed them into a wobbly sandwich of giggles.

"Look at you, how smart you are!" he exclaimed. "Soon you'll be reading everything in the shop, just like Hélène."

"Dinnertime!" Elisabeth called, and they scrambled and squealed into a pushing, shoving cluster to the table, where Elisabeth stood with her eyebrows raised and her wooden spoon raised higher. They quickly quieted down and took their seats, but not without a stray giggle.

"I've been thinking," Max said, flipping through the handmade reader on the table before moving toward the kitchen. "Could you make a patriotic one? To sell in the shop? You know, *B* is for *Bastille*, things like that? I could send it to the printer and see how it does. What do you say?"

Of course, I said yes. We printed it under the name Jean-Luc Michel, and I stood behind the counter taking people's money for my work, none of them having any clue that I was the author. They sold out in a week, and we went to a second printing, and then a third.

By Christmas of 1791, we were going to a fourth, and I had stopped the old woman peddling used clothes along the Pont Neuf to buy a few tricolor dresses, a heavy winter shawl with a fur muff, and some soft gloves with the extra money. Elisabeth cut my hair fashionably short in the front with soft puffs on the side.

I looked the part of Citizeness Hélène Michel.

I tried to forget everything—my home, my name, my family, my ghosts. It almost worked. Almost.

|||| |||| ||||
|

The corridor rustles with whispers. Something is happening outside.

The whispers crescendo as the streets rattle with carriages.

I boost Marielle up so she can see down through the slit between the stones to the Boulevard Saint-Germain. "In the midnight mist, the streetlamps are wearing halos," she says. Like angels watching over the seven, eight, nine priests being yanked out of the carriage and made to walk.

Next, some women dressed too nicely. One of them screams, and Marielle can see no more.

Snow floated down in big, soft clumps, whitening the streets and rooftops. It was morning, still dark, and a piece of licorice was slowly dissolving in my mouth. I was on the sliding ladder, decorating the shop for Christmas with sprigs of holly and some paper stars I'd made with Sophie and Adèle the night before.

I knew that as soon as we unlocked the doors, there would be no time for decorating, sitting down, or daydreaming. I liked it that *way now.*

Political pamphlets were flying off the presses again, as attempts to shut down the clubs and presses had failed. People had gotten a taste of power, and they weren't about to let it slip through their fingers. Page after page detailed the steady stream of royal vetoes, arguments about Coblenz, and what to do about the émigrés, who were certainly plotting with Austria and Prussia. I waited, knowing the future of my family and the safety of my secret hung in the balance. The threat of war from Austria and Prussia was pointed at Paris like a loaded gun, following our every move.

But it was almost Christmas, and we all decided to decorate and sing and try to forget. I had bought little treats for each of the children, and I had painted a portrait of them together and gotten it framed for Max and Elisabeth.

Elisabeth came in and unlocked the door, flipped the sign from *Closed* to *Open.*

"It looks lovely in here, Hélène," she said from below me. "You're always making things so pretty."

I climbed down, smiling, but her eyes were serious. "What's wrong?"

"We're having a little family party here. On Christmas Eve."

So much for forgetting, I thought, glancing up at the paper stars. It was wrong that they didn't shine.

She bit her lip. "So, would you like me to bring your dinner upstairs for you, like last year? Or . . . would you like to join us?"

"I'll eat upstairs," I said quickly. "Thank you."

"I don't want you to feel unwelcome."

"You never make me feel that way," I promised, putting my arm around her and squeezing her shoulder. She did everything she could to ease my nagging ache of picturing Théo with Lucille, but it would never be enough. I glanced toward the street. I needed to be busy. I needed to forget.

"It's just . . . it's *Christmas—*" She squeezed me back as the door jangled and a slight man with huge eyes entered. He muttered good morning, his bony shoulders hunched against the snow, large flakes glistening on his black hair and dripping off his nose.

And then, he looked up.

Forgetting was clearly not an option.

It was Jacques Bennette.

He stopped dead in his tracks when he saw me and blinked. Despite the chill blasting through the open door, I flushed hot.

"Hello," he said, a smile tugging at his lips as he moved toward the counter. "I believe I know you."

I panicked. "I have one of those faces," I said quickly, but he didn't look away.

"No. No, I never forget a face I've drawn," he said, wiping the melting snow from his face and hair. He smiled, and his eyes were gentle. "Art over artifice. Isn't that right, Mademoiselle d'Aubign?"

I smiled nervously but held his gaze hard. "I'm sorry, mons—I mean citizen. I'm Citizeness Hélène Michel. You are mistaken."

He paused for a second and then nodded. "I see. It appears I am. It's just that I didn't think I'd see you—err, *her*—again. Especially . . . not here."

"You know what they say, life is full of surprises," I said, and he smiled. Flipping through newspapers, he kept throwing glances and smiles over his shoulder at me, until he finally brought a single paper up to the counter. He rummaged in his overcoat pocket for coins.

"The papers somehow got the notion that you were dead," he said. "But now that you're not, I think I should be offended."

"I'm sorry if my being alive is offensive to you," I snapped, my eyes flashing up at him.

"No, no, that's a very pleasant surprise. But you never took me up on my offer for lessons."

"Oh!" I said, with a short laugh, embarrassed. "It's a long story. Please, don't be offended."

"All right," he said. He grinned, leaning on the counter. "On the condition that you have dinner with me tonight and tell me the whole, long story."

I opened my mouth, but nothing came out. Glancing at Elisabeth, I saw her eyebrow shoot upward with intrigue. He rested his chin in his palm, curling his fingers against his lips. "What time are you finished here?"

"I can't tonight."

Elisabeth winked over her shoulder, and the words tumbled out before I could stop them. "But I could tomorrow night. That would be fine."

"Tomorrow night is Christmas Eve."

"Right," I said, bringing my hand to my face in embarrassment. "Sorry. You probably have plans."

"I didn't, but I do now," he said, smiling. "Five o'clock?"

My head tingled with something between terror and hope as I nodded.

"Here?"

"Um, yes, I live upstairs."

He dropped coins into my hand and smiled, nodding his head to Elisabeth and then looking back at me, saying, 'Merry Christmas,' as he braced himself for the cold again.

Elisabeth came up behind me, resting her chin on my shoulder. "He's lovely," she whispered into my ear, then straightened a disheveled stack of pamphlets and welcomed another customer.

I nodded and crunched the last bit of hard candy between my teeth.

I found myself telling the story of our escape from Château des Cygnes in a lonely café across from Jacques Bennette on Christmas Eve, the dull lamplight bright in his black eyes. Outside, a man played "Noël nouvelet" on a mournful pochette, and the few customers inside were sad-looking drunks without families to invite them to dinner.

"So, what then? Where did you go?"

"I stayed with family in Grasse, then in Germany . . . until I ran away."

He lifted a mischievous eyebrow. "By yourself?"

I nodded.

"That's impressive, citizeness—what was it, again?"

"Michel."

"Hélène Michel," he said, rubbing his chin and trying it out. "That's quite pretty. So you ran away to pursue your lifelong dream of working at a bookshop?"

I laughed, but then swallowed hard, looking out the window at a halo of lamplight swirling with a vortex of snow. "No. I actually . . . um . . . I actually came back to find my fiancé."

"The old fellow?" He lifted his eyebrow again.

"How do you know so much about me?" I asked, half amused, half concerned.

"I read the papers," he said, shrugging.

"Well, no. Not the 'old fellow.' I was never going to marry Monsieur Foix."

"Well, that's a relief. So, who was your other fiancé? A bookseller?"

"A jeweler's apprentice."

He frowned thoughtfully. "So, what happened to him?"

I sighed. "You weren't the only person to think I was dead, Citizen Bennette." I looked straight ahead past him, biting my lip. "He married someone else. So, I work at the bookshop. And I enjoy working."

"I wasn't expecting that." He looked at me apologetically, then down at his folded hands. "That's some bad luck. I'm sorry for you."

"Yes, well, life's surprises aren't always pleasant ones," I said, drumming my fingers on the table. I wanted this conversation to be over.

He nodded silently, looking at something far off. I watched the little indentations press into his smooth, long cheeks, the slow, thoughtful rise and fall of his eyelids, the perfect symmetry and fine lines. He wasn't just handsome or attractive—though he was those things too. His face was beautiful. I didn't know what to say, but I knew I had to say something. "I hope I didn't take you from other plans this evening."

His eyes jumped back to mine, and he smiled. "Ah, no. My friend Guy Miles always invites me for Christmas, but it makes me feel bad, you know? Barging in on someone else's holiday, being invited because they feel sorry for you. I don't like feeling like a charity case."

"Didn't you have any siblings?" I asked, remembering he had said his parents were dead. "Or any other family here in Paris?"

"No family left," he said, and I nodded, knowing the feeling all too well. "I came to Paris to get work after my father died, and my mother died the year after."

"How old were you?"

"Ten."

"You must have been afraid."

He puffed a sad little laugh and nodded. "I was terrified. I became a servant to an investor in Paris. I kept a little to myself, though, so that I could afford to buy paints, and when I was fifteen I did a display at the Corpus Christi festival on the Pont Neuf. That's when Guy Miles noticed my work, said I was better than a street-corner painter."

"I agree. You're brilliant."

"Well, thank you," he muttered, blushing.

"Is he an artist too? This Monsieur Miles?"

"No. He's a lawyer. Veteran of the American war. He shattered his leg at Brandywine with Lafayette. He needed a part-time assistant, to run errands, to do some tasks his leg wasn't up for. He offered me a job that paid five times what my old boss gave me. So I worked and took lessons, started getting more attention. Miles knows someone who knows someone who knows your parents. And that's how I ended up at your birthday fête."

"Did your parents ever get to see your artwork?

He reached into his breast pocket and brought out a tiny nub of a charcoal pencil. "They encouraged me. This is the only thing I have to remember my father by. It was the only Christmas gift I ever got. He gave it to me when I was nine years old, a few months before he died. I was always drawing pictures on the dirt floor, sculpting with mud and sticks and snow. My father saved up a few coins and bought me this pencil and a sketch book. I'd never felt so special in all my life."

I pulled the key up from my neck and stretched the chain toward him. "My father gave me this for my birthday. It opens a little box where I keep my favorite things. I like to remember him that way, smiling at me. Happy."

He nodded, and his voice lightened. "So, what does an aristocratic Christmas look like? Gold? Frankincense? Myrrh? A fatted calf?"

"No. Ham," I laughed. "The whole d'Aubign family would come over to our house, and my father would give my mother jewelry, my mother would pretend to like him, and they would all get along until about the fifth round of *lait de poule*."

"And then?"

"People started saying what they really thought of each other. My grandmother told my mother she was crazy, my mother told my grandmother she was a nasty old gossip, and my uncles told each other they were ugly. But they were too drunk to remember what they'd said the next morning, so it didn't matter. I remembered, though."

"What about your mother's side of the family?"

"I never knew any of them—until we went to Grasse. And even now I don't understand the ones I met. They couldn't get along, either. I had an aunt and a little cousin who died, and another aunt who disappeared, and I don't actually know what happened to them."

"Strange."

"Some say they were murdered. I have my theories, but no one will tell me the truth."

"That would drive me crazy."

I laughed. "Yes. Me too, actually."

"Do you know their names?"

"Vivienne du Maurier. She was an opera singer. And the one who disappeared was her sister, Josette. A ballerina."

"Maybe I can find out," he said, stroking his chin thoughtfully.

"What?"

"I know people who know people. I can't make any promises. But I'll try."

"Well, that's kind of you. Thank you."

We talked until after midnight, and as we approached the shop, warm lamplight spilled from the windows onto a crust of fresh snow. We came to a halt just in time to hear laughter burst through the opening door, and to see two figures waving goodbye, the man's arm around the woman's waist.

Théo turned at the sound of hooves and jerked his arm down to his side, the golden light warm on his hair and hot in his eyes as he looked at me and then away. An explosion of anger, sadness, and jealous heat went off in my chest. He hurried to help her up into their cart just as Jacques Bennette took my hand to help me down.

"The jeweler?" Bennette asked, studying my face. I nodded and looked away.

I couldn't sleep that night. I was cold, restless, and tired—tired of holding on to a future that I could never have. I thought about his laughter and the way it stopped when he saw me. In the icy, indigo dawn of Christmas morning, I decided I was done ruining Théo's life.

And done ruining my own.

HHT HHT HHT
||

THE ABBAYE PRISON
AUGUST 28, 1792

There are three of us now. Me, Marielle, and a new girl named Élodie.

Élodie is huddled in the corner, still trying to keep her pretty dress clean. Ugly boot prints stain her lower back, and though she can't see them, she surely still feels them.

"They've gone mad," she says, picking at a frayed silken hem in a daze. "They've even taken the princess!"

"Are you the princess?" Marielle asks, eyes wide, and Élodie laughs sharply.

"I'm her handmaiden," she says, and explains how she was pinning Princess de Lamballe's hair when the police broke down the door. "Her hair was only half-finished when they cut off her head."

The mob divided her body up and paraded each part through the streets of Paris to show the whole city what becomes of Marie Antoinette's dear friends.

Outside, Élodie tells us, armed men bang on all the doors, looking for suspects, incriminating documents, and firearms. Everything and everyone now belongs to le patrie. The guillotine sings in the Place du Carrousel, and the people of Paris dance around it. The gutters flow with blood.

"Look," Élodie says, reaching inside her skirt pocket, then handing me a folded placard. "Can you read?"

I take the paper, carefully unfolding it. I take a breath. *By Citizen Fabre d'Eglantine.* Like his friend, Citizen Marat, he considers himself a friend of the people, but I know from the newspapers Max reluctantly sold in the shop that he is no friend to people like me. Men like Marat and Eglantine have no time to consider the many shades between black and white—they would just as soon paint us all red.

The blood rushes and swirls to my head as I start scanning silently, but Élodie shakes her head and commands, "Read it aloud."

A hush comes over the entire corridor as I read the brutal words of Citizen d'Eglantine:

"Once more, citizens, to arms! May all France bristle with pikes, bayonets, cannon and daggers, so that everyone shall be a soldier; let us clear the ranks of these vile slaves of tyranny. In the towns let the blood of traitors be the first holocaust to Liberty."

Gasps ripple down the corridor, followed by whispers.

"Where did you get it?" Marielle asks, trembling, and Élodie puffs a silent, bitter laugh.

"They're plastered all over Paris. I guessed it said as much. They mean to kill us all, you know. They say the prisons are full of spies."

I shake my head quickly to tell Élodie, *Enough. I'll read no more.*

PARIS

JANUARY 1792

"You won't believe this."

Bennette dropped a stack of hastily gathered papers on the bookstore counter, his eyes bright with excitement. He'd been browsing aimlessly, obviously waiting to talk to me for the last fifteen minutes, and for the last fifteen minutes, I could hardly breathe because of so many customers.

"What?"

"There are two reports."

I looked from his face to the papers and back again.

"Not in there. No. About your aunt. There are two reports."

I glanced around cautiously at the momentarily empty shop and leaned closer.

"A friend of mine works in the Palais de Justice and got into the records department for me. Are you ready for this?"

I was ready to reach across and pull the report out of him. He flashed a grin and began.

"The police report says one thing, and the medical examiner's report says another. The medical examiner says that Vivienne du Maurier died suddenly of a hemorrhage after childbirth. But the police report says that neighbors initially reported hearing shots. Rumor had it that Vivienne du Maurier died of a gunshot wound to the chest. But then no one would talk."

"What? How is that possible? Which one is true?"

"That's the crazy thing. Nobody knows."

"But one of them is fake."

"Yes."

"How does that happen? I mean—"

"The truth can always be changed. For the right price."

"What does that mean?"

"It means the question is, who had the money to change it?"

"But wouldn't the family have known? Wouldn't they have known if she had a . . . a wound in her chest?"

"Not necessarily, no. I mean, someone could have patched it up. Also for a price. See?"

"Why wasn't the other record destroyed? Wouldn't someone get rid of it?"

"Do you know how disorganized they are down there? Nobody even noticed. There was no investigation. It just slipped through the cracks. Happens all the time, unless someone hires a lawyer and pursues it."

"And no one did."

"Apparently not."

"You think she was shot?"

"Maybe. Maybe not."

A vision of my mother holding a smoking gun slithered into my mind like a snake. I didn't want to believe that she'd hurt the baby too. I could believe I was the daughter of a murderer, but not of a monster. "What about the baby? Did you find a record on her?"

"Only one report there. Died suddenly in her sleep. Happens to babies sometimes."

A wave of relief washed over me, leaving another theory in its wake. "Well, what if Vivienne killed herself? I mean, if the baby died, and she was distressed, then the family might have covered it up. They wouldn't have called a lawyer. But they wouldn't have wanted that in the papers either, right? Not a suicide."

"It's possible."

"So, how can I find out?"

He shook his head slowly.

"Then I have to find Josette. She knows."

"She is presumed dead," he said grimly.

"What does that mean?"

"It means basically that she disappeared."

"But that means she could be alive somewhere."

"It means she's probably long dead and unidentified," he said softly, tucking a stray hair behind my ear. "Or alive and trying not to be found. Citizeness . . . Michel, I think, maddening though it is, this may be a mystery better left unsolved."

He was right. Of course he was right.

The past was finished. Done. Gone. And dangerous. I couldn't change it just by knowing. I couldn't change anything, but I couldn't let it go either. I wouldn't. I needed to know.

"Thank you for trying anyway," I said, sighing heavily.

"I had an ulterior motive," he whispered, winking at me. "Are you busy this evening?"

Panicked and elated, I shook my head no.

"Would you like to have dinner?"

"Yes, sure." My heart was pounding so hard I couldn't assess my own volume. We hadn't stepped out together since Christmas Eve, and I was beginning to worry he wouldn't ask again.

He promised to come back for me at seven, and when he did, the first thing he asked was, "Would you like to see my studio first? Or are you too hungry?"

"Um, all right. Yes, we can stop there first." I wasn't sure why this terrified me. It was exactly what I'd been hoping he would say.

Taking my gloved hand in his, he led me up a rickety staircase that snaked behind the Dancing Bear Tavern to a large room covered in messy drop cloths, easels, empty glasses, burnt candles, a half-finished sculpture, and gorgeous paintings of Greek gods and naked women.

"Do you always paint women this way?" I asked, smirking as I examined a voluptuous brunette stretched out on a chaise longue.

"Whenever I can, yes," he said, lifting a bony shoulder and smiling mischievously.

"Is that why you became an artist, to look at naked women all day long?"

"No," he said, tossing a cloth over the lady in question. "No, it's the difference between art and fashion, see? People try to cover all their imperfections with makeup and clothes and jewelry. But it's fake. I paint people this way because they're truly themselves—nothing to hide behind, no makeup, no secrets. That's how people are most beautiful."

"So, it's all professional, then?" The pang of jealousy surprised me.

"Usually," he said, smiling sheepishly.

"I see. Well, I hope you didn't bring me here to do . . . business."

"I wasn't really hoping to have a professional relationship with you."

Why couldn't I think of anything to say? Why did his smile have to be so symmetrical, his eyes half closed and dreamy, like he was always thinking about something incredibly beautiful or painful or metaphorical?

"I was thinking more along the way of . . . friendship?" he clarified, his cheeks pink. "But you can tell me your secrets," he added, grinning.

"You can be yourself. I do know who you really are, after all. And I won't tell anyone."

I pushed my hair out of my face nervously and smiled at him. "Thank you, Citizen Bennette." What a stupid thing to say. My heart was racing, my hands were jittery. What did he mean, *friendship*? Do men really want to be friends with women? Did I want to be friends with him, or did I want to be something more?

"Call me Jacques. No more 'Citizen.' How's that for a start?"

I laughed, feeling ridiculous for being so nervous. "Sounds like a very good start. But only if you call me Hélène."

"Do you want to take a ride with me, Hélène? To get some dinner?"

I hesitated for just a second. "All right."

"You can trust me, you know," he said.

"How do I know that?" I smiled sideways at him, and shot a glance at his nudes for his benefit.

"You do know it, or you wouldn't be here." He extended his hand, and I took it. His fingers interlaced with mine, and the blood rushed to my head.

Two weeks later, he took me to meet his friends. Around a marble-topped table at the Café de Foy, sipping at hot chocolate and alcohol, a noisy, mismatched group of men and one extraordinarily beautiful young woman glanced up at us.

"Everyone, this is Hélène Michel. Hélène, meet DuPonte, Goullet, Chagall, Tomlin, and . . . Simonne Asselin," he said, gesturing one by one. Simonne smiled up at me with painted, slightly tipsy lips, her eyes flicking from me to Jacques and back again.

"It's nice not to be the only lady for once," she said, and rose to kiss me on both cheeks.

The men stood and generally nodded, murmuring hello. There was only one empty chair, as if they were expecting Jacques to come alone, but Simonne pulled another chair to the table.

"Sit here," she said, scraping it along the floor and wedging it beside hers. Her hair was sleek and long, her eyes a multifaceted hazel. Several large, dark moles were visible on her chest and arms, and one stood out beside her lips in a distinctively beautiful way. She leaned in against the man beside her, Goullet, whom I took to be her lover.

"Only war will bring peace," Goullet said calmly, pursing his lips around a pipe and puffing smoke above our heads in a thick stream. He was a handsome, thirtyish man with curly chestnut hair tied up in a red silk ribbon. He appeared to be perennially relaxed. "Only war will bring the nation together as one."

"They're amassing troops, while that Austrian bitch is sending letters begging her brother for more," Chagall snarled, chewing a thumbnail. "What sort of cowards would we be if we let the émigré princes take back what we've earned? I'll sooner die than see that happen. War is the only way."

"War is idiotic," Simonne snapped, waving her thin hand at them, and all heads turned toward her. "Don't you understand anything? Robespierre is the only one with any sense. If we win, we'll have a military dictatorship. If we lose, everything will go back to the way it was, with the king reinstated."

"Don't we have a duty to liberty, to France, and to mankind, my sweet?" Goullet asked, smiling flirtatiously at her, as if amused.

"Don't we have a duty to keep our citizens alive? And as for the rest of Europe, 'No one loves armed missionaries.' That's what—"

"Robespierre says," they all finished in chorus, laughing.

"Goullet, my friend, I think you should be jealous of Citizen Robespierre," Chagall said, arching an eyebrow.

"He may have words, but does he have chocolate? And we all know that chocolate is the way to a woman's heart."

As he leaned in to kiss her cheek and pop a truffle in her mouth, Simonne rolled her eyes, but smiled. "Hélène?" she said, turning to me. "What do you think will happen if we go to war?"

"I think you're right," I said, smiling at my own boldness. "War is a terrible idea. It always is." The men glanced from me to Bennette, who waited expectantly.

"See?" Simonne said, sitting back in her chair with her arms crossed smugly over her chest.

"But," I added, and her eyebrow flew up. "We also can't sit by and do nothing."

"We have to do *something*, sure," she said, nodding. "Just not—"

"Someone's got to do something about those bloodthirsty émigrés," Chagall said, still chewing his nails. "They're ready to slit our throats under the blessing of their priests. If we sit around waiting, we'll all be dead."

The men kept on talking about war, but Simonne waved them off, shaking her head. She propped her elbows on the table, leaning her lips toward my ear. "Bennette says you don't like to talk about your family."

I gulped. "Um, no, not really."

"That's all right. Neither do I. He said you paint. Do you like talking about that?"

"Yes," I said, breaking into a relieved smile.

"So, what do you paint?"

"Lately I've been painting my landlord's children. I do portraits of them, but I also draw to help them with their reading. I used to draw the lake near my home . . . in, um, Dijon. Do you paint too?"

"No," she laughed. "I'm the painted, not the painter. And I sing a little, when I need the money."

"I sing too—well, not in public though," I said, laughing a little.

"You're lucky," she said over the rising din of the café. It was getting so loud that none of the men could hear us, even though we were practically shouting. "He doesn't even look at me anymore. He never looked at me like he looks at you." She leaned her mouth lazily on her fist.

I tried to hold her glassy gaze as it drifted toward him. Suddenly, she looked like a disappointed little girl as she laughed again and downed the last of her drink. So close to her, I realized that under all her makeup, she was just sixteen or seventeen.

"But I like you, Hélène," she said, putting her thin hand on mine and turning to smile at me, suddenly bright-eyed again. "So it's all right. I want you to come over to my place and visit me. Would you? I live in the Halle aux blés, just across from the Corn Market. Do you like chocolate?"

"Chocolate?" I shouted, and she nodded. "I love chocolate!"

"Good!" She clasped my hand. "Sunday?"

"Sunday? Yes!"

"Two o'clock?"

"Perfect."

She scrawled her address on a receipt and passed it to me just as a man stood up on his chair behind us and the crowd turned as one toward him. He began to sing the familiar tune of the "Ça ira," but the words had changed since I'd sung them in the carriage on my way to Paris. In an instant, the Café de Foy was on its feet reverberating with song— Simonne loudest of all. Jacques glanced at me, distressed and obviously embarrassed. He started singing along, but the words died on his lips as his friends stood and belted the tune while swaying and lifting their glasses, promising to break the aristocrats. To burn us. To hang us from the lampposts. And this, they sang would make everything right.

Someone punctured a large cask of wine with the tip of a pike, and the crowd pushed and shoved to fill their cups as the floor swelled red with the overflow. My shoes became soggy, the hem of my dress turned crimson.

It was my blood they wanted, and my house they burned.

"Well, I think we'd better be going," Jacques said, downing the last of his drink hastily as the crowd settled down again. He drew an uneasy breath as he pulled his jacket on and then helped me with my shawl.

"Simonne?" Goullet sang in a velvety-smooth voice, turning toward her and touching her cheek. "Shall we?" he asked, standing and pulling her chair out gallantly. She wobbled on her way up, and he caught her by the hand. "Good night, all," he said, and steered her toward the door. Simonne waved at me, mouthing *See you Sunday*. The company broke up after that.

"I'm sorry about the . . . the singing. I hope my friends didn't bother you too much," Jacques whispered on the way out, throwing a glance over his shoulder. "They mean well. They don't know, of course, and I didn't know Simonne would be here, and I . . . they just, well, anyway, are you all right?"

I nodded and smiled at him. "Yes."

"Sorry. I shouldn't have brought you. I wasn't thinking."

"It was fine," I said. "I'm fine."

He lifted an eyebrow and smiled at me curiously. "Really?"

"Really."

We rode back to his flat, chatting easily before settling into chairs in the studio.

"Could you show me how to work with oils sometime?" I asked. "I've really only ever worked with watercolors."

"Any time," he said. "Name the date."

"I'll check with Max about my work schedule," I said, and he nodded. Silence drifted over us then, like a cloud full of questions we wanted to ask each other. I went first.

"So, were you and Simonne—?"

He puffed a sigh and rubbed his face. "No. Not really."

"She certainly seems to like you," I teased, accepting the fact that now I truly felt jealous.

"I know," he said. "It was nothing. Nothing on my part, anyway. Did she say something unkind to you?"

"No, not at all. She actually invited me for chocolate. I just . . . I just wondered, that's all."

"You have nothing to be jealous about," he said and brushed my fingers with his.

"She and Goullet are—?"

"For now," he said, grinning wryly.

"Do you think it's all right for me to go to her flat? Is it safe?"

He went into the other room and came back with a sketch of Simonne. "The real Simonne Asselin," he said, and passed it to me.

Fresh, young, and almost angelic, she wore no makeup or clothing. Her glossy hair was arranged simply around her shoulders and softly gleaming in the distant light. She sat in a Roman garden at dusk, gazing at something in the distance as she cupped her chin in her palm. Her fingers covered her lips, and her other hand hovered over her heart.

"She looks so different," I said. "So . . . sad. As if she's lost something."

He nodded his head, the hint of satisfaction on his lips.

"A part of herself."

"Exactly."

"It's beautiful."

"Hélène, she's just a scared sixteen-year-old girl who's in over her head. You have nothing to fear from her." He motioned for me to join him at the table, where he filled two glasses from a decanter.

I took a sip, gathering my courage. I pushed the words out before I could change my mind. "Why did you paint Helen of Troy for the display at the Louvre?"

He scratched the back of his neck. "You saw it?"

"Yes."

He looked down, color rising adorably in his cheeks, then met my eyes again, shaking his head. "This is somewhat embarrassing," he laughed. "I . . . I couldn't stop thinking about you. When I heard your château had been attacked, well, I was devastated. I had thought you might really come for lessons. Maybe for . . . more than just lessons."

"I'm here now," I said softly, sliding my hand across the table. I brushed my fingers against his, and he held my hand. His fingers were long and thin, like he should play the piano. A fleck of blue paint clung to his thumbnail.

"I need you to understand that whenever I'm with you, I find myself wishing my entire life before you didn't exist." He said it softly, his eyes fastened on mine over his glass of wine. I blushed.

"Perhaps we can forget the past together, then."

He raised his half-empty glass and said, "To forgetfulness, then. And the future."

I raised mine but pulled back before clinking it with his. "How about, to forgetfulness and right now?"

"To now."

We took a walk in the snow that January night, when the year was new, when the snow was fresh and yet so old, as old as the universe. Snow, like love, always feels that way, I thought, as Jacques pulled off his gloves and bent down in the snow to sculpt a frosty white rose for me.

Returning to the studio, I warmed my hands by the fire as he brewed coffee. A steaming cup in each hand, he sat beside me on the braided rug. Leaning in, he kissed me as gently and slowly as the snow falling outside the window, behind the reflection of the dancing flames in the hearth.

He put his arm around my waist and we sat quietly after that, watching the ever-changing patterns of the fire.

Maybe there was a little truth in Grand-mère's words. Maybe to be happy was to be a realist. Maybe life didn't have to be everything I'd imagined. Life, like people, didn't have to live up to every ideal to be good.

For so long, I thought it had to be one thing or another: dead or alive, good or bad, real or pretend. One thing must end before another can begin. Three o'clock ends when the clock chimes four. My governess had to have been right—there was one true love for each person. But what if it wasn't so simple? What if you could be broken and fixed at the same time, starting and stopping, all at once? What if more than one person in this world could love you, and you could love them back? What if it didn't have to be perfect?

By the time I closed the door to the bookshop behind me, I had made up my mind. Max looked up and smiled as I passed into the dim salon. Pipe smoke swirled around his head, and a worn Bible lay open on his lap.

"You're back late," he said, lifting a brotherly eyebrow.

"Things all right at home?" I asked, trying to push the smile off my lips and out of my voice as I pulled my gloves off.

"Mm-hmm. Everyone else is in bed. But I couldn't sleep."

"Brooding?" I teased, and he laughed.

"You know me."

I pulled my cloak off and hung it over the back of the chair opposite him. "About what?"

"You," he said, stroking his chin, looking at me over his large hand.

I lifted my eyebrows and sat across from him, waiting.

"Elisabeth said you know Citizen Bennette. How well do you know him?"

"Um, fairly well I suppose."

"He knows who you truly are."

"Yes. We met several years ago."

Max nodded thoughtfully, still rubbing his chin. "And you trust him?"

"Yes."

"Then I do too. But Hélène, do you remember what I said to you before, about being careful?"

I nodded, my stomach tightening.

"It's not him, Hélène. It's the man he works for, Guy Miles. I know him. He was my commander in the army. The two of us, we didn't get on. He called me a coward, and I thought he was the kind of man who would do anything for money and power. He's an assemblyman now. He and Monsieur Chevallier still get on well, and he rents the flat above the jewelry store, the one your father used to rent. Just . . . just be careful, Hélène. He shouldn't know who you are. I don't trust him. I'm not saying that Bennette is like him, or even knows of all his business. It's just that, well, are you sure he won't tell Miles who you are?"

"He's promised not to tell anyone."

"Good. Good. Just . . . be careful. You mean so much. To all of us."

I rose and put my hand on his shoulder, glancing down at the book of Psalms he was reading. "I'm always careful. I promise."

He patted my hand. "I know. You're a smart girl."

"Good night, Max," I said, starting upstairs, then stopping with my hand on the bannister. "You can stop brooding about me now." He laughed good-naturedly as he closed the book and bid me good night.

As I climbed the stairs to my room, I remembered it was Friday. And for the first time in almost two years, there had been no licorice on the counter.

|||| |||| ||||
|||

THE ABBAYE PRISON

AUGUST 29, 1792

Marielle steps over Élodie to sit beside me cross-legged on the filthy floor, leaning her head against the cold stone wall. "I keep thinking about what that paper said. A *holocaust* to liberty. What does that mean, Hélène?"

"I don't know exactly," I say—a partial truth—putting an arm around her slight shoulders. She reminds me of Adèle and Sophie, the way she looks to me for answers, for comfort. If not for Max and Elisabeth, those little girls would have had the same fate as Marielle. Orphaned children, especially girls, have no future in France. No rights. No hope.

But isn't that what the Revolution was supposed to change?

Yet, here sits Marielle. An orphaned prostitute charged with treason, asking me whether she will be slaughtered for liberty's sake.

PARIS

FEBRUARY 1792

Max insisted on driving me to the Halle aux blés and wandering around the Corn Market across the street while I went upstairs for chocolates. The stairwell was filthy, and I nearly retched at the stench of rotting food and excrement. Muffled behind a door, a man and a woman shouted about money while their baby cried relentlessly. After three flights of creaking, splintered stairs, I knocked.

"Hélène! Come in!" Simonne flung her arms around me and then whirled toward the table with a wave of her hand.

It was a small but pretty room where she lived—linens dotted with little flowers, a bud vase with a rose beside her bed, a delicately painted bureau, and carefully chosen trinkets. A wax effigy of Robespierre stared blankly from beside the mirror, and copies of his speeches and Jacobin newspapers littered the table and floor. She was dressed simply in white muslin and wore no makeup.

"So, how long have you been in Paris?" she asked, flinging a folded napkin open and into her lap as she plunked down at the tiny table, set with chocolates and coffee. I wished I could tell her the truth.

"Almost two years. You?"

"I came after the Bastille fell. I was fourteen."

"Did you come alone?"

"Yes," she said proudly, her chin held high. She popped a chocolate between her teeth.

"So did I."

"Well, my mother and I had a terrible argument," she said, still chewing. "A theater troupe came through town and did this marvelous play about the Bastille and liberty. I went up to talk to the woman who sang with them. She *was* Liberty, and she introduced me to the owner of the company. He said I was pretty, and asked if I could sing. I sang for him, and he said I could have the job. So I left."

"Did you say goodbye?"

"No," she said, her face darkening. "Sometimes I think I should send her a letter."

"Maybe," I said, thinking of my own mother and wondering if she cared what had become of me even though I knew she didn't.

"Maybe I will."

"What about your father?"

She laughed caustically. "My father was a bishop, but my mother was nobody. If I had been a boy, I could've gone to Louis-le-Grand and been a lawyer or something. They look after sons, sometimes. They're proud of them. But what good is a girl? I'm smart enough to be a lawyer, Hélène. I'm smart enough to be an assemblyman. But you know what? It's not the Declaration of the Rights of *Women* posted on the Club walls. It's *Man*. And so instead of telling them what to do, like I should be, I have to sleep with them."

"But Goullet—?"

"Things have improved a little, I suppose. Since I met Guy Miles."

"You know *him* too?"

She laughed. "Everyone knows Miles! He saw me at a performance when the troupe came to Paris. He said he could give me a better job, and he did. But everything comes with a price, and even better pay. And Goullet? His father is a chocolatier. He's handsome too, isn't he? But he doesn't take me seriously."

I nodded and rummaged through the chocolates. I chose a chewy caramel, and she kept talking.

"So, what about you? Did you say goodbye?"

"No," I said, swallowing the sticky sweets and scavenging for a change of subjects. "I couldn't. My parents are no longer living."

"How rude of me! I forgot you don't like to talk about them. Sorry. All right, let's talk about something else. Um ... music? How about Théroigne de Méricourt? Did you know she's been released from prison in Austria and she's back in Paris?"

I shook my head and she gasped, grabbing my arm. "She's coming to the Jacobins to make a speech. Can you believe they're letting a woman give a speech? We've got to go. You're coming with me."

I opened my mouth to say *maybe* in a tactfully noncommittal fashion, but she didn't wait for my reply.

"Do you know that she wears a red men's riding costume? And she's so beautiful. I mean, she's absolutely gorgeous. It must have been horrible in some Austrian prison, but I read that her interrogator was sympathetic to her and helped her to get out. He didn't believe all the terrible things the papers said about her, and neither do I. She's not a spy. She's a heroine of the Revolution. Did you ever hear her sing?"

"Yes, actually, I did," I said, remembering the night with a twinge in my chest.

"You're so lucky!" she cried. "What did she sing?"

I hummed the tune and reached for the words, surprising myself that I remembered them all. The melody brought aching memories of intermission and Théo's kiss.

Simonne sat listening with her hands clasped together under her chin. "Sing it again, please?"

She began to sing along with me as I started over again. Our voices harmonized well, her soprano and my alto, and we began leafing through her stacks of sheet music. She showed me how to play a few notes on her violin. When it was time for me to meet Max again, I was sorry to leave.

Our breath was visible in the cold, black air of the Rue Saint-Honoré. Jacques, Simonne and I pressed into the crush of noisy people, holding hands to stay together. Goullet didn't come. The Club had taken over the quarters of a Dominican convent just a few streets east of Max's house, and it was here that Simonne hoped breathlessly to catch sight of her beloved Robespierre.

Théroigne de Méricourt took the floor, and I noticed the recently formed creases around her eyes and mouth as she told her story.

"Look over there," Simonne whispered, pointing discreetly toward a white-haired woman with piercing, dark eyes. "It's Olympe de Gouges!"

"*The* Olympe de Gouges?" I whispered back, my eyes huge. I couldn't believe I was in the same room as the author of the Declaration of Rights of Woman and the Female Citizen.

"The one and only," Simonne said, her eyes shining with admiration.

"They called me the Whore of the Revolution," Théroigne de Méricourt continued from the floor, her voice straining for volume through emotion. As she paused to wipe her eyes, a rough voice filled the silence.

"How much do you charge?"

She looked at him in horror and disgust, and then another man, from the other side of the room, hollered, "Cook up some dinner and get into bed. That's a woman's place."

Catcalls rang out, and I glanced from Théroigne to Olympe de Gouges, whose eyes could have killed the man. With a nod of her head, she signaled some guards to escort them out.

The room went ghostly quiet. Olympe de Gouges stood to command women everywhere to wake up and demand their own freedom.

"She's quoting from her Declaration of the Rights of Woman and the Female Citizen," Simonne whispered, and I nodded. I had read it all. She claimed rights for illegitimate children and insisted on equality in marriage.

As Olympe sat down, she motioned to Théroigne, who finished the story of her imprisonment without any more heckling.

As the opera singer detailed her release and return to Paris, a voice cheered: "An Amazon of the Revolution!" The crowd went crazy, then sang patriotic songs, clapped, and cried. After the applause died down, she went on to speak passionately about women's role in politics and patriotism. As she finished the sentence "Women, too, should bear arms!" Simonne stood up and whooped and hollered.

A ripple of laughter rumbled among the men, but she cheered all the louder. Jacques glanced at me amusedly. I shrugged and kept applauding, my blood rushing faster. Was it actually possible for women to vote or to be soldiers or to be equal to men?

The baritone murmurs said of course not. What good is the blood of a girl? It was boys who killed each other to save the world.

Did the men really think we didn't know how to kill? Did they really think we didn't know what we wanted? That we might want it badly enough to pull a trigger? Enough to slit a throat?

"Peace will set us back . . ." Max read the words of Madame Roland and sighed heavily in the cool, early-spring morning. "We can be regenerated through blood alone."

Muffled voices filtered in from the street, even though we weren't set to open for another half hour. We were busier than usual. Everyone wanted to know if it was going to happen. When it was going to happen.

"You really think there will be war?" I asked, and Max nodded, covering his face with his hand.

"Soon. You should think about getting out of here."

"Where would I go?" I asked, shaking my head. I couldn't leave. Not alone.

"England? Switzerland?"

"They'll give you an exemption," I said, and he nodded.

"Yes, but not Théo. He'll have no exemption. Not Bennette, either. Not if it comes to a draft."

"But it won't. It won't come to that," I said fiercely, squeezing my eyes closed as I stood.

"You should think about it, Hélène. That's all I'm saying. Start planning ahead."

"We have plenty of volunteers. And plenty of time."

He looked up at me then, frowning a little. "People like things to be simple, Hélène. War will save the Revolution, or overturn it. Either way, war will decide something. There will be a winner and a loser. A right and a wrong. An old and a new. People like crisp, clean lines. They like to think it works that way, that it's simple. But how much time can blood buy? A month of freedom? A year? A century? It's never simple."

I pulled up the shade and opened the door. I wasn't going to leave the bookshop. I wasn't going to leave Max or Elisabeth or the children. I wasn't going to leave Jacques or Simonne. Or Théo. I wasn't going to run away while they were in danger.

I was so stupid. How did I not realize that *I* was putting them in danger?

I should have run away long before. I never should have come in the first place.

|||| |||| ||||
||||

THE ABBAYE PRISON
AUGUST 30, 1792

The prison swells with us. Priests. Aristocrats. Servants to aristocrats. Swiss Guards said to have taken part in the royal counterplots. A couple of prostitutes and thieves. They all come with news.

Outside, Marat's placards scream to the people that the prisons are full of spies. The rumor is that the departure of the next round of troops will serve as a signal for the prisoners to unify and revolt. To violently stop the Revolution. To put the king back on his throne.

There are five of us sharing this little cell now. Five women. All of us scared. None of us with anything remotely resembling a weapon.

PARIS
APRIL–JULY 1792

That spring, we sent our soldiers to kill Austrians, Prussians, and Royalists. Blood was going to set us free, once and for all. We couldn't keep the shop stocked or clean, it was so busy. Desperate news from the front was all over the papers: mutinies and massacres. There was an intelligence leak. Everyone suspected the king and his spies.

When the papers called for more soldiers, boys lined up. Pamphlets screamed at the people to slit the throats of Royalists and spies, to spill the blood of aristocratic and Catholic traitors. Fingers pointed toward Coblenz, and then fingers pointed across café tables.

But I hid my hands in my pockets.

"It's intoxicating," Simonne whispered one day in June, leaning against the bookshop counter while scanning a newspaper. She visited me at work several times a week, staying to talk for hours, whether I had customers or not. She always left with the current issue of Marat's *Friend of the People*, each one more radical than the last.

"What are you reading about now? Wine?"

She laughed. "No. Optimism. It's intoxicating, isn't it? To feel like you might actually have a future. That you might *live*, not just . . . survive?"

I smiled weakly. "Do you think we can actually win this war?"

"Of course we can," she said, her eyes fiercely bright, her lips tight with determination. "We have to. Listen to this: Yesterday, a mob stormed the Assembly carrying the Declaration of the Rights of Man. An anonymous shopkeeper carried the bloody heart of a calf on the tip of a pike with a sign: 'This is the Heart of an Aristocrat.'"

"And this is optimism?" I asked, trying to laugh as I shivered. It was my heart. My blood they wanted. It didn't matter that Mademoiselle Girard had called me a Revolutionary. It didn't matter if I called myself by a different name.

"Of course it is. We're showing them who's boss. And it's not that stupid, fat king!"

A customer was ready to pay, and I nodded my head sideways to signal Simonne to stop talking. She left, promising to come back with two lemonades.

We had extended our hours, especially in the evenings, but late into the night, Max wrestled with what to do about the papers. "The press must be free," he'd always said. "If you restrict the press, it turns to oppression. People must be free to speak their minds, and free to disagree. True freedom is found in the mind, freedom to choose for oneself between right and wrong." But then there were things that troubled him, things he wasn't sure he wanted to distribute. Things he thought were wrong.

Simonne came back, slid my lemonade across the counter, and picked up another paper while I tended to the customers in line. I glanced up to see her nodding in silent agreement with whatever she was reading. "Coblenz isn't the real threat," she said, drumming her fingers on her chin as I finally locked up the shop for the night. She leaned on the counter as I counted the money. "It's the people right here. I mean, how do you know who people really are?"

I shrugged and lost count of the coins. Blinking, I started over.

"Anyone could be a spy. Anyone could be pretending to support the Revolution while sending information to the king, or to Austria. How do you know who to trust? How do you know who anyone *really* is?"

I opened the cashbox, but I lost my grip and sent coins jangling and rolling all over the floor.

"Oh, Hélène!" Simonne exclaimed, falling to her knees beside me. "Let me help you. Are you all right?"

"I'm fine. I'm just . . . I haven't eaten enough today. I'm a little shaky, that's all." I quickly shuffled the receipts together before locking the cashbox.

"Well, something smells good in there," she said, tipping her head toward the door that led to the kitchen. "I'm going to meet Goullet for some dinner of my own. See you tomorrow."

Spy. Pretty little spy, the fédéré had called me.

I wished Coblenz would disappear from the face of the earth. I wished I could disappear too.

"I'm going to join Théroigne," Simonne declared casually over the buzz of the Café de Foy. Goullet laughed out loud and slapped the table, wiping July sweat off his forehead.

"Join her doing what? Singing?"

"Fighting."

All the men burst out laughing. Her fair face went red, her hands balled into white-knuckled fists. "Why shouldn't the women fight too? Isn't it our country, our homes, and our families?"

"Leave the fighting to the men," Goullet said, stroking her hair and running his index finger down her slender arm. She squinted at him and yanked her arm away.

"You're afraid of me, aren't you?"

He laughed again. She jumped to her feet. Her chair scraped the wooden floor.

"The only thing scarier than a woman who reads is a woman who knows how to use one of these, right?" She opened her jacket and whipped out a pistol.

"Put that away! What—is it loaded?" Goullet laughed, but his eyes were bulging. There was a collective leaning back.

"Yes, it is loaded. And yes, I know how to use it. Do you still think I'm so *hilarious*?"

"Where did you get it, Simonne?"

"I told you I was joining up with Théroigne. You don't ever listen, do you? She's starting a regiment for the women. And there are men who will train us. Men who don't laugh at us. So I won't be needing *you* anymore." She spun on her heels, shoving the gun back into her jacket. Goullet sat there stupidly, watching her go.

"Are you going to go after her?" Jacques asked him, stroking his chin in amusement.

"What, and let her shoot me?" Goullet exclaimed, his face a mixture of idiotic surprise and genuine fear.

A half hour later, my hand was in the crook of Jacques's elbow. Sweat rings stained the underarms of his jacket, and my hair frizzed uncontrollably. The blazing sun was finally going down, but it was still sweltering. Simonne was nowhere to be found, and despite the heat, I shivered as we walked away from the Café de Foy and toward the Champ-de-Mars.

"What do you think about Simonne?" Jacques asked.

"I think she wants to be taken seriously."

"Well, Goullet will never take anything seriously," he laughed.

"She said they had a fight the other night," I said softly, glancing over my shoulder. "She asked him if he was ever going to marry her. He laughed."

"Well. He's not exactly the husband type."

"And what about you, Jacques Bennette?" I poked him in the ribs playfully. "Will you have to be taken to the altar at gunpoint?"

"Definitely not." He kissed me on the cheek.

I squeezed his arm affectionately, but I held on because I was scared too. The city was becoming an armed camp of soldiers, guardsmen, and ragtag local militias. The lines between them were blurring, as the Commune had ordered all citizens with pikes to enlist. Fighting was everywhere—as much at the borders as inland—while they tried to figure out who was still loyal to the king.

Conscription tents covered the Champ-de-Mars, and I glanced at the long lines of men and boys snaking through the green terraces, searching for faces I knew.

Searching for one face.

I still thought I saw him everywhere, all the time—in cafés, on the sidewalk, passing through a doorway—and it never failed to throw me off balance. But it was never him. I was relieved and disappointed every time.

"It's getting dark," Jacques said, glancing up at the sky above the Tuileries. "We'd better head back." Golden light glinted from his fist for a second. He was clutching his switchblade.

We crossed the Pont Neuf, and gruff shouts echoed off the water. I glanced down to see a fédéré holding a National Guardsman by the collar, smashing a fist into his face. Splashing, moaning, heavy footsteps running away. I dug my nails into Jacques's arm.

"Should we go down?" I whispered, glancing over my shoulder at the crumpled guardsman on the bank of the Seine.

He shook his head. "We should have taken the cart." I heard the click of the switchblade in his fist, and he picked up his pace.

"He needs help," I whispered, my throat thick.

"Not from us. Come on."

I glanced over my shoulder once more. He tugged my arm.

We could hear them before we saw them, their shouts and squeals echoing off the bookshop. I smiled as we rounded the corner, knowing Etienne and his friends would be chasing a ball around the alleyway. But then, a deep voice whooped, and Etienne whined.

"Oncle Théo!" he cried. "No fair!"

"I learned that maneuver from you," Théo laughed, but then he looked up and froze.

I stopped in my tracks, and Jacques stiffened. He looked from me to Théo and the group of gangly boys gathered around him.

"Well. I'd better be getting home," Théo told Etienne, resting a hand on his shoulder and holding my gaze. The boys glanced between the three of us, not sure whether to giggle or go home.

"It's almost dark," Théo said, frowning at the sky. "You played a good game, boys."

Simonne wore bright-red trousers, beaming on the arm of a muscular, devastatingly handsome, uniformed fédéré. "This is Gerard," she said, adjusting a new tricolor scarf around her shoulders. "Gerard, this is my friend Hélène."

After he nodded politely to me and turned to peruse the papers, she whispered, "He's one of the trainers. He taught me to handle the pistol. And isn't he *gorgeous*?"

I glanced at him over my shoulder, raised my eyebrows, and nodded. She grinned.

"Speaking of gorgeous, just look at this." She slid the pistol out, and it gleamed in the light. "Touch it!"

Hesitantly, I ran my index finger along the smooth ivory handle. It was cool but promised heat. Promised blood.

"Here, hold it!" she urged, dropping it into my palm.

I held it. Nobody else was in the shop then, which was rare. Simonne and Gerard kissed in the back corner of the shop, open-mouthed and sloppy, and I held her pistol and thought about what it could do for me.

The bell jangled as the door opened, and I quickly hid my hands under the counter. I looked up directly into Lucille Leroux's eyes.

"Is Elisabeth here?" she asked, picking up a pamphlet and pretending to read it so she wouldn't have to look at me.

"No," I said, the gun warming to the temperature of my hand. My finger stroked the trigger under the counter. "No, she's gone to the market with the children. She'll be back in a bit." I didn't drop my eyes from her. She squirmed under the strength of my stare, and I enjoyed it.

"Oh. Fine. Tell her I was here, all right?"

I nodded. I didn't breathe. She turned her back, and it would have been easy. It would have been quick.

"Time to go if we don't want to be late," Gerard said, smiling flirtatiously at Simonne. The door jangled again, and Lucille was back on the street. A shudder ran through me as I realized what I could have done and how much I wanted to do it.

I put the gun on the counter and slid it toward Simonne so I could take the coins Gerard held out to me. He kissed her on the neck. She giggled.

"You should join us, Hélène," she said, fingering the barrel of the pistol before slipping it back into her waistband. "It's amazing how strong it makes you feel, how powerful! The trousers are fantastic too."

"I'll think about it," I promised. She waved goodbye from Gerard's thick arm. I rubbed my eyes and put my head down on the counter. I knew Max kept his own pistol locked in the drawer beside me. Just in case.

I knew I couldn't point a gun at someone I didn't know, didn't even hate, and pull the trigger. It wouldn't make me feel strong. Only afraid of myself. Ashamed.

But what about someone I did hate? Could I pull the trigger then? The realization that I had even thought about it was appalling. So easily, with such a small movement, I could have done it. And that terrified me.

When I closed my eyes, I saw my mother, her eyes wide and frosty blue. Did she feel strong, just for a moment? Did she think she had won?

‖‖ ‖‖ ‖‖
‖‖

THE ABBAYE PRISON
AUGUST 31, 1792

When I open my eyes, I see what it must have felt like inside of Madeleine d'Aubign's head.

Like cold stone and darkness and locked doors.

Like voices without bodies.

Like no escape.

PARIS
AUGUST 1792

Jacques sat with his knees hooked over the arm of his favorite chair, reading, while I pushed oil paint around a canvas distractedly, wearing one of his old shirts over my dress. He put down the pamphlet he was reading about freedom for Black slaves and then picked up the *Friend of the People*.

Something inside of me snapped. "Don't you realize that it's my blood he wants?" The words tumbled out low and hot, and my breath came heavy and hard.

"No, no," he said soothingly, standing up and walking toward me. "You're one of us."

"But I'm one of *them* too."

"Nobody knows that," he said, resting his hands on my shoulders gently. "And loyalty is what counts. I promise, nothing is going to happen to you. It's the Royalists, traitors conspiring a counterrevolution. And can't you see that they must be stopped by any means necessary? Or everyone will starve. We'll be massacred by the Austrians and Prussians, and everything will go back to the way it was. People will die either way, so it's better to keep the innocent ones alive. Don't you think?"

"I don't like having to decide who should live and who should die," I said, biting my lip. "People don't always fit into neat categories, you know."

"But their ideas do," he said, smiling tensely and squeezing my hand. "So don't let anyone but me hear you say something like that. You could get yourself in serious trouble."

The hairs on the back of my neck prickled as I nodded.

"What do you say to the Café Procope?"

"Sure." I wondered if he had to force his smile too, as I briskly scrubbed a rainbow of paint off my fingers and out from under my nails.

"Miles wants me to bring you over for dinner," Jacques said casually over dessert later that evening. I couldn't hide my surprise. In the months I'd spent with him, never once had he offered to introduce me to his associate, friend, and mentor. I had never asked him why.

"Well, that's nice," I said, tracing the water rings on the table.

"Yes. He said next Sunday. How does that sound?"

"Fine."

"You sure?"

I pretended to smile again. "It's fine. Yes. I'm just a little tired. I think I'm ready to go."

Back in the Vendôme, he patted the horse and then helped me down.

"Do you want me to walk you up?"

I shook my head, my hand already on the knob of the bookshop door. "I'm tired. I'll just go to bed."

He kissed my cheek and stepped up into his cart. As I watched him go, I noticed another cart out front.

Théo's.

He was sitting alone at the kitchen table. Darkness rimmed his eyes above an unshaven face. He smiled weakly at me. "Hi."

"Um, hi."

"Want some coffee?"

"Sure."

He rose to fix it for me, and I sat down at the kitchen table awkwardly, looking into the salon.

"Where is everyone?"

"At my mother's," he said, his back to me. He turned his head slightly to address me. "Do you still like a spoon of sugar and a little cream?"

I nodded, smiling sadly.

"Max told me about you and Bennette."

I said nothing. He sat down and slid the coffee across the table to me. "That's good. It's good for you to be taken care of."

I took a sip of the perfect coffee then stared into it, wrapping my fingers tight around the warm cup. Silence threatened to separate us, to pull him away from me to his cart, out of my life again. "How are you, Théo?"

"I'm fine. I want you to be happy. To be taken care of."

"No, that's not what I asked. How are *you*? Really."

He looked up and met my eyes again, and it went to my head like too much champagne. The corner of his mouth tipped up into a sad half smile. "Hélène. You know how I am."

I looked at my skirt, pressing my lips tight, trying to breathe.

"How are you?" he said, attempting a lighter tone.

"I'm . . . I'm scared," I said, marveling that I'd never said these words to Jacques.

Théo reached his hand across the table and squeezed mine just long enough that I could feel the pulse in his wrist, long enough that I felt cold when he moved it away. He said, "I have a surprise for you. Up in your room. Come on."

The door to my attic room was locked. He pulled the key from his pocket. There, on my bed, sat Marie, with a child sleeping beside her on my pillow and a pug in her lap. Dulcet barked and ran toward me for a belly rub.

"What are you doing here?" I gasped, looking from her to Théo then rushing to embrace her.

"I'll leave you two alone," he said, but I stepped back near him as he moved toward the door. Neither of us knew what to say. We just stood there, looking at each other, while Marie and my room and the rest of the world disappeared. I almost touched him. And then he was gone. Again. I struggled to regain my balance and turned to Marie.

"We've left him," Marie whispered. "I've had enough. I want to be free."

"You left him in Coblenz? How did you get here?"

"No," she cried, her voice high and thin. "He's here. He's here in Paris, advising the king. We're at war, Hélène. They're preparing to invade. They've got an army in Coblenz. We came to Paris together, but I promised myself I wouldn't go back with him. I promised myself I wouldn't sleep in the same house as him ever again."

"It's all right. It's the right thing. To be safe."

"This is Giselle," Marie said, nodding toward the sleeping child on my bed.

"She's beautiful." I sat beside her and touched a golden curl, then covered Marie's hand with my own. "Just perfect."

"What happened?" She pointed toward the door, as if Théo were still there.

We talked all night, until Elisabeth finally knocked on the door with a breakfast tray and said that Max had agreed to shelter them. Scooping up little Giselle, she told me and Marie to get some sleep. That everything would be all right.

I didn't tell Jacques about Marie and Giselle. I felt them like a tether, pulling my heart back toward Paris as we passed through the gates of the sweltering city to Guy Miles's country house for dinner and fresh air. I hadn't forgotten Max's warning. But I was more afraid to act strangely, to refuse to see them. Especially with Marie and Giselle in my room.

"Is there anything I should . . . know?" I asked Jacques, anxious as Paris disappeared behind us.

"Just be yourself," he said, and then winked at me. "Well, you know what I mean."

"Will he ask a lot of questions?"

"I doubt it. Don't worry. I'll be with you. You'll be fine. He'll adore you."

"And his wife? What's she like?"

"She'll love you too. Relax."

I sighed and reached for the jar of water I'd brought along. Rummaging around at my feet, my fingers happened upon a blanket, and under the blanket was a book.

"What's this?"

His eyes darted to it and back to the road again too quickly. "A book."

"Right."

An envelope slipped out from the back of the book and into my lap. I reached to replace it, but Jacques jumped on it. "Ah! Thank you," he said, grabbing and tucking it into his breast pocket. "I was looking for that. You found it for me."

"Welcome! Welcome!" The voice of Guy Miles boomed down the lane at us as we approached the house. He limped down the walkway and pulled his watch from his pocket. "Right on time!"

We slowed to a halt, and an icy wave of anxiety washed over me.

"And you must be Citizeness Michel!" Reaching up and grinning, he took my hand and helped me down. "I've heard so many good things about you."

"Well, Citizen Bennette only has good things to say about you, Citizen Miles. Thank you for your kind invitation."

Jacques walked around the wagon and shook hands with Miles, who leaned close to his ear and asked him some unintelligible question.

Jacques nodded and said, "Yes." His hand went to his breast pocket, and Miles broke into a wide grin.

"Come in, come in. Claire is waiting in the salon."

Claire Miles sat on the piano bench with her back to the keys, facing the doorway. She smiled at us with striking composure. Her dark hair was swept up neatly from her neck, and her dress was fashionably simple. Her posture was perfect, and she rose gracefully to kiss me on both cheeks.

"Welcome," she said. "Please, feel comfortable to call me Claire."

"Thank you. Please call me Hélène."

She was an impeccable hostess, polite and warm, but I couldn't shake the feeling that her eyes were staring into me, looking for something she couldn't find. Dinner was relaxed and pleasant, and surprisingly, politics didn't even come up. There was only easy conversation about the weather and the benefits of country life.

As Miles wiped his mouth and sat back to pat his full belly, he said to his wife, "Bennette and I have a bit of business to discuss, *mon amour*. Would you show Citizeness Michel around a bit?"

"I'll take her to the gallery," Claire said, turning to me with eager eyes. "Hélène, you'll truly enjoy our collection. Of course, some of Bennette's work is there. But we have a David, and a Grueze too. My husband brought back a Turner from across the English Channel—specially commissioned. Follow me."

I followed, glancing over my shoulder at Jacques, who nodded encouragingly.

We perused a wall of portraits and pastorals, but then one made me stop dead in my tracks.

Nemesis and Zeus.

It was signed Jacques Bennette.

I froze in front of it while Claire moved on to the next painting to discuss Turner's tumultuous, gray sea. I couldn't unfasten my eyes from the depiction of a man-sized swan with outstretched, graceful wings embracing a beautifully fierce woman with ebony hair and smoldering eyes, draped only in a white scarf. She turned away from him, but he moved toward her with desire, catching the edge of her scarf in his beak.

"Do you know the story?" Claire asked, and I shook my head without looking at her. "Zeus desired Nemesis, the goddess of divine retribution and revenge. But she spurned him. And so, he turned himself into a swan to seduce her. After he had his way with her, she became pregnant and laid an egg. Helen of Troy was inside," she said, smiling amusedly at me.

"But I thought Leda was Helen's mother."

"In most versions, she is. But there is an alternative version, in which Nemesis's egg was rolled to Leda, who became her surrogate mother. Would you like to tour the gardens and view the sculptures?"

I nodded dumbly. *Nemesis. Nemesis.* Was Grand-père honestly trying to tell me that Madeleine d'Aubign was not my mother? He had called me Vivienne's child. But what did that make my father, Zeus? I didn't want to believe he was like Alexander Evereaux. He may have had lovers, but they were lovers. Not victims. Grand-père was confused. Mad. Wasn't he?

My mother's words followed me as I followed Claire silently into the garden.

I always thought your father did it . . .

Did he fool you with that charming grin?

Claire prattled on about the sculptor and gardener, but my thoughts were a maze. Greek gods and Roman warriors stared out over rosebushes and between fragrant trees heavy with fruit. My dress clung to me, and strands of hair were plastered to the back of my dripping neck. Nothing that I looked at registered. The eyes, were they a symbol of love? Or of possession?

We finally returned indoors to the salon for fresh lemonade.

As I set my glass on the end table beside me, I noticed a statuette on top of the piano. A ballerina.

"Do you enjoy the ballet?" I ventured, my heart pounding. If she liked the ballet . . . if she knew the names of the dancers.

"I do," Claire answered, then took a sip of lemonade, her eyes not moving from mine. "Have you been to the ballet since coming to Paris?"

"Yes, yes I have. Jacques and I went together a few times."

"And did you go to the ballet in Dijon?"

"I didn't go then. No. Not in Dijon."

"Is there a theater there?"

"I, um, I don't think so. No."

"Isn't there? That's surprising. It's a large city, after all."

I shrugged, wiped the sweat off my neck with a handkerchief. I'd never even been to Dijon. I was being foolish.

Nemesis. Nemesis.

I scrambled for something to say. "My grandfather used to talk about a dancer, his favorite. From a long time ago. I wonder if you've heard of her? Her name was Josette du Maurier."

She blinked thoughtfully and then frowned, shaking her head. "I don't think I have. Was she from Dijon?"

"Ah, no. Well, I don't know. But she danced in Paris, I think."

"Hmm. Haven't heard of her. But I'm intrigued. What do you know about her?"

Sweat trickled faster down my temples and I fluttered my fan. "Just that she disappeared. Almost twenty years ago."

"Strange," Claire said, reaching for the ballerina. With the dancer's feet in her palm, she twirled it with her fingertips and smiled.

"What was your grandfather's name?"

"Joseph."

"Joseph Michel?"

"Um, no. No, he was my mother's father. He was Joseph, um, Joseph Petit," I lied, feeling like a small animal backed into a corner by her steady eyes.

"Hmm," was all she said, then turned and began to pick out a tune on the piano. I sat still and listened. The heat and Claire's perfume plus dozens of roses on end tables made me woozy. Glancing at the clock, I wondered what sort of business was taking Jacques away from me for so long.

Finally, the door burst open, and Miles beamed at the sight and sound of his wife at the piano. He leaned his bulk against it and nodded his head gently to the tune. Jacques moved beside me, smiling apologetically, and asked, "Did you ladies have a nice time together?"

"Of course," Claire said without turning, and finished up the song. "Yes, we were discussing the ballet. Darling, do you know of a ballerina by the name of Josette du Maurier? Hélène was asking about her, and I've never heard of her. I thought you might have a better knowledge than I concerning ladies of . . . that sort," she said, her mouth and eyebrow tipping playfully.

He turned his face up to the ceiling and laughed aloud. *"Mon amour,* you know you're the only woman in the world for me. And no, I haven't heard of her. Is she new?"

"No. No, she was Hélène's grandfather's favorite ballerina, it seems. Her grandfather from Dijon. But the lady vanished."

I glanced at Jacques. His mouth was tight, the indentations all wrong, and he gripped his chair with white knuckles as Miles shook his head. "Well, you know how girls like that are. Here today, gone tomorrow."

Claire laughed, but her eyes kept prying.

"Well, we'd better be going," Jacques said, rising and taking my hand. "Thank you both for such a lovely evening."

"Yes, yes, thank you," I managed, my head burning.

"We'll have to do this again sometime very soon," Claire said, smiling composedly and kissing me on both cheeks. "We have so much in common."

"Yes, yes, thank you." Before I knew it, we were in Jacques's cart waving goodbye.

Jacques was silent for half a mile, his face growing increasingly red, the vein in his temple bulging. When he finally spoke, his words were rushed and hot. "What were you thinking, Hélène?"

"I . . . I don't know. I just . . . I saw her ballerina, and it came out. I'm sorry. I didn't say anything else, though. I—" Suddenly, tears were spilling down my cheeks.

"You just can't let it go, can you?"

I shook my head, speechless.

"Why can't you just let it go?" he shouted. "The past is over. There's nothing you can do about it! Hélène, it could get you killed."

"But I don't know who I am," I snapped. How could he not understand how much it mattered?

"You're whoever you choose to be. The past doesn't mean anything! You're Hélène Michel."

"But I'm not."

"You have to be."

"I just—I need to know. I'm sorry. I shouldn't have said anything. I just—"

"They already think you're a spy."

His words crawled up my spine like a spider, and I jumped. "What? Why didn't you tell me? I asked you if I should know anything. Why didn't you tell me?"

"Because I didn't want you to be nervous. I didn't think you'd say anything."

"I didn't say anything! I just . . . made up a name for my grandfather. That's all."

He huffed and nodded. "All right. All right."

"You told them I'm not a spy right? Didn't you?"

"Of course I told them you're not."

"So, it's all right then?"

"No, no. You don't understand, Hélène. They didn't believe me. They said I was blinded."

"Blinded? By what? What does that even mean?"

His face softened and he sighed. He slowed the horse and pulled to the side of the road, where we looked out over the fields of a small farm. "They said I was blinded by love." He wiped the tears from my face with his thumbs, smiling gently, and he took my hand. "They were right, Hélène. I mean, right that I love you. I do love you." He paused, as if I were supposed to say something back, but I couldn't. He'd never said these words before. "That's why I wanted to take you there today. To let them see why—why I want to leave France with you."

"Leave?"

"Yes, leave. You. Me. Switzerland. England. America?" he laughed, and closed his hands around mine. Another wave of panic rippled through me.

"What do you mean? I don't understand what you're talking about," I stumbled.

"I want you to marry me, Hélène. I want you to be my wife. I want to get you out of here, to take you somewhere safe. Anywhere you say."

"You already told Miles? Is that what the envelope was about?"

"No," he said, scratching the back of his neck. "No, that was business. I'll tell him once you give me an answer." He fidgeted, laughing nervously.

"What was in the envelope then?"

"Nothing for you to be worried about. So, what do you say? I would recommend *yes*."

"Um . . . I don't know what to say. I'm just . . . I'm just surprised. I . . . I mean . . ."

"Well, think about it," he said, his voice tight and short. "Think about it for a week. Next Sunday, you can give me your answer." He started the horses again. "It's nothing to rush."

I nodded silently.

"And Hélène?"

"Yes?"

He looked at me and smiled. "Say yes."

When I got in, I found Max sitting with his arm around Elisabeth on the chaise, their heads touching, speaking in hushed tones with Victoire sleeping between them. At the sound of the door closing, Elisabeth motioned to me. I sat down on the rug in front of them.

"How are they?" I whispered, lifting my eyes toward the attic.

"Fine," Elisabeth said. "Just fine. How was your day?"

I shrugged, felt my throat thickening. "I don't know. Apparently they think I'm a spy."

"They said so?" Max exclaimed, his eyes bulging, startling Victoire.

"No. No. Jacques told me. He said he told them I'm not, but they didn't believe him. And then she was asking me questions about Dijon—" With shaky hands, I rubbed my eyes. Elisabeth shifted Victoire to Max's lap and sank down on the floor beside me.

"We've been talking about leaving, Hélène. It's time."

I looked up at her through the blur of tears. "Jacques says he wants to marry me. To take me away, someplace safe."

"And what did you say?"

"I couldn't answer him. I . . . I told him I would give him an answer in a week, but I don't know what I'm going to say."

"Is it Théo?" she whispered, and I bit my lip.

"I don't know. It's . . . it's everything."

She nodded. "Max and I are going to London. We'll take Marie and Giselle with us, and you are of course part of that plan, if you want to be."

"Are Théo and Lucille going too?"

"We haven't spoken to them about it yet," said Max, rubbing his chin. "We'll talk to the family soon."

"When would you leave?"

"In a week or so, as soon as we can get the paperwork taken care of," Max said, standing with Victoire in his arms, ready to carry her to bed. "I'll work on getting papers for you either way. You need to get out soon, whether you leave with us or with him," he said, and slipped into the children's room.

|||| |||| ||||
|||| |

I count them. Twenty-one.

I have been here twenty-one days, which means it is September now. Are the leaves changing color? Has it rained? Do the nights begin to chill?

September was supposed to be so many things, but it was never supposed to be this.

Adèle shook her head, tossing long, stringy bangs into her eyes, and stomped hard enough to make the dishes rattle. Her arms were folded tight across her chest.

"Come on, now, *ma chérie*, let's go see Grand-mère," Elisabeth coaxed, but Adèle sprang toward me, wrapped her arms around my waist, and squeezed so tight it took my breath away, her green eyes flashing fiercely at her mother.

"She can stay with me," I said, gently loosening her grip. "I don't mind."

Adèle's mouth curled into a crooked little smile as Elisabeth sighed in exhausted resignation, raising her hands in surrender. She hurried the other children to Max's mother's house. It was a family meeting of sorts, to announce their plans and try to convince the rest of the family to leave with them for London.

"Let's get our friends some breakfast," I whispered to Adèle after the door was firmly closed and bolted. Together we took bread and cheese upstairs and unlocked my room. Adèle was enamored with Giselle, though Mal was less than enamored with Dulcet. The girls made funny faces at each other and laughed. Adèle picked the littler girl up and cuddled her, braided her hair, and gave her ribbons for the cat to chase. Marie and I sat on the bed, smiling at the girls.

"What are you going to do?" she whispered.

"I don't know."

"I don't want you to make your decision based on us," she said, covering my hand with hers. "I want you to do what you want to do. If you have a chance at happiness, I want you to take it. We'll be all right."

I smiled and hugged her, but I didn't say anything.

As Giselle grew sleepy, I took Adèle's hand and led her back downstairs. I hid the key to my room in the bottom of an empty teapot, and turned to Adèle.

"Want to play hide and seek?"

She grinned, bright-eyed, nodding. I hid first, behind the curtains, and she found me easily with a giggle.

"Your turn to hide," I said and covered my eyes as she scampered off. "*Un . . . deux . . . trois . . . quatre . . . cinq!*" I began looking in her usual hiding places: under the table, under the covers of the bed she shared with Sophie, and behind the chaise. "Adèle?" I glanced in Max and Elisabeth's room, where the children weren't supposed to hide. "Are you in here? Adèle? You shouldn't be. Come on out, all right?" Silence. I kept looking, turning the salon inside out and then searching the bookshop—under the counter and inside empty book crates. "Adèle? I give up. Come out! You win!" I called, but there wasn't a sound as I moved back into the kitchen. The door was ajar. I panicked. "Adèle! You were supposed to keep the door locked!" I scolded, poking my head through the door to the courtyard. "Come back inside, now, and I'll read you a story. Adèle?" Fear pulsed through my veins as I stepped into the courtyard. "Adèle?" I knelt to peer under a bush, and as I stood again, my blood went cold.

"Hello," he said casually, as if we were friends. "I think you have something I'm looking for."

"I don't think so," I said, gazing as steadily as I could into the pale blue eyes of Alexander Evereaux.

"Where are they?"

"Where are what?"

He laughed coolly and reached inside his coat. When his hand reappeared, it was wrapped around a pistol. "You know what. My wife. My daughter."

"I haven't seen your wife since I left Coblenz," I lied, trying to determine if I could get around him and to the street, into public view before he pulled the trigger. I took a side step. The barrel followed me.

"You're not a good liar, Hélène," he said, cocking the hammer. "Take me inside. I know they're here." Pressing the barrel into my breastbone, he nodded with his chin toward the open door. Frantically, I scanned the courtyard once more for Adèle while stepping backward, stumbling at the doorway and grabbing the doorpost for balance.

"You can look around if you want," I said, "but you won't find them. They're not here." I took a step away, motioning with a flourish for him to search the house, but he shook his head.

"You're coming with me." The gun pulsed, pressed against my heart's throbbing rhythm. He grabbed me roughly by the shoulder and spun me around, jabbing the barrel between my shoulder blades. "You lead."

Squeezing my eyes closed, I breathed deeply. "This is the kitchen," I said petulantly. "Would you like to search the cabinets?"

"Open them."

I opened each cabinet door slowly, displaying dishes, flour, and bags of coffee, refusing to even glance at the teapot.

"You're wasting my time, and your own."

"I told you I don't know where they are," I snapped, and led him into the next room. "The salon. Would you care to look under the pillows?"

I gasped as the barrel stabbed hard into my spine. "Upstairs," he whispered.

I thought I would be sick as he followed me up the creaking stairs. After the first flight, he stopped and pressed me against the wall, running the tip of the barrel along my jawline, twirling his fingers in my hair. "This haircut suits you," he said, his lips close to my ear, then pointed with his chin toward the stairs and pushed me in front of him again. I led him up the final flight and pressed my back against my door, waiting. "Well?"

"I don't have the key," I said, cornered. It was true.

"Then get it."

"I don't know where it is. This isn't my house."

"I'm afraid I'm going to have to search you then," he said, a grin slowly spreading across his smooth face. "Come on," he said. "Undress."

Marie and Giselle were silent, but I knew how easily sound leaked under the crack of the door. I prayed Marie would keep quiet and Giselle would sleep through whatever was about to happen. Slipping my skirt off slowly and deliberately, I prayed that Max would come back in time to help me, and then I prayed that no one would come back so no one else would get hurt.

"No need to hurry," Evereaux said, smiling as I undid the buttons of my blouse. "I'm enjoying this."

"How did you find me? How did you know I was here?"

"Wouldn't you like to know." He laughed, and then, with two syllables, everything changed.

"Papa?"

His head jerked toward the sound of his daughter, and Dulcet barked from behind the door.

"Giselle?"

"Papa!"

"Is Maman in there with you?"

"Yes, Papa."

"*Shhh!*" Marie hissed loudly, and I could hear the little girl whimpering through the hand over her mouth. Dulcet's nose was at the crack, and from the pitch of her growl, I knew she was baring her teeth at him.

"Marie, open the door," he said calmly.

She said nothing. Giselle began to cry.

"Open the door, or I'll shoot Hélène and break it down. Do you hear me?"

My fingers were frozen on a button. He meant it. I could see the blue veins pulsing beneath his pale skin, the rage in his tight-pressed lips. His hand was steady on the gun.

Then, the kitchen door hit the wall with a thud. Evereaux kept the gun steady, but peered down the stairwell. He put his finger to his lips menacingly.

"Hélène?" It was Théo's voice, Théo's feet pounding on the stairs.

"No!" I screamed, but he was halfway up the steps. Evereaux whipped the gun from me to him, and an ear-splitting explosion knocked him backward to the landing.

Just then the bedroom door burst open, framing Marie with the knife from my drawer high in her hand. In an instant, it was in Alexander Evereaux's back, and he was stumbling down the stairs cursing, stepping over Théo, trailing blood through the house as he ran away into the street. Max appeared, clumsily loading his pistol, glancing in horror from the bloody intruder to his slumping brother.

"Théo! No!" I clambered down the steps to where he crouched on the landing, his back against the wall. He clutched his shoulder, blackish-red blood trickling between his fingers. "Max, get Elisabeth! He's been shot!"

Max finished loading the pistol and took off as quickly as he could, without a word.

I scrambled beside Théo and eased his sweat-soaked head in my lap. My white petticoat went deep red. I yelled to Marie to give me my skirt, which lay crumpled at my door. I pressed it into the wound, and he groaned. "I'm sorry. I'm sorry. I've got to stop the bleeding."

"It's all right, Hélène," he whispered, his eyes barely open, his forehead dripping with perspiration and my tears. "It's all right." Blood soaked the skirt in no time. His eyes drooped, and his head became heavier in my lap as he slipped out of consciousness.

"Get something else!" I shrieked to Marie, who was frantically trying to comfort her child.

"I . . . stabbed . . . him." Her eyes were glazed and wide as she tossed a white nightgown down the steps, covering Giselle's eyes.

When Max, Elisabeth, and Lucille appeared, I was pressing my nightgown into his shoulder, whispering in his ear, "Don't die. Please, please don't die. You can't die. I need you."

Max, Lucille, and Elisabeth lifted him off my lap and carried him to my bed. Elisabeth rushed past me to fetch tweezers and her sewing box. Max led Marie by the hand and carried Giselle into the cellar and locked the door.

"Come on," he said gently, and helped me up. He wiped my face with his handkerchief. "That woman saved my life. She'll save *his* too. She knows what she's doing." After helping me wash my hands and arms in the basin, he pulled out a chair and sat me down at the table opposite Lucille.

"Do you need help?" Lucille asked, her voice trembling, but Elisabeth shook her head no.

Suddenly, I remembered. "Adèle?" I lunged toward the kitchen door, but Elisabeth turned and grabbed my arm.

"She's with Max's mother," she said, looking steadily into my eyes. "She's fine."

"I was looking for her and I couldn't find her, and then—"

"I know. She *told* us."

Adèle had given up her silence. She had given it up for me.

She'd been hiding under another bush all along, and once I was inside she ran down the street. She told them that a bad man was trying to hurt me. Their jaws dropped at the sound of her voice, and Théo and Max took off running. Max's leg slowed him down, and he had told Théo to wait until he fetched the pistol under the bookshop counter, but Théo didn't listen. He ran up anyway, unarmed.

Now, in my room, bleeding into my bed, it was Théo who was silent. What had he given up for me?

I heard the clock punctuating every long minute into sixty unbearable ticks. Lucille and I sat with our arms crossed, turned away from one another on opposite sides of the table. Max paced from window, to door, to window, his fingers wrapped around the pistol, his knuckles white. I turned and glanced over Lucille's head at the clock, and her eyes darted into her lap. It wasn't quick enough to hide the heat in her stare, the accusations. I was the reason he was going to die.

At the sound of Elisabeth's foot on the first stair, we were both on our feet.

"You can go up to him now," Elisabeth said, sighing in exhaustion as she dried her hands on a towel and then used it to wipe her forehead.

I took a step, but at the turn of Lucille's head, I stopped myself. Of course, Elisabeth didn't mean me.

"Is he awake?" Lucille asked stiffly.

"No. No, he's asleep. But the bullet's out. He was lucky."

"So, he'll be all right?" she asked, exhaling and starting toward the stairs.

"I don't know. But I've done all I could do. He's lost a lot of blood."

Lucille went home to get fresh clothes, and I was allowed to go upstairs to gather my things. Théo was frighteningly pale and mumbling something in his sleep as he jerked restlessly, soaked with sweat. I slid my drawers open and gathered a nightgown and clothes for morning, and then I reached for my jewelry box. I removed the brown eye and held it up to my eye in the mirror again. It could have been mine, he had said years ago. A token of secret love. Dangerous love. Gently, I opened his clammy hand and lay it in his damp palm. He groaned, but didn't open his eyes. I closed his fist and brushed my lips against his fingers. I only hoped he would wake and find it before Lucille took it from him.

When Adèle came home, she ran to me and flung her arms around my neck. "I helped you," she whispered. "I helped you."

"Yes, you did. You were so brave. So brave. You helped me, Giselle, and her mother."

"I didn't help Oncle Théo, though," she said, the sound of her voice so new and lovely and sad.

"Your mère is helping Oncle Théo."

"Will he be all right?"

"Yes," I whispered. "Yes, he'll be all right."

"Will you sing to me, Hélène? I'm scared."

I sang. I sang until Lucille came back.

"Don't stop!" Adèle protested, and I swallowed down my shame and continued softly as Lucille glanced repeatedly at me over her shoulder.

Stretched out on my stomach on the floor in the children's room, I listened to the sound of their breathing as they slept. I wedged a chair under the handle and placed myself between them and the door. I had endangered them all. And Théo was still unconscious upstairs.

I imagined Alexander Evereaux lying dead in the street, the knife in his back. I imagined him in a doctor's upper room, being stitched up and getting stronger. I imagined him back at our door, or crashing through a window. I thought of his wife and daughter in the dank, dim cellar. I thought of my family in Coblenz and Grasse.

"Hélène?" It was Elisabeth's voice. "Can you come out for a minute? It's safe. I need to talk to you."

I wiggled the chair away from the door and slipped out into the kitchen, breathless.

"He's awake," she whispered, her smooth brow furrowed and plastered with sweaty, black ringlets.

"Is he all right?"

"He has a fever. I'm going to try to get it down. But I thought you should know," she pressed her lips together, considering whether or not to keep speaking. "The first word out of his mouth was your name."

She tiptoed into the kitchen and filled a bowl from a pitcher of cool water. On a tray she piled strips of cloth and some various dried herbs from her medicine cabinet. Before going up to him, she stopped and smiled bravely at me. "Try to rest. I'll wake you if anything changes."

I prayed with all my might that my name would not be his last word.

Optimism is just hope by a different name.

Looking at the closed eyes of the children, their sweet faces illuminated in the soft light, gleaming with August sweat, it was hope that I needed, and hope that I clung to, whether it was insanity or not.

For two days and two nights, Théo burned with fever. Elisabeth didn't sleep. Lucille nodded off on a blanket on my bedroom floor, and I stayed with the children through two sleepless nights of my own. Max opened the shop but worked alone with his pistol in his jacket. I was to stay behind locked doors at all times, and I tried to distract myself by becoming useful: cooking meals for the family, reading with the children, bathing and dressing them, and caring for Giselle and a dazed Marie, who stayed in the dark, damp cellar.

The shop was packed and noisy, but Max said little of the news. I didn't understand what was about to happen. I almost didn't care.

On the morning of August 9, Théo's fever broke. He ate a piece of bread and drank some coffee, Elisabeth announced, her eyes bright despite her obvious exhaustion.

"He's turned the corner, then," Max said, putting his hand over his heart as he exhaled heavily. Elisabeth smiled, pouring herself a cup of coffee. She sank into the chair beside Max, who kissed her head. "You're an angel," he murmured.

"Now, tell me what's going on outside," she said, leaning her head against his shoulder and closing her eyes.

"An insurrection is planned for morning. The sections are going to try to depose the king and set up a new government."

Her sleepy eyes widened. "Oh. Oh my."

HHT HHT HHT
HHT II

"So, what did you do?" Our newest addition has asked us each in turn, and now her dark eyes are on me.

I clench my teeth. She's too curious. "Nothing."

"I mean on the outside. Your hands are soft," she says, and starts separating my fingers with her own darkly stained ones. I jerk away, glaring at her. She taps a long, blackened nail against her lips. "Let me guess . . ."

"Bookshop. I worked at a bookshop."

"What about the *Sun of the French*? Did you carry that newspaper?"

I nod.

She grins, but there's bitterness in her eyes. "Why, thank you."

I lift an eyebrow.

"It was my father's paper. I typeset it. Before these bastards shut it down and threw us in here. What delightful freedom the French now enjoy. Ah, sweet liberty," she says mockingly, and stands up to stare through the grate of our door.

The *Sun of the French* always sat just above Marat's *Friend of the People* in the shop, but it didn't sell nearly as well, and suddenly it strikes me as funny the way we used to organize everything. Fiction in one section. History in another. Science here, religion there, philosophy to the left, and newspapers right down the middle. Who told us what went where? How did we know?

And here we are, stacked three floors high, each of us full of stories. But who will decide whether our stories are fact or fiction? Who will tell us where to go?

PARIS

AUGUST 9, 1792

The shop and street were chaotic, full of anxious and bizarrely merry people. To be a hero was something to celebrate, even if it meant death. It meant you mattered, at least for once in your life. Pikes, pistols, muskets, kitchen knives, spikes from railings mounted on broom handles, and cudgels were gathered and carried into the streets to be distributed. I thought of Simonne and her pistol, of the professional soldiers she'd be up against.

Drums banged, each to their own rhythm, and scattered verses of "La Marseillaise," sung by voices deep and high, young and old, seeped through the shuttered windows and into the unbearably stuffy house. We sat quietly watching the children play, hushing them now and again, but mostly wanting their laughter to overtake the sounds outside.

Lucille came downstairs in the afternoon, choking back tears. "I'm going to see my father. I want to see him before he goes."

Max nodded. "Of course. Of course. We'll look in on Théo."

The tocsin began to ring, calling the people to report to their section leaders for instructions. Elisabeth woke and changed shifts with Max as the singing outside grew louder and stronger, punctuated with women crying as they kissed their men goodbye, while others sang as they marched beside their husbands, pikes in hand. Some brought their children too, singing and armed with whatever sharp things they could find.

> To arms, to arms, ye brave!
> The avenging sword unsheathe!

March on, march on!

All hearts resolved on victory or death!

I sent a tray upstairs for Théo and Elisabeth and then sank into a kitchen chair, pushing my food around with my fork, unable to bring any of it to my lips.

"Papa, why is it so noisy outside?" Adèle asked. "Why are the bells ringing?"

Max's fingers fidgeted beside his plate, and he crumpled his napkin into his fist. "People are upset, *ma petite*. They're getting ready to fight."

"Why?"

"To be free. They'll fight to be free."

"That's bad, Papa!" Sophie exclaimed. "It's bad to fight."

Étienne nodded, glancing at Pierre. They had been told so more than once.

"Yes," Max said slowly. "Yes, but sometimes, people are left with two choices, and neither one is quite right. Both are bad, but people must decide which choice is the better one, the less bad one."

"So fighting is the less bad choice?"

"Today, it seems to be. Yes."

"Are you going to fight too, Papa?" asked Étienne, and Pierre's eyes grew wide with excitement as the girls protested.

Max shook his head. "My arm and leg are no good for fighting. I'm finished with that."

"I'm glad," said Sophie, snuggling up to him and kissing his unshaven cheek. "I want you to stay here with us. I'd be scared if you had to go fight."

"Me too, my Sophie. Me too."

Was anyone in Paris sleeping that night? It took hours to get the children to bed. Everyone was carrying weapons, singing and shouting, or lying awake listening . . .

Now, now, the dangerous storm is rolling,

Which treacherous kings confederate raise!

The dogs of war, let loose, are howling,
And lo! Our homes will soon invade!

The knock at the door jolted Max to his feet, pistol in hand.

"It's probably just Lucille," he said, raising a calming hand. Peering around the curtain, he heaved sigh of relief. "Oh. It's for you, Hélène. It's Bennette."

My stomach lurched. Was he here for an answer? It wasn't Sunday yet. I wasn't ready.

Max unlocked the door and nodded to Jacques, who entered in the uniform of the National Guard with a pistol on his belt. After locking the door behind him, Max excused himself and went upstairs.

"You're going?"

"Of course. I just came for a good-luck kiss." He smiled, and I looked into his eyes, so dark and sad and familiar. He cornered me against the door, his hand on the wall, and kissed me long and hard, like we might never see or touch or taste each other again. Or like we might spend the rest of our lives kissing like that. "Everything is all set," he whispered against my cheek. "Sunday we leave. I have the papers ready. As soon as you give me the word."

"Sunday," I repeated, and he smiled.

"Sunday."

The tocsin rang again, making me jump, and he straightened his uniform and reached for the doorknob.

"Jacques? Please, please, be careful."

"I'm always careful." His lips brushed against my cheek one last time. "I'll be fine."

"Watch out for Simonne."

He laughed. "She's got her pistol, and her fédéré. She'll be all right."

"Jacques? You look . . . beautiful. In your uniform. And all the time."

He smiled with his teeth, which he almost never did.

"I love you, you know," he said.

"I know," I replied, because I had felt it in his kiss, how much he cared for me. And I thought back to that night in the snow, realizing that

I could feel two things at once, that nothing was ever simple. "I . . . I love you, too."

"I know you do," he said with a wink, and then he left. Smiling.

That smile pierced my heart, because I hadn't lied. And yet, I knew I wouldn't leave Paris with him. I couldn't.

The street was a great river of armed people. Jacques Bennette's voice drifted away from me, blending into the crowd, their voices strong and frantic, their feet in rhythm with the beat . . .

> O Liberty, can man resign thee,
> Once having felt thy generous flame?
> Can dungeons, bolts, or bars confine thee,
> Or whips thy noble spirit tame?
> To arms, to arms, ye brave . . .

"Do you love her?" I'd asked Théo so many months ago when he'd told me, tears in his eyes, that he'd married Lucille.

"I never stopped wishing it was you, not for a single day, not a single hour," he'd said, without really answering my question. And yet, as I made my bed on the children's floor, knowing I wouldn't sleep in it, I realized he had answered the question for both of us.

Elisabeth knocked softly. "Has Lucille come back?" she asked.

"No. Not yet."

"Hélène, I'm tired. It's your shift."

"My shift?"

"Your shift."

"Does he need medicine or anything?"

"No," she said, slipping an arm around me. "No, he just needs you."

I weighed nothing. I was a cloud walking up the steps on sunbeam legs.

Théo's eyes were closed. The fresh bandage around his arm and shoulder was still white. I tiptoed to the chair beside the bed but didn't sit. I just stood there, thinking about war.

There are wars between kings and countries, churches and states, heads and hearts, hearts and souls. But all are the same. War is nothing but a desperation, a time when it suddenly becomes necessary and maybe even right to do something wrong. Sometimes you must kill to save, destroy to build, take to give. Sometimes it takes one wrong to make everything else right. Sometimes lines shift, at least a little. Maybe even a lot.

I knelt and brushed the damp, curly hair off his forehead. His eyelashes fluttered, but he didn't wake up. "Théo."

If this was war, I was going to win. *We* were going to win. I bent over and kissed his lips, salty with summer sweat. *I never stopped wishing it was you.*

His mouth opened and curved into a half smile against mine. "I haven't shaved in almost a week," he said, his voice slow and tired. "I can't believe you just did that." I laughed and he brushed my cheek with the back of his hand. "You're my night nurse?"

"Yes. How are you feeling?"

"Better now. Much better now." He smiled and closed his eyes. I squeezed his hand, and he squeezed mine back.

"I'm sorry. This was my fault. I'm so sorry."

"No," he whispered, opening his eyes. "I'm sorry, Hélène. I should have listened to you that night on the river. We should have floated away on that little boat and never looked back."

"You didn't know."

"Still," he said, shaking his head against the damp pillow. "We should have gone. I thought we'd be in America by now. Where will you be in a week, Hélène? When do you leave with Bennette?"

I squeezed my eyes tight, bracing myself. "I'm not leaving with him."

"You're going with Max then?"

"Only if you are. If you're going, I'm going. If you're staying, I'm staying." I swirled my finger across his knuckles, tracing the bones in his hand.

He smiled and tried to push himself up with one arm. Surrendering, he laid his head back on the pillow and curled his index finger toward himself. I rose from the floor and perched on the edge of the bed, but he pulled me closer. It was like that night on the river. As if no time had passed since then. As if nothing could ever tear us apart.

"Where have you been sleeping while I'm taking your bed?"

"On the floor, with the children."

"I can't approve of that," he said, half smiling. "You should sleep in your own bed."

Carefully, I curled against him. He quickly fell asleep, but I lay awake for a long time. My head on his good shoulder, my hand on his chest, I absorbed the steady rhythm of his heart. As long as it kept time, all the melodies in my head could untangle themselves and make sense. It was safe to be Hélène d'Aubign for the first time in what felt like an eternity, and I finally fell asleep.

The first cannon fired, close enough to rattle the walls, and set off a chain of howling dogs. Muskets and cannons exploded, tinging the air with sulfur. Women screamed and wailed. Children cried as vibrations and screams rippled toward us from the direction of the Tuileries. The morning sky was hazy with smoke as we lay awake together in the stifling heat, waiting for Elisabeth to tell me my shift was up.

Lucille came back late, and Elisabeth was with Théo by then. I lay down on the children's floor again that night, trying to find the words to tell Jacques no. I hadn't lied to him. I did love him. But I think, deep down, we both knew we were like two people trying to play the same song in different keys.

"We're leaving before dawn," Max said. By Saturday, the fighting had stopped, but the air still smelled of smoke. He held Giselle in his lap on the cellar floor, making Sophie's doll dance floppily while he spoke to us. Marie's hands trembled in her lap.

"What about Théo?" I asked.

"He has a passport. It's up to him and his wife, once he's well enough to travel. But we have to go."

Him and his wife. Did I imagine this phrase was directed at me? It seemed almost like Elisabeth's idea, to allow us to be alone together at last, but what did Max think?

"So, are you coming with us?" he asked me.

I shook my head. I couldn't make my mouth say no.

His shoulders fell and he extended an envelope toward me. "Then here are your papers."

"But I'll see you in London," I said hastily. "We're coming to London. I'll see all of you soon."

"Good. Good. That will make it easier on the children. When do you and Bennette leave?"

"I . . . I don't know."

"Once we have an address, we'll leave it for you at Child's Bank."

Marie grabbed my hand, her eyes wide with panic. "I'm sorry, Hélène. I'm sorry for coming here. I'm sorry for everything."

"It's all right. He'll be all right. Giselle needs you. Be strong for her."

It was pitch black and damp, that dreary hour between Saturday night and Sunday morning when no one should be awake. Victoire sucked her thumb and clutched her blanket, and Pierre hadn't even protested at getting dressed. Sophie, Adèle, and even Étienne were crying, and Elisabeth stiffly shushed them, wiping her own tears away.

"We'll see Hélène in London. Enough. Enough. Let's go."

Adèle shook her head and stomped, clinging to my waist.

"I'll see you soon," I said, kneeling beside her. "Be a good girl and go. I promise I'll see you very soon."

"Promise?"

"Promise."

As Sunday morning light filtered through the bolted windows and under the crack of the door, I waited for Jacques Bennette. I promised myself I would keep my promise to Adèle, having no idea how I was going to do it. We didn't have a plan. Lucille was upstairs with Théo, and I was alone.

I paced. I scrubbed at the cracks between wooden floorboards. I folded and refolded the few pieces of clothing I had packed, ready for whenever we could leave. I counted my money, counted the stripes on the wallpaper, checked the locks on the doors, and washed my hair. I cooked and carried food upstairs.

As I handed the tray to Lucille, her voice was full of shadows. "When is your fiancé coming for you?"

"I don't know. I thought he'd be here by now."

"Well, in case we're sleeping when you leave, goodbye," she said, her blue eyes icy.

Monday morning. No sign of Jacques. I opened the cupboards for breakfast, but there was nothing but a bit of old cheese.

I knocked on my bedroom door.

"Yes?" Lucille's lips were close to the crack of the door, but she didn't open it.

"I wondered if you might be able to go to the market this morning? There's no food."

"You don't expect me to leave him in this condition, do you?" she snapped.

I squeezed my eyes shut, desperate. "I'm not supposed to leave the house. Max said so."

The door swung open. She squinted at me. "Well, Max isn't here. You didn't go with Max, remember?"

"Fine. I'll go." I glanced over her shoulder. Théo was sound asleep. "What would you like to eat?"

"Doesn't matter to me. Perhaps you can find Bennette on your way."

I smiled stiffly as the door closed in my face. I pulled on my bonnet, arranging the lace and flowers, tying the yellow ribbons distractedly. I was hungry. And I was scared.

I followed Lucille's advice. I went to Jacques's studio, snaking behind the Jacobin Club and into the Bibliothèque. "Jacques?"

No answer.

"Jacques, are you home?" I jiggled the knob and it turned. Dirty dishes littered the table and floor, and it reeked with the stench of food scraps baking in a closed-up, hundred-degree flat. I peeked into the bedroom and called his name, but it was empty. After scrawling a quick note on scrap paper, I left.

The market had the feeling of a box filled to the brim, ready to explode. People were purposefully minding their own business, whispering, their eyes darting around corners and under wagons. I bought a loaf of bread, cheese, and three apples, trying to be invisible.

"Flowers!" a wispy, young girl called, extending a snow-white lily toward me. "Flowers for the dead. For the heroes of the Fatherland!"

I bought one, making her smile, hoping it wouldn't symbolize any of the people I loved. I walked to Simonne's flat.

Laughter filtered through the crack in the door as I knocked.

"Simonne? It's Hélène," I called, and heard her moving toward the door.

She flung her arms around me. "Oh, God, what a night! What a horrible night!"

"You're all right? You're both all right?" I exhaled and peered over her shoulder at Gerard, stretched out on her couch, bare-chested.

"Thank God, yes! What about Bennette? How is he?"

"I hoped you knew. I haven't seen him. I'm worried."

"Have you gone to see Miles? If anyone knows, he does."

I shook my head slowly, unable to explain why that was not an option. "No, not yet. Let me know if you hear anything, please?"

"Of course," she said, hugging me again.

"Here." I handed her the flower. "I bought it at the market. It'll look pretty in your room."

Her face lit with a smile and she turned to get a little cup. "Do you want to stay for some coffee?"

"No, no. I've got to get back," I said, glancing again at shirtless Gerard. She waved at me from the table and blew me a kiss.

I trudged home with my basket, desperately hoping that Jacques would be sitting at the table waiting for me, desperately afraid of it at the same time.

He wasn't.

I carried the bread, cheese, and apples up to Lucille and Théo, trying to catch his eye unsuccessfully.

I tried to eat. Tried to make my hands stop shaking. Tried to tell myself that it was the righter wrong. Tried to think of how to get Théo alone for just five minutes, and how to explain it to Jacques. I tried to tell myself Jacques Bennette was alive, that there was a perfectly good reason for him not being home or here. That he would somehow understand and not hate me.

That it *was* the righter wrong.

When the fist banged on the door, I sprang out of my chair and flung the door open wide. The sentence was ready on my lips. *Jacques, I'm sorry, I'm so so sorry, but I can't—*

But it wasn't him.

It was two National Guardsmen. "Hélène d'Aubign?"

I nodded dumbly.

"You're under arrest."

This is the end, I thought. *The end of everything.*

Twenty-three days ago, it was Tuesday, August 12. On that day I was taken unceremoniously to the Abbaye Prison in a cart jammed with prisoners. I couldn't say goodbye, couldn't tell Théo where I was going.

After five days, Simonne came to see me, and it cost her an argument with Gerard and who knows what to bribe the guard. When I begged her to tell me what was happening outside, she made me sit down.

"It's Bennette," she said, and my heart broke. "He didn't make it Hélène."

"What? Are you sure?"

She nodded slowly. "I'm sure. I saw him."

"No."

"Yes."

I felt her light hand on my shoulder, heard her breath coming in shaky bursts.

"It was quick. And mostly painless. Miles was with him, so he wasn't alone. It was one of those damned Swiss Guards—" She cut herself off, her clenched fists white as porcelain, her eyes wild and wet.

"No. No. No." I said it repeatedly, my head falling onto my arms as I crumpled onto the desk.

"He loved you," Simonne said, perching on the edge of the desk and lifting my chin. "He was brave."

"I don't want to be brave anymore. I just—I want it all to stop. I can't—"

All I wanted to do was turn the clock back to August 9, when he was alive and in the salon, asking me for a good-luck kiss and telling me he was always careful. I wanted to say *I love you*, just one more time. I wanted to lock him in and keep him safe. His eyes should be open, he should be painting, thinking of everything beautiful and painful and metaphorical—no, no, he should just be thinking of everything beautiful. And not thinking of me. I was going to betray him. To tell him *no*, even though I had just told him I loved him. I hoped he didn't think of me at the end, that he thought of his parents, or Simonne, or the sunrise—anything or anyone but me.

"Shh, shh." Simonne held me close and rubbed my back as if I were a child. "I don't think I'll be able to come again. It's crazy out there now," she said, and told me in whispers that the royal family had been imprisoned and a new commune ruled the dark and shuttered city. Fear of counterrevolution gripped people like never before. A guillotine had been set up in the Place du Carrousel, and there were calls to exterminate the Royalists, to irrigate the soil of a new France with their blood.

"What's your secret, Hélène?" she asked. "Tell me everything, and I'll try to help you."

She promised to believe me.

She said she was my friend.

But that was weeks ago.

‖‖‖ ‖‖‖ ‖‖‖
‖‖‖ |||

THE ABBAYE PRISON
SEPTEMBER 3, 1792

"What is it?" Marielle cries.

We are all on our feet at the sudden ruckus outside. There are screams of alarm and pain. Shouting and curses. Violent sounds of metal and bone.

"What's happening?" everyone asks at once.

The Swiss Guard from across the corridor, the one with the turret window, is the only one who can see.

"They're slaughtering priests in the street." He steps away from the window to vomit. "It has begun."

|||| |||| ||||
|||| ||||

THE ABBAYE PRISON
SEPTEMBER 4, 1792

Who decides where the line between right and wrong falls? Who decides when it must shift? The strongest? The loudest? The bravest? The wisest? The holiest? The ones who have nothing to lose, or the ones who have nothing to gain?

Outside, a mob kills the prisoners. We sit together, waiting our turn, holding hands with strangers. The brave ones look outside and decide the quickest way to die.

"It goes faster, I think, if you put your hands behind your back," a solemn voice declares over the cacophony, a voice that seems accustomed to overcoming noise and evil. "They stand them upon a slippery heap of the dead, and make them swear to the Fatherland. I saw one woman go free. There is hope." When he says this last bit, he presses his face to the bars and looks into my eyes. He's a priest who wouldn't take his vows to the nation over the pope. Through the opening in his cell door, he comforts the small ones who are weeping and trembling. He reminds them that death is not an ending, but a beginning.

We wait, listening to the screams, to clanging swords and sharpening knives, to the chant of the "Ça ira," and to the names being called ten at a time to come to the makeshift tribunal for trial. I feel like a criminal, like a person whose life is over before it's even begun.

They say it is a necessary evil. The righter wrong.

Marielle and Élodie and the others scream over the frenetic singing that arrives outside our door, and then enters our cell.

The warden is shoved in at pike-point. A filthy, crimson crowd backs him up as he hoarsely reads the names of my cellmates:

Marielle du Champ.

Élodie Brodeux.

Delphine de Roche.

Anne Baton.

Marielle clings to me, and I promise her it's going to be fine. The judge will understand. Just tell the truth. But one of the wild-eyed, blood-soaked men pulls her off me like she's a dog. He shoves her in line and commands them all to walk out into the corridor.

Delphine shoots me a death look. "What about her?" she says, and I know what she thinks: *Spy. Filthy spy.*

"Her time is coming," the warden says, and jostles them out into the corridor. He hands Marielle, Élodie, Delphine, and Anne to the singing butchers.

And then, he locks me in.

||||| ||||| |||||
||||| |||||

THE ABBAYE PRISON
SEPTEMBER 5, 1792

The bloody work of the mob goes on through the night. The Swiss Guard from across the corridor has met his own fate, and no one gives me news. I want someone to tell me that Marielle made it out alive, but the corridor is silent. All the noise has moved downstairs. And outside.

As the key turns in my door, my heart explodes in my chest. Is it my turn?

But it's not a wild-eyed man ready to deliver me justice.

It's not even a man.

The dim light of a single candle paints dark half circles under Claire Miles's penetrating eyes, turning her soft features angular and harsh. "Hélène d'Aubign, do you know why you're here?" she asks.

"No."

"No one's told you anything?"

"Nothing."

"I always thought you were a spy." Her back is to me now as she walks around my cell.

"You thought wrong. I'm not."

"Simonne told me your story," Claire says, not turning to look at me.

"She came to see you?"

She smiles over her shoulder. "Yes. She works for me. It's not only Royalists who have spies."

"*She* accused me? Simonne?"

Claire looks at me, squinting, her eyes so pinched I can decode nothing but suspicion, and lifts her chin. "Why did you ask me about Josette du Maurier?"

"She's my aunt. I wanted to find her."

"Why?"

"To ask her for the truth about my family. And to tell her I'm sorry for whatever happened to her. I wanted her to know that her father loves her and would give anything to see her again."

She presses her lips together tightly and takes a deep breath. "And how do you know this?"

"He told me. My grandfather told me in Grasse. His name is Joseph du Maurier, and he lives in Grasse, not Dijon. That's the truth. Look, he gave me this." Quickly, I unpin the blue-eyed brooch from under my skirts, and pray it will mean something to her.

She steps closer to me, staring at the eye in my palm.

"I'm telling you the truth, I swear!"

"Yes," she says slowly, and her face softens. "Yes, I know you are. I'm going to help you. I'm going to help you because it was the dying wish of two people that I loved dearly: Jacques Bennette, and your mother."

"My mother? My mother is dead? How do you know that?"

"I know a great many things you don't know. Things it's time you knew. Not least of all, my name. Hélène, I . . . am Josette du Maurier."

Screams echo off the walls from the street, but the sound of my breathing, the sound of my own heart in my ears momentarily shuts them out. Josette du Maurier glances at the barred window and shudders, shaking her head.

"My husband became suspicious when Bennette inquired about the du Maurier sisters at the Department of Justice. But no matter how much we pressed him, he insisted you were Hélène Michel from Dijon. Bennette fell in love with you, and so, Simonne became necessary. Still, we could obtain no hard facts, no proof that you were my niece, and no proof that you were looking for me for friendly reasons. For all I knew, you were under the influence of Madeleine and her family and the court. For all I knew, they had convinced you to work for them, for Coblenz, trying to find me and my husband. They would love to get their dirty hands on him and everything he knows. And Madeleine, I'm sure, would love to silence me once and for all. Finally, after your arrest, Simonne brought me your true name and motives. And I began to work on assisting you. It hasn't been easy."

"I don't understand. Please—?"

"I caused trouble. Too much trouble. I believed that Madeleine murdered Vivienne. I believed it with all my heart, and I still do. I've improved in my ability to keep my mouth shut, but back then, I couldn't. How could I? Of course, Madeleine's mother, sister, and her brother would have nothing of it. And besides, there was the medical report. Who could argue with that?

"Antoine told me to shut up. He told me that if I made any trouble for the family, he would have me imprisoned. He said he'd have someone break my legs in the night so I'd never dance again. But I couldn't be quiet. I had the baby to think about."

"But I . . . I thought the baby died."

She squeezes my hands in both of hers. "A baby died. But not Vivienne's. It was Madeleine's baby that died. I knew it. I was certain. Vivienne's baby had dark hair and dimples."

Gently, she touches my hair, brushes the indent of my cheek. "But the baby that we buried was fair. I told my father, but neither he nor I knew that Antoine had been given power of attorney. Papa had been declared mentally unfit to rule his own estate. And so, Antoine had me arrested instead of Madeleine, and I never saw my father again. I sat for three months in the Bastille, waiting, writing to your father for help.

"I was angry, grief-stricken, and ill. Your father finally wrote to me, telling me he found Vivienne at the bottom of the stairs in a pool of blood. She was already dead, and he was broken. He believed it was an accident, that she must have tripped, but I knew Madeleine must have been responsible for her fall. One way or another, I *knew* she did it, and I wanted justice—but your father wanted something more. He wanted a good life for you. He wrote me that Madeleine's child had indeed died, but that he wanted to keep you. He wouldn't give you up. And so, the babies were switched, and he made me swear not to tell you or anyone else that you were Vivienne's—not to speak of it again.

"If it became known that you were the daughter of an opera singer, you would have no future. Your father meant well, and I kept my promise in exchange for freedom, but he was wrong," she says flatly. "Everyone deserves to know the truth of who they are."

She reaches inside her shawl and hands me a wrinkly, worn envelope addressed in gracefully swirling handwriting. "I've carried this for too long, and learned only that it proves nothing. It's yours now. Keep it. Maybe it will be enough for you."

Carefully, I unfolded the letter and began to read.

My Dear Josette,

Madeleine knows. He told her he's leaving her, that we're going to Monaco, and she's livid. "You'll never have him," she said, and I saw violence in her eyes—I know it. I can't sleep for fear she'll do something terrible.

She has always hated me, and now I can hardly blame her for it. But hasn't she been a cruel and miserable wife to him? Who is guilty, and who is innocent? What is there to do but beg God for mercy and forgiveness, and start anew? I do pity her, but I fear for myself and my sweet baby!

She looks more like Jean-Luc every day. She's beautiful—dark-haired with his dimples, but her eyes are like mine. Wait until you see her, Josette! You'll be under her spell. I told Jean-Luc I want to name her Hélène. It carries the meaning of light, and that's what I want for her. Light, beauty, and goodness. We will leave this darkness behind us.

Promise me, Josette, promise me that if anything happens to me,

you'll look after my little girl. Tell my Hélène I love her always and
always. And God willing, I will see you and Papa and Maman soon.
                                      Always,
                                      VEdM

It sinks in fast, heavy, and hard, like a stone, sending slow ripples
through me.

"It's a promise I intend to keep," Josette says. "To look after Vivienne's little girl."

My vision blurs the swirling ink into a great black smudge, and I wipe
my eyes with the heel of my hand.

"You take after your mother," she says, smiling, tucking a stray hair
behind my ear. "You never thought *that* would be said as a compliment,
now did you?"

We both laugh despite our tears, and I shake my head.

"I wish I could have been with you all of these years to tell you that."
She wipes her own eyes and sighs, her heavy breast rising and falling.

"I'm so glad to have finally found you, to know—"

"Yes," she says, stroking my hair and nodding. She opens her mouth
to say more, but a drum begins to beat wildly outside my window, and
voices like gravel chant the "Ça ira."

She draws an anxious breath and squeezes my hands so tightly, my
bones rub together. "Your fate is in the hands of the people now. And
they want blood today. But they're fickle. They can be swayed. I've seen
them save some. I've done everything I could possibly do to ensure that
you will be one of them." She smiles bravely and rises, moving toward
the door.

"Don't leave me," I beg. "Please. I don't want to be alone!"

"There are things that must be done. I must go."

"But who accused me? What are my charges?"

She presses her lips tight again, considering. "I think it's best if you
don't know that yet. Not until you need to. Just . . . trust me. And my
husband."

HHt HHt HHt
HHt HHt I

THE ABBAYE PRISON
SEPTEMBER 6, 1792

"Prisoner 2247, Hélène d'Aubign. Step forward."

I can't breathe. I can't feel my hands or feet, but I think I'm still holding Vivienne's letter. I think I'm stepping forward, but the world is spinning and I've lost my sense of direction. I squeeze my eyes tight and try not to be sick.

Somehow, I've descended to the inner sanctuary of the Abbaye, into a dim and smoky corridor lit by torches and candles. I face my judges, a group of rough-looking men from the neighborhood, their sleeves rolled up to expose bare arms covered in blood and tattoos. They sit at a worn wooden table strewn with empty flasks and bottles.

More men stand along the wall, swords at their sides, wearing red woolen caps and dirtied butcher's aprons. More still make up an audience, men and women whose eyes are scared and furious. Frantically I look for Claire and then remind myself to call her Josette. But I don't see her. She's not here, and neither is her husband.

In front of the judges' table, a blond man is being held by the wrists and the collar, pulled up for his trial. He's yanked roughly to face the other prisoners, and my mouth falls open.

Alexander Evereaux.

LINDSAY K. BANDY

Our gazes lock, and for once, his blue eyes are not cold, haughty, or lustful. Just wide with an intense animal fear.

"Hélène!" he cries desperately and cranes his neck toward the judges. "Look, she knows me! She'll tell you I'm not a traitor! She'll tell you I'm loyal to the Revolution! Tell them, Hélène!"

He's crying, crystalline drops sliding down his chiseled cheeks, and I shake my head as the tribunal and spectators all follow his gaze to me. "No," I whisper. "No, I won't lie for you."

"Please, Hélène, tell them the truth! Save me!" he cries.

"I won't lie for you!" I say, my voice growing stronger. He's whirled around to face the men that declare him guilty. The red-capped men with swords drag him outside.

I don't feel satisfaction or joy. I don't feel grief, either. I only feel sick to my stomach.

I am ninth in line. One by one, my predecessors are declared guilty. I look around for Marielle, but there is no sign of her or Josette, and I am afraid I will faint.

"You—the friend of Evereaux. What's your name?" a judge tattooed with the symbol of a hammer calls to me roughly, shuffling through a scrawled list of names.

"Hélène d'Aubign." My voice is small and wobbly, echoing in my own ears. "And he's not my friend. He's not my friend at all."

"Ah. Yes, d'Aubign." He runs a thick finger down his list and then stops. "Your charges are conspiracy against the Republic and espionage. How do you plead?"

"Not guilty," I whisper, and they all laugh as if I've told a joke.

A runner bursts in, a boy of twelve with tattered pants and toes sticking out of his shoes. He taps the judge in the middle on the shoulder, whispering in his ear. The middle judge straightens and motions slightly toward himself with each hand to the others, whose sweaty heads cluster against his.

"Stand aside, d'Aubign," the tattooed man says, squinting. "We're waiting for your witness."

Witness? None of the others have had a witness. I stand against the cold wall, torchlight dancing manically on either side of me, and close my eyes as prisoner after prisoner is declared guilty. How long does this go on? How many are taken? Time has been warped into a slow bend of unbearable unreality, only it's real.

I think about what I am guilty of. I think of Jacques, of Théo, Lucille, my mother, my father, our château filled with jewels, and maybe I do deserve to die. Maybe that's the only way to make anything right. Maybe my blood will make someone else free.

"D'Aubign?" the rough voice jolts my eyes open and makes me gasp. "Yes?"

He motions toward me, his tattoo flexing, the dried blood crusting in the folds of his skin. A door is opened, and I turn to see Guy Miles.

"This had better be worth the delay, Miles," the head judge scowls.

"I assure you, it will be." Miles nods respectfully toward the judges, then toward the guards. "May I present the witness: Citizeness Lucille Leroux."

She slinks, pale and wide-eyed, between the stained swords of the guardsmen. Suddenly, the world stops spinning around me. Suddenly, everything is perfectly clear.

"You, Citizeness Leroux, have filed charges against this Hélène d'Aubign, who was operating under the false name of Hélène Michel. Is this true?" Miles inquires.

"Yes," she says, her chin pointed upward with determination. Her eyes come nowhere near me.

"And what evidence do you have of her conspiracy against the Revolution?"

"Letters, Citizen Miles. Many letters from Coblenz."

"*You* stole my letters?" I blurt, and her eyes flit to and from mine. "It was you?" My blood goes from icy to boiling. I want to run at her and grab her, shake her, hurt her, but I'm held back by strong hands.

The judge scowls at me and bangs his meaty fist on the table. "Silence!"

Miles rubs his hands together and turns toward Lucille once again. "Were these letters addressed to you?"

"No. No. To my husband."

"And what was the content of these letters?"

"Intelligence. Military details from Coblenz."

"I see," Miles grumbles. "How very damning. Citizeness Leroux, show the tribunal one of these treacherous letters, that they might see it with their own eyes before they execute their justice upon this traitor to our great Republic."

Lucille trembles. She swallows. She takes a shaky breath. "I . . . I cannot."

"You cannot?"

"No," she whispers. "I cannot."

"And why not?" Miles asks, his voice growing louder and echoing in the shadowy chamber.

"Because I burned them."

"You burned them?" his voice is high and intentionally incredulous. A murmur goes up among the judges and prisoners.

"Yes. I burned them. They were evil letters. Wouldn't you have burned them?"

Miles stops to suck his teeth, screwing his mouth up thoughtfully for a moment. "No," he says slowly. "No, if I were in possession of treacherous letters that endangered my national security, the last thing I would do would be to burn them. No, I wouldn't do that at all."

He stares at her silently for a long moment, and she looks as if she'll faint. She grabs hold of the judges' table for balance. We hold our breath as Miles's voice slowly increases in volume, as his bulging eyes bulge wider than seems humanly possible.

"Do you know what I would do with letters like that? I would deliver them to an authority the instant they arrived. Especially if I worked below the flat of an assemblyman," he adds, his eyes shrewd, his movements sharp. "Yes, I would report such a letter—such a person—immediately. When did you intercept them?"

"Um, it was, ah, between 1789 and 1790."

"But you did not report these letters until August the twelfth of the year 1792. Three years. Three years! Did it not occur to you that you should report a person you suspected of espionage and treachery, a person living above a bookshop always full of influential people and information? Did it not occur to you that you, yourself, were committing a crime by allowing this spy to do her work?"

"I . . . I didn't commit a crime, citizen," Lucille whimpers.

"Then defend yourself!" he booms. "Why did I overhear you telling the former prisoner, Alexander Evereaux, where to find this prisoner if you were not assisting them in their espionage?"

She gasps as her eyes flicker to mine. She told him. She told him where to find me. She's tried to kill me twice.

"I . . . I don't really know anything about her. I just . . . I didn't have any information to report to you, Citizen Miles. I knew where she lived. That's all. I didn't know who that man was or what he wanted, not really. I was just being helpful."

"Until August the twelfth?" he interjects accusingly, and she takes a step backward. "Tell us the true contents of the letters in question, or face your death, Citizeness Leroux!"

"They were love letters," she sobs, tears streaming down her cheeks. "Love letters to my husband."

"So she is a whore, then? Your husband's lover?"

"It was . . . before we were married. She was engaged to him."

"Your husband was engaged to a spy! Shall we bring him here for trial too?"

"No!" she shrieks, shaking her head emphatically. "No. I was just . . . She's not really . . . a spy. She's just—he was in love with her."

Guy Miles laughs loudly, and his laughter echoes in the silent chamber. "Jealousy," he says slowly. "And so, Citizeness Leroux, do you, upon pain of death, swear to it that this woman is not a counterrevolutionary spy, and that you did not obstruct justice by withholding her letters from the authorities? That you merely obstructed the union of two young people in love for your own wickedly selfish reasons?"

She collapses onto her knees, nodding, her face in her hands.

"Do you swear it?" he bellows.

"I swear it! I swear it!" she sobs repeatedly.

For the first time since he entered the room, Guy Miles looks at me, his eyes bright with satisfaction, his rough face curved into a smile.

"Citizeness d'Aubign, your name has been cleared." He turns to the onlookers. "But what shall we do with the real criminal? This thief?"

The room is silent. Rage swirls behind my eyes. The words *kill her* form on my tongue. *Take her out and kill her.* I want to scream it, to see her meet the fate she wished on me, to see the swords red with her blood. But I feel the soft envelope against my skin, under my dress. I hear my voice, feel my lips moving. "She hasn't wronged the Republic. Only me."

Miles turns and smiles oddly at me, then faces the judges again. "Then cannot this marriage founded on lies and treachery be annulled by the state?"

They shrug and nod.

"Good," Miles says, and papers are shuffled, documents are signed. Lucille is hoisted up to her feet by the guards, who shake her, instructing her to hold up her own weight. She can't, and crumples to her knees again. They leave her there, sobbing, refusing to look up.

"Hélène d'Aubign, do you swear allegiance to the Republic of France?" Miles asks me, his face deadly serious.

My clammy hand is over my banging heart. "I swear it."

"Then, d'Aubign, you are free to go," barks the tattooed judge with a nod. Calloused hands grab my arm from behind. I'm pushed up stairs made slick with blood, then through a dim hallway. I'm shoved toward a door, and then discarded.

The blood is draining from my head. I feel like a wrung-out rag. Dizzy and weak, I push the door and it *opens*. I stumble and blink in the sudden burst of light, missing the step down to the street. But he's here. Before I hit the ground, Théo catches me up in his arms.

"Hélène," he whispers into my hair. "Oh, thank God, Hélène. Thank God."

He checks me all over for bruises. Blood stains my white nightdress, who knows whose blood? But it's not mine. I'm whole and alive—and free. He steadies me, holding me close, and then I see Simonne, her bright-red pants rolled up to the ankles, her crimson cap fastened sideways to her gleaming, dark hair. She runs to wrap her thin arms around me.

"Thank you," I whisper and kiss her on the cheek.

She kisses my cheek and then takes me by the shoulders. Her dark eyes wide and intense, she looks from me to Théo and whispers, "Get her out of here before they change their minds."

Théo nods. "Let's go."

We're halfway to his cart when the Abbaye door scrapes stone again. A wail pierces the air. We turn toward the sound, and it's Lucille, skinning her knees and palms on the rough stone step as she falls into a heap in the sunlight. I feel Théo tense, but he shakes his head and keeps moving.

"Her father will come for her," he whispers tersely, and helps me up into his cart. His voice low and hot, he explains how Miles came to talk to him after my arrest, telling him it was Lucille who had blocked my letters, not my mother. It was Lucille who had told Evereaux where to find me. And it was Lucille who had accused me.

Théo submitted an official legal statement. He filed to have their marriage annulled without telling her. If not for the riots, there would have been a formal trial. And he would have taken the stand. But instead, he drove her to the prison. He took her there to testify and then left her.

And now, he's taking me home. Home to the bookshop.

He helps me up and lights a lantern, and I stretch my stiff legs. His arm is better, still a little sore, but better. Our footsteps echo across the salon floor and into the kitchen. I blink at the light and hold my aching head.

"Why don't I get you a hot bath?"

"Do I smell that bad?"

He laughs softly. "Yes, actually."

"I feel disgusting."

"A bath, and then some food. All right?"

I smile tiredly. "All right."

I wash my hands in a basin as he heats the water for the bath, the first I've had in nearly a month. I throw my filthy nightdress into the fire and step into the steaming water, soaking in up to my chin. The smell of soup wafts in from the kitchen.

"Doing all right?"

"Yes."

"Can I come in?"

"Um, yes. All right." I arrange the soap bubbles strategically and sink lower.

He falls to his knees beside the tub and rubs my hair with chamomile and rosemary. "How's that?" he asks, his fingers circling around my sore temples.

"Good. That's good," I sigh, closing my eyes and sinking up to my chin in the glorious hot water. "Théo? Tell me I'm not dead one more time. Please."

"Not dead."

"Promise?"

His mouth is on mine, and then I'm sure. I'm sure I'm alive.

"I'd better check on the soup," he whispers against my wet skin, and tosses a towel over the back of a nearby chair.

"Wait, give me your watch?" I ask, and he gives me a funny look while reaching into his pocket.

He hands it to me, and I stop it.

Then, I start it over again.

PART III

Liberté, liberté chérie . . .

—"La Marseillaise"

ONE

The September air is crisp and cool, carrying the sweetness of autumn leaves as it drifts over our skin. We are a warm tangle of arms and legs, afraid to let go. I slip my hand inside his shirt. I can't be close enough to him.

The sun keeps climbing higher in the sky, but we don't get up. *It must be noon*, I think, squinting at the golden dot gleaming through the threads of my curtain.

And then, I hear something.

"Théo? Did you hear that?"

"Hmm?"

"Knocking?"

"No."

"Yes."

"Ignore them," he whispers, wrapping his arm across my middle and snuggling close against me. "Stay with me."

But I hear it again.

I sit up, my heart pounding. "That was definitely a knock."

"I'll look. Don't go away," he mumbles groggily, and slides his lips across my bare neck and shoulders.

I catch his hand. "What if they're coming back for me?"

"They're not." He buttons his shirt and touches my cheek, his eyes steady. "It's all right. It's over."

Heart throbbing, I move for my robe and glance in the mirror. Splashing cool water on my face with trembling hands, I hear footsteps on the stairs.

"Hélène, it's your aunt," he says. "Are you dressed?"

"Yes. Yes, come in." I open the door, and her warm arms pull me into a soft embrace. She holds me out in front of her, staring at me and smiling, then wipes her eyes. She opens a worn leather satchel.

"This is for you. It's from Bennette. He wanted you to have it," Josette says, and thrusts a sealed envelope into my hands.

"What is it?"

"Open it and find out."

I break the seal and find two sets of travel papers with names I don't recognize, one male, one female. Behind them is enough money to buy two fares to London.

"I can't take this," I whisper, my throat thickening. "I shouldn't—"

"He left this with me on August the ninth," she says, nodding. "He made me promise to give it to you if anything happened to him. You'll make it through the city gates with those."

I feel Théo's hand at my back. She looks at him and nods in approval. "Take care of my niece." She reaches out her hand to shake his, but he wraps his arms around her.

"Leave soon," she says over his shoulder. "God knows what will happen next. A day or two, you don't have more than that. I won't see you again, I'm afraid."

"Tante . . . Josette? Can I give you something?"

"Oh, my. You've given me enough."

I slide a drawer open, unlock my box, and take out the folded sheets of music. "L'Espérance." "Would you like to have this?" I ask.

Her dark eyes scan it, clouding with tears. "Where in the world did you get this?"

"I found it. At Château des Cygnes."

"And do you know what this is?"

"Only that it was Vivienne's . . . my mother's."

"Can you sing it?" She listens, smiling softly, and when I've finished she says, "You sound like her. She wrote this herself. She wrote it in her own hand. Perhaps you should keep it."

"No. I have it memorized. You gave me her letter. Let me give you her song."

EPILOGUE

BALTIMORE, MARYLAND

APRIL 25, 1793

White sails flutter in the Baltimore harbor, and the salty springtime air is full of promise. The water is cold, but soon, it will be warm enough for swimming. Théo and I sit on a hill overlooking the water and I sketch the sugar boats, the men tugging at nets of oysters, and the glittering midafternoon sun on the water.

"That's pretty," Théo says, looking up from his novel and at my sketch.

"Thank you. You're next."

"You can sketch me any time. Today is your day. Why don't we go home for some dinner before moving the furniture around?"

"We don't really have to move the furniture around, Théo."

"Yes, we do. Some traditions are worth keeping."

"All right," I laugh. "Just let me finish up here. I have a little more shading to do."

He smiles and stretches out on the blanket to read a few more pages.

"Here," Théo says, handing me the key when we get back to the house. "I'll get the packages. You get the door." He juggles boxes of paint and brushes, two canvases, and a pack of watercolor paper while I turn the key.

I hear a stray giggle and then, "Surprise!"

Adèle, Sophie, Étienne, Pierre, Victoire, Giselle, Marie, Max, and Elisabeth cluster in my kitchen. The table is set.

"Happy birthday!" the children squeal, rushing toward me with their small hands full of flowers.

I look over my shoulder at Théo, who grins as he sets the packages down in the hall. Elisabeth reaches up into my cabinet for a vase. Max gives me a book from his new shop, a collection of prints by American artists. Marie hands me a bag of marzipan candy. Adèle hangs back, but once my hands are empty, she brings me a small box wrapped in yellow ribbon.

"Open it," she says, and I sit down to untie the bow.

"Adèle, this is a perfect shell." She grins her crooked little grin, and I lift the conch shell out to touch the spiky white points jutting at even intervals, the smooth, pink curve on the inside.

"Listen to it," she says, and holds it up to my ear to hear the swishing sound. "It sings the song of where it's come from. The ocean's song."

"I love it," I say, hugging her. "I'm going to put it right here on the windowsill, beside the flowers."

There was a time when I would have locked it away in my box. But not today. Today, I keep my favorite things where I can see them.

Setting the shell on my handkerchief with the crooked, pink *H*, I catch my own reflection in the darkening window. Today, I see the things that have been there all along—my mother's imaginative eyes and my father's easy smile. I see the courageous hope that kept my grandfather alive in India and brought him home to the gentleness of my grandmother's fingers at her harp, and the love that was my beginning. I see the light in my own eyes, the love that I know will last beyond endings.

Today, I think about the ocean and the tide, how in the end, there are things you throw back, things you let the undertow pull down to the bottom of a forgetful, forgiving sea. You open your hand, and you're free.

And when the tide changes, bringing shells, stars, and tiny creatures of happiness that make their homes in the hollows of your heart, those are the things you keep.

The things that keep you.

Forever.

ACKNOWLEDGMENTS

I would like to thank . . .

My dynamite agent Cate Hart and sage editor Holly Rubino, as well as the wonderful team at Blackstone: Rick Bleiweiss and Josie Wood-bridge.

My husband, Clay, for his tireless support and optimism, and our daughters Eva and Sarah for their patience with and enthusiasm for the worlds inside my head. My mom, Lori Fisher, for all those bedtime stories we made up together and for letting me make creative messes I had to clean up myself.

My earliest readers—Genevieve Abravanel, Michele Lombardo, Eva Polites, and Bernadette Ziemba—for the late nights at Panera filled with coffee, muffies, and all the right questions. Kristen Strocchia for her priceless feedback and patient mending of my French grammar. Heather Flaherty for showing me how to fearlessly make broad and sweeping changes to improve my craft. Sandy Asher, a dear mentor and friend.

Amanda DeWitt, Tom Hoover, Tracey Enerson Wood, Christine Cohen, and Jen Fahey, whose feedback, wisdom, virtual tissues and hugs have talked me down from countless ledges and prevented dastardly plot turns and word choices. And the trusty Herd: Summer Spence,

Rachel Rear, Julia Walton, Emma Berquist, Lauren Nicolle Taylor, Hope Cook, Ava Woolf, Michella Dominici, Amy Merrill Wyatt, and Kate Wakefield.

Everyone at the Society of Children's Book Writers and Illustrators who has helped make this dream a reality: Alison Green Myers, Kim Briggs, Donna Boock, Rona Shirdan, Virginia Law Manning, Berrie Torgan-Randall, and Laura Parnum, to name just a few. Thank you for welcoming me into your warm, bookish family and giving me the resources, encouragement, and opportunities I need to continue to grow as a writer.